Whistle Down the Wind

Sibelle Street

Whistle Down the Wind
Book One of the Mystic Moon Series
by
Sibelle Stone

Published by Moon Valley Publishing
Copyright © 2012 Deborah Schneider

All rights reserved. Except as permitted under the U.S. Copyright Act of 1976, no part of this publication may be reproduced, distributed, or transmitted in any form or by any means, or stored in a database or retrieval system, without prior written permission of the publisher.

This book is a work of fiction. While references may be made to actual places or events, the names, characters, incidents, and locations are from the author's imagination and any similarity to actual living or dead persons, businesses, or events is coincidental.

Published in the United States of America
Moon Valley Publishing, P.O. Box 1357, North Bend, WA 98045
ISBN 978-0-98391-033-6

For Dave, my handsome hero.

Prologue

twilight shadows chased Catlin Glyndwr down the cobblestoned streets of Shrewsbury. The mist reached out to snatch at her, like skeletal hands creeping across the graveyard when the moon is dark.

I'll never reach home before dark. Catlin pulled the velvet cape tightly around her shoulders and quickened her step. Her heart thumped like a bodhrán drum.

Danger lurked in the darkness of Shrewsbury. Hunters searched for those who dared leave the safe confines of their homes to wander at night. These hunters were especially interested in any woman bold enough to walk the streets after dusk. Such women quickly came under suspicion.

Catlin had planned to make her visit to the tiny, shabby hut brief. But the Widow Holton was too feverish to rise from her bed. After glancing around the dingy one-room hovel with no fire to keep the Widow and her three children warm or to cook, Catlin couldn't turn her back on the impoverished family.

She'd prepared a stew from the foodstuffs she carried in the basket with her herbs and tonics. She even took the time to stir up a pot of porridge for the next day. Then she promised the Widow she'd return soon.

Catlin stumbled on the rough cobblestones. She adjusted the basket on her arm just as a glimmer of light diverted her attention.

A warning?

She didn't have time to respond as a thick arm shot out from the darkness, grasped her around the waist, and pulled her into the shadows.

A leather-gloved hand covered her mouth, smothering her scream. Her stomach heaved, in danger of purging her hastily eaten meal.

Not that screaming would do any good. Lately, the good people of Shrewsbury kept their doors barred and their shutters fastened after the sun set. They'd grown accustomed to hearing screams in the night and accepted that sometimes women simply disappeared without a trace.

Fear made them silent allies in the sick drama being played out in the lanes surrounding their homes and businesses. Too many living in the village of Shrewsbury chose to look the other way, or to pretend that whatever happened 'twas God's will.

"Stay silent," a voice warned from behind her as the sharp prick of a knife blade pierced the skin at the side of her throat. She felt a trickle of blood slide down to wet her collar.

The arm dragged her farther back into the alley. Catlin knew any effort to resist the man holding her captive could easily result in her death. She fought the tremors making her so weak, if she wasn't held so tightly she'd collapse.

As a candle passed before her face, Catlin tried to shrink back from the stinking hulk holding it. He leered at her with a toothless grin.

"One of dem Glyndwr sisters, Bodwell."

A muffled laugh echoed behind her. "Then 'tis a good night of hunting indeed, Scapes."

Symon Bodwell, the witch hunter, was not known for his compassion or fine manners. He was probably the most despised man in Shrewsbury, yet the license dispensed from the Bishop had given him power and authority over almost everyone in the village.

The iron grip holding her prisoner slackened. Huge hands shoved her roughly against a wall. She crumbled to her knees, and tears washed the back of her eyelids.

I must not be afraid, for fear is the thing that feeds creatures like Bodwell, she silently reminded herself.

"Leave me alone," she finally gasped. Her arm ached from the assailants grip and her ears still rang from her collision with the wall.

Symon Bodwell, his thin lips formed into a sneer, glared down at her with a hatred so fierce, if she wasn't already forced against the wall, she'd have clamored away from him.

"You are not in a position to give me orders, witch."

Catlin tried to swallow her fear. The man couldn't possibly have proof of his accusation. She and her sisters were careful about practicing the craft. Their celebration of Imbolc, in the quiet of her sister's home, had been modest compared to their rites back home in Cymru.

"You've attacked an innocent woman, Bodwell, and I can assure you I shall complain to the Justice of the Peace about this treatment." Her voice echoed high and thin with fear.

Bodwell's mouth twisted into a cruel smile at her words.

"Save your ink and paper, for Lord Cranbourne is soon headed to the grave from what I hear," he snarled. The tone of his voice was as harsh and cold as the winter winds that blew in from the ocean near her ancestral home. "He'll not help any such as you, witch." Catlin shivered at the menace in the man's words.

"I've done nothing wrong," she protested, hating the weak tremor that entered her voice. Her stomach clenched again, and Catlin feared she would humiliate herself by spewing. She couldn't help it, deep down, she was terrified. She was sure these men could hear the staccato beat of her heart, banging in her chest.

Symon Bodwell hovered above her like a specter for a moment, then grasped the fabric of her cape and pulled her roughly to her feet.

"There are ways to escape the gallows." His other hand slipped beneath the velvet cape to roughly grasp the fabric covering one of her breasts. He yanked her even closer, so his face was only inches from hers. The pungent odor of onions clinging to his breath made her gag. She swallowed to keep her stomach from spilling its contents on his boots.

Catlin gasped as he continued to squeeze and mangle her breast before his hand moved lower. Ice spilled through her veins as she realized his intention.

"Lean back against the wall and spread yer legs." He pushed her backwards again. "If ye please me, I might let ye live so's I can enjoy ye again."

Catlin tried to scream, but the gloved hand covered her mouth again. Bodwell released his hold on her arms to yank at her gown and petticoat, lifting them to bare her legs.

The man planned to ravish her, and he thought she'd meekly acquiesce to his demands. The chill of fear quickly turned to white hot rage. Death couldn't be worse than allowing this monster to steal her virginity. Catlin balled her hands into fists and prepared to lash out and fight the man intent on raping her.

"Leave her," another man's voice called out from the darkness. "You were told to capture her and I'll not have the goods sullied before you hand her off to me!"

The accent was polished, deep enough to reverberate in the alleyway. She recognized beneath the words lingered an ugly, evil thread of dark magic. She sensed the greater threat came from the man hidden from view.

Bodwell turned away from her, his gaze scanning the night surrounding them like a funeral shroud. "I wasn't expecting ye here tonight, milord," he said, backing away from Catlin. His arrogant sneer had turned to a simpering whine.

She seized the opportunity to quickly draw a sigil in the air before closing her eyes to gather her power. She cleared her mind of the fear and drew on the ancient and familiar words she'd learned from her mother. Energy spiraled through her body, making her fingertips tingle and her heartbeat slow to an easy rhythm.

She called on her *sylphs* for help, and a quick breeze assured her they'd heard her plea. Within moments, the breeze transformed into a whirlwind that gathered dust and dirt to pelt her attackers with debris.

The two men who had cornered her started to cough and hack, giving her the chance she'd been waiting for.

Gathering the magical power building within her, she hurled it at her captors. Bodwell slammed backwards into the man holding the candle. They both toppled to the ground, spitting and swearing.

Catlin sketched a different sigil in the air and small dots of light began to flicker around her. She pointed her finger at the two men and chanted in the ancient language of her ancestors.

"Doethineb, cryfder, ammddiffyn rhag!"

Wisdom, strength, protection. An ancient spell.

Sparks of light flew from every direction and attacked the men, making them swat at the air around them as if warding off angry hornets.

Catlin circled away from her attackers, working hard to keep her trembling body under control.

"I'll see all ye Glyndwr sisters dancin' at the end of a rope. Wait and see." Bodwell's voice trailed behind her, his vile threats laced with swearing.

"You fools," the stranger howled, "she's escaping!"

A spiral of dark magic followed Catlin as she stumbled away from her attackers. Her *sylphs* acted as a shield, protecting her from its evil touch. Fear gripped Catlin's heart as she slipped through the murky ink of night, toward the safety of her sister's shop. Away from the immediate danger, but she sensed a terrifying malevolence hunted her and her family. She had managed to elude arrest for now, but she knew the Witch Finder wouldn't give up so easily. She was now terrified that she'd led the monster directly to her sister's door, and she didn't know how to protect those she loved from the approaching horror that could reach out and snatch them all away.

Chapter One

Shrewsbury Gaol
England, 1664

death stalked her in the deepening gloom of early evening. Glancing around the dank, windowless cell, Catlin suppressed a shudder and maintained the slimmest pretense of control. Three men stared at her with cold eyes. The dull, bored expressions on their faces informed her they'd grown hard enough to dispense with all emotion, especially pity.

The stench of decaying hay, human waste, and rank body odor emanating from the gaoler standing closest to Catlin made her stomach churn. Rumor alleged once an accused witch was imprisoned in Shrewsbury Gaol, escape was impossible.

Closing her eyes, she repeated the familiar calming chant of composure her mother had taught her long ago.

Protection, love, strength. Mother of us all, hear my plea. The comforting words reassured her as her breathing slowed from ragged gasps to a slow, measured pattern of air moving in and out of her chest. A few moments later, a strange new voice filled the silence of the cell.

"Cranbourne, I never thought you foolish enough to be taken in by gossip and old wives tales."

She heard a gasp, a quick shuffling of feet and then the scraping of a chair across the cold stone of the floor. When Catlin opened her eyes, a tall stranger stood with the group of men. His broad shoulders and long legs made the cramped cell feel even smaller.

Catlin studied the dark broadcloth suit of clothes the stranger wore beneath a huge sweep of woolen cape. She considered his appearance for a moment longer before dismissing him as a clergyman. Likely he'd been called here to read the charges against her with the Justice of the Peace. She defiantly lifted her head to stare back at them. They were all men and so they would all be against her. She had no doubt.

"I have no stomach for these foul affairs, Griffin, but duty requires I read the charges against all those accused of witchcraft in my district." The chair squeaked across the floor again.

"Then read these foolhardy charges, dismiss them quickly, and release this poor woman to her family so we can be off to enjoy our evening of pleasure."

The hair on the back of Catlin's neck rose. The stranger returned her stare, and she trembled as he stepped closer.

"Or perhaps we can entice her to join us at the *Raven's Beak* for a pint." A dimple formed near the corner of his mouth as he smiled. "She seems comely enough, though I swear in the dimness of this light I could be deceived." The stranger gave a deep, rich laugh.

Catlin's cheeks warmed at the remark. How dare this stranger make such a crude jest at a time when her very life stood in jeopardy? Didn't he know during the last full moon Old Nonnie from the Glen had been chased from her home and branded as a witch? Witch fever gripped the people of the region. Each fortnight brought new charges against more women accused of consorting with the devil or casting spells.

Lord Morgan Fitz-John, Viscount Cranbourne, who served as the Justice of the Peace, and the new arrival whispered across the room. She tried to focus, but she couldn't discern their words. Another bold laugh erupted from the stranger who had entered the cell. Catlin tried to control the flash of anger that snapped through her. It didn't work and she sent a scalding look of disdain in his direction.

He laughed again.

"I believe I've made your little witch angry, Cranbourne. Shall I throw myself upon her mercy and beg to be freed from her spell? Or shall I submit and see what pleasures she can offer to bind me to her?"

"You might be amused by charges of witchcraft, Griffin, but in this parish they are taken seriously. 'Tis an offense punishable by death," Lord Cranbourne growled. "I assumed my duties with reluctance but even you should be aware of the grim consequences should this prisoner be found guilty."

Catlin's heartbeat quickened at the deliberate tone and words spoken by the man representing the law. She was in this predicament because she'd reacted too hastily against Symon Bodwell. How she wished she could draw back the angry spell she'd cast when he'd cornered her in a dark alley the previous night. She'd responded without thinking and lashed out with magic against the most dangerous man in the village.

Catlin's mother had warned many times that her quick temper would be her undoing. But the hated witch hunter had forced her to defend her virtue and use her powers. Escape had been foremost in her mind.

Bodwell had been quick to bring his men to her sister's door with a warrant for Catlin's arrest. His vindictive smile had widened when her younger sisters pleaded for Aelwyd to do something.

The charges leveled against her included malfeasance, the intention to harm another human being—the most serious allegation that could be made for the use of magic.

Her arrest brought her to Shrewsbury Gaol to be charged with consorting with the devil. Bodwell spread gossip throughout the village that suggested to cross Catlin would result in immediate and harsh punishment dispensed by the Prince of Darkness himself.

She did possess powers, by rite of blood and through the ancient heredity of the women of her clan. It didn't matter to any of these people if she held to the ancient creed of harming none with her magic, lest she invite the darkness to possess her. Any witch was evil in their eyes, even one who practiced white magic. Their fear of powers they didn't understand made death the only suitable punishment for such a vile creature.

And the one exception to the creed was that if someone was trying to harm her, she could protect herself.

"Will you swim her then? Bind her foot to hand—toss her into the canal and determine she's innocent if she drowns and guilty if she floats? Hardly a fair choice for her, eh?"

Catlin grew more intrigued. The man named Griffin made jests, but he seemed to be championing her in a very odd way.

"Leave me to perform my duties, Griffin, and I'll meet you at the tavern when I finish questioning this woman." Lord Cranbourne removed his glove to wipe his brow and gave a deep sigh of resignation. "Your interference isn't making this any easier."

Griffin strode across the room and paused before her. His name invoked the image of a creature combining the intelligence of an eagle with the courage of a lion. What business would bring such a man to a filthy cell on such a murky and moonless night?

When Griffin leaned forward to study her more carefully, one of his fingers gently toyed with a thick dark curl that had escaped from the arrangement she'd so artfully arranged earlier. A quiver passed through her. Not fear, not exactly excitement. Warmth spread up from her belly to her breasts, then heated her cheeks.

"God's tears, Cranbourne, this shouldn't be easy for any man. Her very life is at stake and you'd best proceed with gravity and caution." He stepped away from her, yet his masculine fragrance lingered, a pleasant combination of sandalwood and tobacco. A small mischievous gleam in his eye caught her unaware and she fought the urge to smile back at him. Then she recalled the seriousness of her circumstances and her knees trembled.

He was taller than any man she knew, even taller than her father had been. Dark, wavy hair brushed his shoulders, and a large felt hat with a huge black plume for decoration sat upon his head. He stood with authority, his posture signaling he was proud. Perhaps even a bit arrogant. He wore a leather jerkin, dark breeches tucked into high black boots, and a heavy woolen cape that swept almost to the floor.

He was handsome, and if the circumstances were different, she'd be tempted to flirt with him.

"Be off, Griffin, because I'll get naught done as long as you're here making me the object of your jest. Let me finish with this and then we can enjoy our dinner and toast your imprudent adventure to the New World." Lord Cranbourne urged.

The New World? Catlin's attention shifted back to the Eagle-Lion Griffin. For months she'd dreamed of traveling to the colonies. She imagined it a place her family could escape the pestilence and superstitious fears of those stranded on this cursed island. And now only inches from her stood an adventurer ready to embark upon a journey that had consumed her daydreams for months. She cursed her own bad luck and ill timing.

"'Tis a foul deed to condemn her because she's as fair a maiden as I've seen in many a day. Couldn't you release her to me for questioning, Cranbourne? I think I might force her to confess her sins. Or perhaps she will bewitch me and I'll find myself transformed into her familiar by morning."

Catlin warmed again as Griffin's gaze swept down the length of her body. As his frank perusal ended, their gazes locked. Eyes as dark as a sky before a thunder storm flashed with intensity, his mouth tipped up at the corners and he winked at her.

She momentarily forgot the danger, as her breathing quickened and her heart lurched. A strange heat swirled through her body, dispelling the chill of the stone cell surrounding her.

"If you tire of your questions, bring the maid with you to the tavern. I swear she'll be more pleasant company than you this night," Griffin said.

The guards laughed. As one of them took a careful step closer to Catlin, his eyes widened. "I'll be. He's right! If me old eyes ain't playin' tricks on me, this one's no ugly hag. I say we strip off her clothes to search for the Devil's Mark."

The gaoler's thick fist grabbed her bodice. With one swift movement he tore the front of the heavily embroidered cloth open to her waist. Catlin screamed and wrenched against the leather straps binding her hands. Fighting to twist away from the men, tears filled her eyes and shame washed through her at being exposed. Her mind spun and the protection spell came to her lips unbidden.

Griffin spun and shielded her with his body. "How dare you touch this lady?" he snarled.

Within a heartbeat, a thin, keening wind whistled into the room and scattered the dirt on the floor, making the men cough. The bleak light of the rushes in the hallway flickered. As the wind built to a howling scream, they flashed out, and the room plunged into total darkness.

The sound of the wind echoed throughout the stone prison, as a tempest whipped through the room and slapped the men against the wall. The door blew back on its iron hinges to hit the stone with a loud boom that reverberated in the cell.

The doors imprisoning other inmates banged open one after another, sounding like musket fire on a battlefield.

The storm howled through the ancient prison. A fierce, wailing wind screamed like a banshee stealing across the night to capture the souls of the dying. Finally, a cold, lonely silence echoed through the cell, as if the wind had escaped out into the night.

"Find the head gaoler and get us some light." Griffin put the tone of command into his voice, despite his uneasiness. He'd heard the groans of men dying on the battlefield, the weeping of widows, and the cold, harsh cry of an enemy entering battle. But nothing had ever unsettled him like the screaming wind that had just swept through the jail. He prayed he would never hear such a sound again.

He brushed away the prickle of fear that had raised the hair on the back of his neck, swallowed hard and cleared the dust from his throat with a loud cough.

A wavering voice finally broke the silence. "There ain't no fire in the grates. That hellish wind musta put it out. I'll have to get some hot coals from down below." One of the gaolers called out.

Griffin swore beneath his breath as he wrapped his cloak more tightly about him. "Be quick about it, then. This place is a tomb to begin with and made even more so in this suffocating darkness."

The scuffle of footsteps grew faint as the man went in search of flame to rekindle the torches.

A deep, hacking cough reverberated from within the confines of the cell, and a lancet of fear pierced through Griffin.

"Take care, Morgan, this dust cannot be good for your lungs. Find a chair and once the rushes are lit again, we shall leave this cursed place. Let this witch be free or be damned, 'tis too dangerous for you to remain here tonight in the dampness and cold."

Lord Morgan Cranbourne responded with another wretched, lingering cough. Griffin regretted his interference with his friend's duties. Why should he be concerned if this maiden were found guilty of the crime of witchcraft? He had only a few precious hours to spend with his best friend, and he'd squandered some of it on a petty argument about a woman he cared nothing about. Tomorrow he'd head to Bristol, and within the week board a ship to cross the ocean to Jamestown in the New World. He might never see his oldest and dearest childhood friend again. How foolish to quarrel about a strange woman and her fate.

The gaoler returned carrying a small candle that shed a paltry light into the dimness of the hallway. He roughly pushed aside a queue of prisoners who had left their cells and were attempting to get out of the narrow hallway and up the stone steps.

"Get back into your cells ya mangy beasts, or I'll get me whip and beat ye."

Griffin winced at the man's threat and the obvious pleasure the lummox derived from terrifying the poor unfortunates lined up around him. He wanted to pummel the man, but he heard Morgan gasping weakly for each breath.

Griffin grabbed the candle and held it closer to his friend's face. A wide band of fear clenched his heart at the image the candlelight revealed. Morgan was deathly pale, blue tinged his lips, and the shadows that circled his eyes looked as black and blue as bruises. Most frightening of all, a thin trickle of blood edged the corner of his mouth. Lord Cranbourne was fatally ill, and Griffin knew he needed to rush his friend back to Mabley Hall and put him under the care of a physician as soon as possible.

"You there—" He pointed at the other gaoler, still plastered against the wall where the wind had planted him. "Help me here."

The command was lost on the man, as he wordlessly pointed to the timber where the accused witch had been lashed to an iron ring with leather straps and held prisoner.

Griffin's gaze followed the man's pointing finger. His mouth went dry as the meager light of the candle illuminated the darkness. Two thick leather straps lay empty against the pillar. "The devil's work," cried the man, still posed frozen against the wall. "She'll bring the evil one's wrath down upon us all."

"God's teeth," whispered Griffin. "Perhaps she truly is a witch." He shook his head to clear the thoughts that whirled about in confusion. "That cursed wind has put us all in an odd mood. 'Tis likely someone forgot to close the upper doors and the storm outside sought refuge within this stone keep." He turned back to his friend. "She took advantage of the chaos."

"She has escaped," gasped Morgan. "I shall be held responsible for this, I know it."

Griffin wanted to reassure his friend, but before he could utter a word Morgan fell forward and would have collapsed at his feet. Only Griffin's lightening reflexes, honed by years of military training, saved his friend from crushing his nose against the unforgiving stone of the floor.

Chapter Two

Griffin grasped his best friend beneath the arms in an attempt to haul him to his feet.

"To hell with this witch folly, Morgan. This wretched place is bound to kill you if we stay."

Glaring at the gaoler, Griffin shoved at him with his free hand.

"Clear a path out there so I can get Lord Cranbourne away from this hell-hole."

Morgan's complexion was ashen as he gasped for each precious breath of air. Griffin knew his friend's episodes of lung fever had increased of late, but he was shocked at the severity of this attack. When he pressed a handkerchief to Morgan's lips, more blood tinged the cloth. Morgan tried to take a deeper breath, but fell into another fit of coughing.

As Morgan leaned heavily against him for support, Griffin was astonished to discover how thin and wasted his friend appeared. Dragging the ailing man with him down the damp stone hallway, Griffin began to regret his plans to leave Shrewsbury so soon. But passage was booked and arrangements had been made for him to claim the tobacco plantation he'd recently inherited. More was at stake than his eager desire to get away from England. Much more.

Thin, boney hands stretched toward them in the dim light as they made their way down the hallway. Voices crackled with pleading, for help, for freedom, and some simply for pity.

They were poor wretched prisoners, more likely to die from illness and starvation than the hangman's noose. Griffin tensed his muscles, threw back his head, and bellowed a rough order to get back. The ragged army of damned creatures smashed themselves against the wall. Griffin hauled Morgan's limp form up the stairs of the gaol.

"Who goes there?" a smelly hulk questioned, barring their way. His feet were planted at the top of the stone steps as he brandished his sword.

"Lord Cranbourne is deathly ill, and if you do not let me pass I will drop him only long enough to remove your head from your shoulders, you horse's arse."

The man quickly stepped aside. "I'll open the doors for ye, milord."

Griffin's stomach clenched at the sour odor of the jailer as he stepped to the massive oak door blocking the way to the entry hall. "Be quick about it then, for he needs fresh air." Near as much as I do at this moment he thought, nearly gagging. His stomach roiled at the foul air surrounding them.

The guard fumbled with the keys. Griffin shifted the weight of his friend and glanced down at him. Morgan's eyes were closed, his face like a mask of death, his chest rattled. Death rattle? It was a terrifying thought.

The door swung open, and the guard shuffled out of the way. Griffin could hardly see in the dim light stretching to the end of the entry hall. The strange wind must have howled through here too, although the idea confused Griffin. How could a draft seep under a massive oak door that was tightly locked and put out all but one of the rushes used for light?

He shrugged off the question as he struggled to get Morgan out of the damp, cursed darkness and home to warmth and the care of a reputable physician.

He paused once again to shift Morgan and reach for the iron handle of the door leading to the courtyard where his coach was waiting for them beyond the outer gate. A soft rustling behind him stopped his hand in mid-air.

"I will heal your friend if you help me escape."

The soft cadence of the woman's voice told him she was Welsh. He turned slowly, and though he couldn't see the figure shrouded deep within the shadows, Griffin knew he faced the witch.

No, his good sense argued with him, the woman accused of being a witch. She stepped toward him, and her features became visible. The arched eyebrows, the slightly tilted eyes a startling shade of blue that reminded him of spring skies. A mouth that was small but so finely shaped, Griffin wished he could lean forward and trace the outline of her lips with one finger.

Despite her efforts to gather the torn bodice of her gown, the soft mounds of her breasts peeked through the rived fabric. Thick russet colored hair curled over her shoulders and framed her heart-shaped face.

"You've been accused of attacking a man using magic. How do you know I won't call for the gaoler and have you thrown back into that cell? And how did you manage to get up here in the first place?"

She took another step toward him and pointed at Morgan, now gasping for each thin breath of air he could pull into his lungs.

"You treasure this man's life, and I can help him. We should assist each other."

Griffin considered her words. "Are you a healer, then?"

A shimmer of silver lit the edges of the blue and her eyes grew brighter.

"Better than a surgeon, who is more likely to kill your friend with his bleeding leeches and purging potions then cure him." She tilted her head.

"The death rattle is in his cough and his lungs are filled with blood. My mother was a healer of great renown, and I've seen this type of illness before."

"Your mother taught you to heal, then?"

She gave him a thin, sad smile. "My mother taught me many things."

The noise of several men thudded up the stairs. Gaolers, from the sounds of the heavy footfalls and rough voices.

When the woman turned her head, bright silver glimmers of light, like dust motes caught in sunlight, formed a halo behind her. The huge oak door slammed shut behind them.

He blinked, and his vision cleared. The wine he'd drank earlier in the evening had affected him more than he'd realized.

"You must decide quickly, there isn't much time."

Her voice was gentle, and it carried an assurance that somehow comforted him. He didn't struggle with his decision, despite his own doubts that this woman could perform any kind of healing on his friend. He simply couldn't abide the forfeit of a life, especially the life of a beautiful Welsh maiden, for the sake of superstition. Witches were a folktale created to frighten children.

Griffin quickly pulled at his cape and tossed it with one hand to the woman. He handed her his hat.

"Cover yourself with these, then you can help me carry Lord Cranbourne to my coach. Stay quiet and say nothing!"

She quickly complied and nodded her agreement.

The door scraped open, and the gloomy night blew into the hall, making shadows dance along the stone floor like ancient wraiths released from the grave. Rain fell in heavy sheets in the courtyard, where one guard stood in a small ramshackle hut before the gate. Just beyond the iron bars, Griffin's coach stood waiting. Carter would wait for him until the hounds of hell arrived, he was that loyal.

"Who goes there?" The guard peered at them.

"'Tis Sir Reynolds of Hawthorne House, and I'm anxious to get Lord Cranbourne to his estate. He's had an attack of lung fever and is dangerously ill." He avoided the small flicker of light issuing from the doorway and walked directly to the huge lock on the gate. "Be quick about this, man, lest he die here and I inform his father, the Earl, 'twas your fault."

The guard stumbled. All of Shrewsbury knew the Earl doted upon his only son. They also knew the old man had a wildly unpredictable temper, and no one would willingly become his enemy. Griffin was counting on that knowlege to help him get away quickly.

The guard found the key and inserted it into the lock. Before they moved through the gate, a large, meaty fist blocked their way.

The guard nodded at the companion on the other side of Morgan. "Who's this then?"

"Lord Cranbourne's servant you fool," Griffin said with authority. "Do you think he'd enter this pisshole without someone to guard his back?"

"'Course, I got to know. Been strange doin's in the gaol tonight." The man's eyes bulged with a fearful look as he pulled the gate open. "There's rumors a witch has called down demons upon us."

Griffin pulled his friend through the space, grateful for the help of the woman on the other side. He paused to reassure the guard as the gate slammed shut behind them.

"I've heard if you rub garlic and chicken fat upon yourself, it will protect you from demons." The man on the other side grunted. "Aye, I believe I've heard the same thing. Thank ye for the advice."

The woman's shoulders shook as she and Griffin shuffled Morgan to the coach where Carter had already jumped down to open the door. He gave them an inquisitive look, but said nothing as he helped them settle Morgan onto the seat.

"Let's be off quickly," Griffin ordered, as he arranged a thick woolen blanket around the legs of his friend who was now unconscious. The woman hovered above the sick man, and with a sudden move she grasped Morgan by the shoulders and gave him a hard shake.

Griffin grabbed her upper arm roughly, "Be careful how you treat him, Miss." She shrugged off his grasp and opened Morgan's mouth, leaning forward to peer inside.

Her brusque manner perturbed Griffin, but before he could pull her away from Morgan the carriage jolted forward, flinging her back into Griffin's arms. She gasped.

Griffin felt of sizzle of heat climb up his leg and settle heavily in the region of his cock. He gave her a mischievous grin while realizing he wasn't immune to the woman's charms.

"A perfect seating arrangement, wouldn't you agree, milady?"

She pushed at his shoulders and a flicker of defiance blazed in her eyes before she lowered her gaze and lifted herself from his lap.

"I beg your pardon, sir."

Her gaze caught his and a flash of curiosity sizzled through him. She crouched before him, one hand on the seat next to Morgan to steady herself.

"I believe 'twould be better for Lord Cranbourne if we stretched him out upon the seat. I think the air might move in and out of his lungs more easily."

He stood, moving Morgan so he now rested across the seat. Griffin covered him more securely with the blanket and sat back to watch as she placed a hand gently on his friend's chest. "His breath moves in and out more easily and he'll rest comfortably without being folded in the middle. I have no doubt he's been bled overmuch. Look at the pallor of his skin."

Griffin nodded. "He's lost a great deal of weight, too." He drew his fingers through his damp hair. "I've only just returned from Ireland, and I'm shocked to see my friend in such poor condition. I swear I don't know what he was thinking to go out to an inquiry on an evening such as this."

The woman lifted her head. "But 'twas an inquiry of witchcraft, so how could he resist? Aren't all men eager to see a witch punished?" The tone of her voice was flat, but defiance blazed in her soft blue eyes.

Griffin pondered the question.

"I admit some men are fascinated by the trials of witches. But Lord Cranbourne is not such a man. If he went out into the storm tonight, it was to insure that you would be given the opportunity for a fair trial."

"And afterwards, he would be sure to see that I was executed swiftly and efficiently." She tossed her head. "I am confident of that."

"Are you a witch, then?"

She gazed up at him from beneath thick, dark lashes fringing her sapphire eyes. A smile formed at the edges of her mouth, lifting the corners.

"Of course. One would never even be accused lest there were irrefutable proof, is that not so?"

Griffin leaned back. "Of course. Well, 'tis good to have that settled. Will you be calling upon demons to cure my friend of his affliction?"

She shook water droplets from her hair as she settled the cloak around her shoulders. A flash of desire whipped through Griffin, and he wished he were the course fabric nestled against those firm, round breasts.

"I suppose if 'tis necessary." She gave him another of her bright-eyed looks. "I've heard you can rub chicken fat and garlic upon yourself to keep them at bay."

Griffin laughed. "I couldn't seem to resist the opportunity to have a bit of fun at the expense of our superstitious friend."

He watched her face in the warm lamplight inside the carriage.

She was comely, but there was a glow about her unlike any woman he'd ever met before, as if she held a candle within her that illuminated the darkest corners of the night.

"You don't believe in witchcraft, do you?" She asked.

Griffin turned his head to gaze out the window. It was shrouded with dark leather curtains to keep the wind and rain howling through the night securely contained outside. He gave a deep sigh before turning back to her.

"I've seen all the horrible and ugly things men can do to each other. I doubt demons could entice us to do worse than that which we choose to do of our own will."

"And so witches and demons are of the same ilk in your mind?"

She shifted in her seat and warmth rose from her skin combined with an herbal scent that enticed him. The hardening between his legs became more acute.

"I have no interest in the arcane arts, so I do not think of such things at all." He leaned toward her, and their gazes locked. "But I am interested in you. What is your name, my lady?"

The tip of her tongue touched her lips, and a warm rush of desire pulsed through him. Perhaps there would be time for play with this minx, once he got Morgan settled into his bed and sent a servant for the physician.

"Catlin Glyndwr," she said and moistened her lips again.

"Catlin," he repeated. "The name suits you."

"And what about you?" she asked.

"Oh, it suits me too."

Her lashes fluttered against her cheek and a deep dimple appeared at the corner of her mouth when her lips formed a puckered smile. "I meant to ask, who are you? I heard Lord Cranbourne call you Griffin in the cell at the gaol."

"So you were paying attention to our conversation? I thought perhaps you had been terrified into a fainting spell." He crossed one leg over the other and leaned back against the seat. "I am Sir Griffin Reynolds, the son of Baron Thomas Reynolds. Since I am the third son, I chose a commission in His Majesty's service rather then genteel poverty. As I told you before, I only recently arrived back home from Ireland."

Catlin Glyndwr trained her gaze upon Morgan. Silence filled the carriage as they bumped along for a few miles.

"I will do as I promised, I swear to it."

Griffin struggled to hear the soft whisper of her words.

"I shall heal your friend in payment for my life, for surely they would have hanged me as a witch."

Anger flashed through Griffin that a woman as gentle and beautiful as Catlin Glyndwr should be caught in a web of outrageous lies and superstitious fear. He could forgive peasants, for they had no education, but for the merchants and aristocracy to be so gullible seemed improbable. While he might call this woman bewitching, he would never accuse her of the dark crimes associated with witchcraft.

"I appreciate the help you've given my friend, but once we arrive at his home, I intend to send for a physician to treat him. He can decide what further measures are necessary."

Catlin turned to him. Silver glimmers of light once again danced in the sapphire depths of her eyes and a sudden calm warmth suffused his body. He had an urge to look away, yet discovered he couldn't turn from her captivating gaze.

"I can cure your friend, if you but give me the chance."

"You can cure him," murmured Griffin. The warmth now enveloped him as the herbal scent surrounding Catlin intensified. Small silver and crystal motes darted toward his friend stretched upon the opposite seat. He wanted to turn away, but the look in Catlin Glyndwr's eyes mesmerized him.

"If you but trust in me, 'twill be done." Her voice held a musical Welsh accent like she was singing an ancient song.

His body was warm, relaxed, and he felt as content as he'd been since arriving home from Ireland. "I trust you to heal Lord Cranbourne," he said.

A rush of wind gusted over him as one of the curtains tore from its tie. A splash of rain hit his face and jerked him from his trancelike reverie.

What in God's name had just happened to him?

Chapter Three

"As I have promised, so shall it be," Catlin whispered. Her voice was soft, but sure.

Griffin leaned back on the seat. His dark glower warned her he wasn't as susceptible to magic as some. Oh, he would do as she wanted, eventually, but he resisted the glamour she'd cast to control him.

He's very strong. Managing him would be a challenge.

She blinked and tried to dismiss the thought. She must protect her sisters, not entertain notions of romantic liaisons or flirting. Her actions had put her entire family in jeopardy, and it was now her responsibility to find a way to keep them safe.

Once word of Catlin's escape spread, her sisters would be drawn into the inquiry concerning her disappearance. Her younger sisters were not yet initiated into their magic, and her eldest sister's magic could be wild and unpredictable when fully unleashed, especially if she were angry.

"What?" He seemed about to say more before glancing away.

The form stretched across the seat opposite them coughed. A pale visage rose like a ghost to face them.

Lord Cranbourne's struggle for each breath now seemed less labored. Good, she thought, relieved. The *sylphs* have done their work and eased this man's suffering.

A small light shimmered like a crystal in response to her thought, and she smiled at the subtle message.

Griffin leaned forward to place his strong, thick-fingered hand on his friend's knee. "Don't try to speak, Cranbourne. God's teeth but I thought you were destined for the church yard before the week was done."

Lord Cranbourne moaned as he put his hand to his chest.

Caught up again in a fit of coughing, he closed his eyes. He struggled for a moment, attempting to sit, then he laid back again on the seat.

"My father will be most disappointed if I choose to exit this world before producing an heir. 'Tis a task he reminds me of religiously since this illness came over me." He paused to inhale. "Even now he is in London, searching for a virgin to sacrifice upon the marital altar in order to guarantee our family line does not disappear when I die."

Griffin examined his friend's ashen face. "The man cannot let you rest even when you suffer so much. A pox on his wish for an heir, Cranbourne. You are ill and should not be considering marriage at this time."

Lord Cranbourne accomplished a thin smile and coughed again before answering. "My father has all but arranged it, and only needs me to accomplish the bedding to be content that at least I shall not leave this earth without attempting to breed him an heir. The old man has been most patient with me, and while he'd hoped his new wife would give him another son, it appears I am his only hope for the family name to continue."

Catlin regarded the two men. "So much talk of death, when men of your age and position should be eager for life and all the adventure it presents."

Lord Cranbourne frowned. "Aren't you the witch? How did you come to be here?"

A smirk crossed Griffin's handsome face as he leaned toward his friend. "She escaped with us from the gaol, and I beg for the sake of our friendship that you won't send her back to that pisshole."

The carriage halted and sent Griffin and Catlin forward, almost knocking their heads against each other.

Another coughing fit struck Lord Cranbourne. "You said—you could—cure me."

He leaned back. His face was still pale, but a bit of ruddy color had returned to his cheeks. He would be a handsome man if his health improved.

"If you trust me, 'twill be done," she promised.

When the carriage door opened, Griffin offered a hand to assist his friend.

The sick man rose, unsteady on his legs. He finally leaned against Griffin's shoulder to stand. "I trust you, witch, if your ministrations can be less painful than the bleeding and puking the surgeons have forced upon me." Lord Cranbourne carefully climbed out the carriage door, reaching for assistance from the coachman. He shuffled up the granite steps to the manor house, using Griffin for support and help.

Catlin sensed there was little time left to help this man. His talk of death might serve as a premonition of his fate.

She cursed the loss of her deerskin herbal pouch, which carried all the necessary items for creating the potions and elixirs her mother had taught her. Tonight she would be forced to improvise. She took a deep breath and tried to push away the dreadful memory of the last time she'd attempted a healing spell. Her life might depend upon her ability to save Lord Cranbourne.

And yet, she knew to do so would put her life, and the lives of her sisters, into greater jeopardy. The authorities would search her sister's home first for her, and Catlin only hoped they wouldn't seize her family and throw them into the goal.

But she couldn't deny this man the help he so desperately needed. Her vows demanded she help anyone who asked for her assistance regardless of concerns for her own, or her families fate.

There was also her own conscience to deal with, for her call to the wind to release her from the gaol had been the reason Lord Cranbourne was suffering from this most recent episode of lung fever.

As she watched the two men climb the steps, she recalled the words of her initiation.

Deny ye none who ask for help and healing. Harm not those who harm not thee. So as it is, so shall it be.

Demonstrating her powers could convince these men that she was in league with the devil and send her to the gallows. Yet to refuse the help Sir Griffin Reynolds requested would test her own vows as an elemental witch.

She could pretend to help with some simple herbal concoctions and a few phrases that might appear to work, if only long enough for her to return to her sister's house. But she sensed from what her *sylphs* had told her that Lord Cranbourne was fatally ill, and only with their assistance had he even regained consciousness. Despite her concerns about the consequences, she would do all she could to heal the man.

Catlin was grateful to enter the shelter of the cozy hall and escape the torrent of rain as they made their way from the carriage to the manor house. She wrapped Griffin's cloak more securely about herself to hide her torn clothing. The steward sniffed, and she understood that after only a few hours in the gaol, she carried its stench of filth and despair.

Sir Griffin Reynolds barked an order at the footman standing nearby.

"We must get Lord Cranbourne into his bed, and then be quick about gathering the things this woman needs. Obey her without question."

She stared in wonder as the men stumbled in their eagerness to follow his directions. Sir Griffin Reynolds had likely served his king well, because his tone left no doubt as to his ability to lead men.

The steward nodded in her direction, and she struggled to come up with items this household might have on hand.

"Can you bring me a silver bowl, hot water, some herbs?"

She gained courage when the man nodded.

"The apothecary has left us well stocked, due to milord's recent illness." He offered.

"Aye" she said. "Then bring me garlic, stinging nettle, butterbur, chamomile and some white lard. Also bring me a branch from a willow tree, a silver handled knife, some green cloth and I will need several porcelain cups and a candle scented with sage, if you have one."

She concentrated, trying to remember all the items necessary to cast a healing circle. Her mother had been a gifted healer, but Catlin had little experience, and after her last attempt, no confidence. Healing was rarely asked of one who could call upon the elemental spirit of the wind. She was a visionary and traveler between the spirit worlds.

As she climbed the stairs, following the group of men carrying Lord Cranbourne she peeked back behind her. The servant stood frozen to the spot, a look of fear sketched upon his face as he crossed himself. If only such simple gestures were adequate for such a task. She wanted to be patient, but the healing spell put upon the sick man was weak and would not hold long without more help from her.

"I believe Sir Reynolds told you to be quick about your business," she snapped. "I would regret telling him you have tarried as Lord Cranbourne expired upon this stairway."

The man bustled from the hallway toward the back of the house.

Her stomach rumbled and she regretted her failure to request a simple ploughman's lunch of bread, cheese, and cider. The casting of spells was hard work. She would need the assistance of her *sylphs* again tonight, and she found their management both a trial and a delight.

Catlin discovered a group of servants assembled outside a doorway near the top of the second floor. Griffin Reynolds issued orders for them to bring warm stones for Lord Cranbourne's bed in a loud, booming voice.

By the Lady, that man was an officious sort. A shiver of fear rolled down her spine. Men who expected obedience always resented women who refused to be easily managed or controlled.

An elderly servant stripped the drenched clothing from Lord Cranbourne. She averted her eyes and pretended to study the decoration of the room. A hot fire glowed in the fireplace, and she stepped forward to warm her hands.

"Hawes, see to it that stones are warmed for his bed, and bring me a change of clothing. I'm fairly soaked to the bone myself."

Sir Reynolds's voice paused, and she felt his dark eyes upon her back.

"See if you can find a dry gown for this lady. She's been caught with us in this wretched downpour tonight and is traveling without her baggage."

Catlin nodded her gratitude to Sir Reynolds. Lord Cranbourne was now settled into the huge cherry wood bedstead with several layers of covers pulled to his chin. He appeared to sleep, although his continued struggle to breathe and the ivory pallor of his skin indicated the spell was wearing off. Time was growing short, she realized, and a small flicker of light appeared near the edge of her vision to confirm her prediction.

He grows weaker each moment, a sweet voice, like birdsong filled her mind. *Ye must work quickly and ye need our help.*

Catlin nodded and proceeded to bargain. *What price?* She asked in the silent language of her *sylphs*.

A loud twittering filled her ears, and Catlin watched Sir Reynolds in terror. Of course, he wasn't an elemental empath, so he heard nothing. Still, the fear was always with her. Since the *sylphs* were so dear and real to her, she feared a *sophor*, a person who possessed no magic, might someday hear one.

Honey and cakes, came the answer. *Silk thread for ribbons, bright colors this time, not drab.* The bargaining continued.

An hour and a day in the Dream Time. And a kiss.

"A kiss!"

When Sir Reynolds turned his head and raised a well-formed eyebrow, she realized she had uttered the words aloud. Her cheeks warmed.

"'Twill be my pleasure, my lady, once Lord Cranbourne is well settled."

His impossibly beautiful mouth lifted at the corners and formed a delicious grin. Catlin resisted the urge to answer his jape. Assuming the role of bitter harpy would not serve her well on this night.

"I must beg your pardon, sir. I was considering the healing and thought perchance a kiss might help revive his lordship."

Sir Griffin Reynolds stood and strode in her direction. He towered above her as she drew herself to her full height to face him, bringing her eyes level with his thickly muscled chest. A glimmer of teasing sparkled in his midnight hued eyes.

"It is such a shame to waste the sweetness of a kiss upon one who cannot enjoy the pleasure of it, Catlin."

He pronounced her name slowly, like honey dripping from a pitcher.

The dampness made his ebony locks curl at their ends. He wore it stylishly long, and this night the stubble of a beard fringed the sharp contours of his face. He looked dark and dangerous, and another flare of something hot and arousing moved through her.

His gaze wandered from her eyes to her bosom. Once again a

flash of heat bestirred her.

She took a step back, fearful his hand might stretch out to squeeze and fondle her, like the Witch Hunter Bodwell had done. She needn't have worried. A parade of servants arrived carrying the items she'd requested from the steward. Sir Reynolds turned away from her to cross the room. He stood for a moment at a small door leading to another room adjoining the bedchamber.

"See that Miss Glyndwr has all she needs." His terse remark had a dazzling effect upon the servants, as they hurried to clear a space upon a huge wood table and set out the items she'd requested.

A young maid curtsied to her and indicated the steaming kettle of hot water would be hung on an iron bar stretched across the fireplace. Another maid set down a trencher of meats, cheese, bread, and several goblets. She placed a large pitcher nearby. Catlin sniffed and caught the yeasty scent of ale.

"Thank you for bringing the food." She gave the young woman a warm smile.

The maid tossed her head and looked in the direction of the door where Griffin had exited the bedchamber. Sensual hunger flickered in the young maid's eyes, and a prick of jealousy seized Catlin.

Lord Cranbourne's valet entered the room with a simple overdress folded across his arm. He gently handed it to her, coughed and bowed in her direction. "If you are not in need of me, I shall be waiting outside."

She struggled to remove the sleeves of her bodice before dropping the tattered garment to the floor. The fabric was ruined. She used a rough towel to dry herself and her linen shift as much as possible. She was donning the gown when she heard steps behind her. She whirled to see Sir Reynolds standing at the doorway, his clothing now exchanged for dry issue.

She yanked the overdress to cover her thin shift, aware the dampness made every soft curve of her body visible. She smoothed the luxurious silk fabric.

Griffin took several long steps toward her. "Does everything meet with your approval Catlin?" He pointed at the table.

She shivered at the way her name slid off his tongue, with an emphasis on the *cat*"

"Yes, thank you. I have the things I need."

"Perhaps it is just my own instincts and your manner of speech that tell me you are a well-bred lady, Catlin." His eyes crinkled at the corners as he smiled at her. A thin shiver of delight coursed through her. She swallowed, aware this man still posed a serious threat to her.

She imagined she could feel the touch of those cursed and beautiful lips as he leaned even closer. "I hope you don't mind if I call you Catlin." The deep tones of his voice, his clean scent and the heat rising from his skin mesmerized her.

Catlin jerked away, bustled to the table and assembled the items she'd requested. She couldn't be distracted when she needed all of her abilities to focus upon the task before her.

What of the kiss? A soft voice chirped in her ear.

"I don't know what you want," she blurted, before realizing again she had answered her tiny elemental *sylph's* out loud.

Sir Griffin Reynolds stood with his back to the fire, his dark breeches tucked into tall leather boots. His black silk doublet stretched across his broad chest and wide shoulders.

"I wish only to be of service, Catlin. You swore an oath to heal my oldest and dearest friend. Since he believes such a thing possible, I ask only that you do your best to ease his suffering."

He gave a deep sigh, and for the first time Catlin recognized he had let down his guard and the pretension of wit that had served to disguise his real concern for his friend.

"I can heal him, but I must be left alone in this chamber."

Griffin turned back to her, his eyes flaring bright with rage. "That will not be possible. I cannot abandon my friend to a stranger, even one as lovely as you."

The now familiar swirl of heat flowed through her. He thought she was lovely?

Then the reality of the situation became evident. If he remained in the room, not only would he witness her casting a spell, but he'd see her do so without her clothing.

"I can be trusted. You only have to remain outside the door until I finish."

Griffin shook his head. "I cannot leave him, for if something happens..."

A surge of sympathy flowed through her. Several small chirping voices echoed in her mind. *Let him stay, for you might need his help.*

Catlin frowned. What could the *sylphs* mean? She'd never heard of allowing a *sophor* to observe the casting of a spell. Still, she had to trust her elemental spirits. "If you remain, you must swear an oath to stand away and not interfere with anything you see taking shape in this room. You must allow me to do what I need to do." The logs crackled in the fireplace.

"Will you be consorting with demons?" He asked.

"Nay, not unless perchance you are one?" She quickly responded.

He raised an arched brow and shook his head. "I have been called worse, to be sure."

"You shall see things that might frighten you," she warned. "I only ask that you let me do what I must in order to heal your friend."

His gaze searched her face for a few moments, then he turned to the man stretched across the length of the bed.

"Do what you can and I shall not interfere, but I warn you—" He paused to stare intently into her eyes. "I do not frighten as easily as some men."

Catlin returned to her chore of arranging the items on the table, then snatched the trencher of food and broke off a large chunk of the hearty dark bread. She handed it to him, and he shrugged away her offer.

"The night has been long and grows longer even as we speak. If I need help I must count on you, and food gives us strength for what we must endure."

He took the bread and cheese she offered. "You make it sound as if we are marching into battle this night."

She chewed her food, broke off another bit of cheese and lifted her chin to stare into his midnight hued eyes. "Never having faced battle, I have no way of understanding what such a thing requires. But I have cast healing spells, and I understand all magic is unpredictable." She sighed deeply. "And there is a high price that always demands payment."

Griffin stared at her. "You speak so freely of magic, when to mention such a thing could send you to the gallows as a condemned woman?"

Catlin poured ale into two pewter goblets and held one out to him. "I tell you that it will be so and we can toast the magic that will heal your friend. You are a soldier who has proclaimed he has little fear of such things." She lifted her goblet.

The corners of Griffin's mouth formed a smile as he held his cup out to touch hers. "So shall we toast, for my words still ring true. Any man who sees the barbarism of war would never again fear the agents of magic."

She drank the ale, enjoying the robust taste. When she had drained it she set the goblet aside.

"Bar the door and then open a window, for once begun, we cannot stop." She regarded the sick man in the bed. "'Twill go foul for him if that happens."

Griffin moved quickly to do as she bid while she assembled the ingredients for her potion on the table.

She took the willow bough and began to sweep near the floor and then into the air. She whispered her incantation for banishing the ill-humored spirits from the room.

Next she lit the candle and the scent of sage suffused the room. She directed Griffin to extinguish all but the candle closest to Lord Cranbourne's bed.

Griffin moved the steaming kettle to a flat stone on the table. She began to sing the ancient words her mother had taught her while sprinkling healing herbs into the water.

Catlin allowed the mixture to steep as she picked up the silver-handled knife and prepared to cast her circle.

"Do not step out of the protected area once I designate the boundary. 'Twill not be safe." She lifted the hem of her gown, and pulled it over her head. Her shift followed and the fabric pooled near her feet on the floor. She shivered as the cool air touched her skin.

She wanted to lift her eyes to see Sir Reynolds's reaction to her nakedness, but embarrassment kept her focused upon the task before her. She sensed his heavy gaze upon her and it burned as she slowly slipped around the young nobleman's bed. Her cheeks warmed.

Using her knife, she carved the circle of protection in the air near the floor. She would need to guard the North, where the ornately carved headboard kept her from extending the full measure of the circle.

She spoke in the old language, taught to all women of her ancient family, renowned for their magic, conjuring and skill. She was descended from a line of strong, independent women marching back to the time of the Goddess.

The circle cast, she faced each direction to plead for help and healing. The music of her *sylphs* captured her as they joined the circle, their sweet, birdlike voices lifted in praise of all the earth, of the Great Mother, of her consort and each guardian and the gift of their element.

Approaching the man stretched upon the bed, Catlin laid one hand gently on his chest. His struggle to breathe had grown more intense, and the death rattle in his chest reverberated throughout the room. Each step was crucial, yet she worried her efforts might come too late. She turned to the table, and with a motion, directed Griffin to bring her the silver bowl. He hesitated for a moment, his gaze sweeping her from head to toe.

"Help me prop him up with these pillows," she said.

Griffin turned away from her. He nodded toward the open window. "The storm has subsided," he said, his voice rough with emotion.

She heard him take a deep breath. Was he growing uncomfortable with the magic? Or with her nakedness?

Catlin concentrated on the sick man lying before her and didn't look at the open window. "So it would seem, at least for the moment."

Once he was sitting up, she draped the green velvet cloth over Lord Cranbourne's head. She held the herbal mixture near his mouth and watched as the steam rose. In a few moments, his breath eased a bit, until his lungs seemed more capable of taking in air.

She handed the bowl to Griffin. "Bring me the cup of lard and the garlic and rosemary, please."

She sliced the garlic and poked pieces into the lard. She added crumbled pieces of dried rosemary and then kneaded the mixture into a paste. With practiced ease she spread the concoction across Lord Cranbourne's chest. Griffin wrinkled his nose, but still remained silent as he watched.

She wiped her hands upon a small towel and handed the cup back to Griffin. Now came the most difficult part of the spell. She had opened the way to his lungs, but this was only perfunctory. If she could not complete a healing, the phlegm would block his throat again and his breathing would be obstructed.

Catlin raised her hands over her head and began the ancient chant, repeating the words over and over again as she concentrated on directing the power of her *sylphs*.

Doethineb, lechyd, amddiffyn rhag. Great mother of us all, hear my plea.

The voices of her elemental spirits joined the song and she closed her eyes. Over and over again, building, building — raising the power until she opened her eyes.

Glimmers of crystal light blinked all around her as small winged creatures darted about her head. Her chanting grew more intense as the light shattered into rainbow hues, bathing the darkness in shadows of brilliant color.

She gently stroked Lord Cranbourne's cheek before leaning over him to carefully pry his mouth open. A cool breeze stirred the warm air in the room as she continued the chant.

The strength of the breeze intensified and circled the room. It sent her *sylphs* fluttering. Power built within her. She shivered as the spiral swept up from her feet, swirled up her legs, making the muscles hard and taunt and settled in the center of her being. She felt strong, nearly invincible when she held the power.

When the breeze lifted the bed curtains, she stood tall, threw back her head, closed her eyes and opened her mouth in silent invitation.

The wind entered her with a spasm of delight that engulfed her body like an impatient lover, eager to be joined with her. Her lungs expanded with power as she worked hard not to let the euphoria of the moment obscure her purpose. With one quick movement she was leaning above the man. He was icy cold and ashen. Touching his cheek again, she put her lips to his, whispering the spell into his mouth.

The glimmers of light circled Lord Cranbourne's head while his chest expanded. Finally a rush of air escaped from his lips. The wind whipped through the room again as the fireplace flickered and the flames danced. The breeze caressed her naked skin one more time before fleeing out the window into the night.

Griffin stood at her side, his muttered oath faint to her ears as she grieved the loss of the wind. She grasped the knife. As she stumbled, Griffin steadied her, and she leaned into his warmth and strength.

With precise measure, she performed the steps of widdershins to release the power of the circle. She discharged the guardians back to their posts while gratefully acknowledging their help. Gazing into the face of her patient, she was pleased to see color return to his skin and his breathing grow less labored with each breath. By all appearances, this healing had been successful. Lord Cranbourne would never again be cursed with lung fever.

She was relieved the outcome had been so much better than her last attempt at a healing spell.

Weakness overcame her, and Catlin stumbled against the bed. Only the silent support of Griffin's arms kept her standing upright. His thick erection poked at her bottom, and flame slid through her veins, the heat of desire finally pooling at the cleft between her legs. Fever seemed to grip her, despite the cool chill of the room upon her naked skin.

Griffin turned her gently, lifted her chin and gazed into her eyes. "I have never. . ." he whispered.

Their faces were mere inches from each other. The *sylphs* buzzed in her ears. *The kiss, the kiss. We want the kiss.*

Her *sylphs* were ever eager for even a small taste of pleasure. She had always disappointed the gloriously sensuous creatures in that respect. Not this time. She licked her lips.

Griffin didn't need much urging. He leaned forward and gently touched his lips to hers. She sighed. She'd grown accustomed to joining with the wind, but this was totally different. The hard muscles of Griffins arms pulled her closer. The heated length of his tarse rubbed against the cleft of her womanhood, and a throbbing need made her spread her legs in invitation. Her nipples hardened against the smooth fabric covering his chest, and the tingle of this kiss was so unanticipated that she could have collapsed with surprise.

The pressure of his lips increased, and emotions she didn't understand swept through her. She opened her mouth to welcome him. His tongue parted her lips, capturing her own tongue to parry and joust like two warriors entangled in a delicious battle.

His hand moved down to gently trace a pattern across the tender skin of her breast. His touch was light, reverent as he stroked her.

It was like standing before a blazing hearth fire, as heat flickered wherever his fingers touched her body. Her arms crept up to wrap around his neck. She wanted to hold him prisoner, to make this moment linger on for hours, yet she wanted more than a kiss. An aching need devoured her good sense, as she pushed away the flash of warning that she was dangerously close to being seduced by this handsome knight.

She moaned, and her response seemed to ignite Griffin, who leaned her back, almost touching the bed that held Lord Cranbourne, to deepen the kiss.

She wanted this moment to last forever. It was enchanting torture to feel his lips upon hers, his strong arms encircling her. Yet the soft edges of sleep began to make her limbs feel heavy, her head was filled with the gentle lullaby of her *sylphs* and knew she was slipping into Dream Time. Warmth suffused her body, and a sweet humming filled her ears.

No, she begged silently. Not yet. Let me enjoy more of this delightful kissing.

Before she could utter a word, the *sylphs* had dragged her into their world of delight. She couldn't resist, despite her desire for one more kiss, and for more of the sweet agony of being touched by Sir Griffin Reynolds.

Chapter Four

When I open my eyes, I discover I'm in the garden at Llithfaen. It was my mother's favorite place, with the scent of roses filling the air, the warm sun splashing the gentle paths and the cool water of the brook meandering through the flowers and herbs. I inhale the familiar fragrance and smile because I know we will soon be spending time together.

Sitting up, I stare around in confusion. Usually when I travel to Dream Time, she's here waiting for me. I turn in the direction of the stone keep, the place that in the real world of Cymru is our ancestral home. Was she still inside, distracted by her duties as the lady of the manor? Would I be forced to wait even in this magical between world? Was I going to be abandoned once more by her need to respond to a call to duty?

Fear always lurks at the edge of my thoughts when I encounter my mother in the Dream Time. Our time together here is always too short, the things I need to ask her overwhelming my ability to hang on to her for even a few moments longer. Of course, I could stay in the Dream Time with my mother forever, but then my body would slowly wither away and die. I would cease to exist on earth.

"You've done well my child." Her soft voice alerts me to her presence. "Healing that man was the honorable thing to do."

I turn, delighted to see my mother dressed in the soft blue gown that favors her sapphire blue eyes and golden hair. I have always regretted I do not favor my beautiful mother the way my younger sister Meaghan does. With my unremarkable, brown length of hair that hangs thickly down my back, I envy the blonde curls of my sibling. The only feature I inherited from her was my eye color. I take the rest of my coloring from my father's side of the family.

"I know it was the right thing to do," I finally reply, "yet he's done much to harm our kind, allowing the Witch Hunter to charge even those without powers." I raise my gaze to implore my mother. "Wouldn't his death prevent others who are innocent from suffering?"

My mother moves with a gentle, sweeping grace to stand beside me. "It is not for us to say how things will turn out for this man. Perhaps he shall change." She shrugs. "We cannot know what the fates have woven into the pattern of his life."

I want to believe it is possible for a sophor to change, yet I witnessed how the people of our own village turned on my mother. Because she was a healer, they blamed her when the plague began to decimate the people in our parish, and they demanded her torture and death because of the pestilence attacking them. In the end, their demands went unheeded, for it was the plague that took my mother from me. Ultimately, it was I who failed her.

I shudder at the ugly memories and work to push them away.

"You have faith that sophors can change, yet I see no proof of such things." I reach out to touch her, yet my hand passes through her, and the cold void recalls a familiar ache of loss deep within my soul.

"We do not judge, Catlin," she reminds me. "We serve the Queen of Heaven. She demands we offer our very lives in her service, if necessary. You must remember the creed."

Her lecture is constant, because I rebel at the idea of sacrificing myself for those sophors who attack my kind. They call us the servants of the Devil and accuse us of heinous rituals and ghastly crimes. Yet my mother has always implored me to look beyond their anger, to the fear and hopelessness that fills their lives. My great burden is to set aside my hostility and learn to care for sophors.

"I'm afraid for my sisters," I offer, in an attempt to sway her from delivering her favorite sermon. "We are all in danger."

"Aye," she says, still watching me carefully. "And who is responsible for creating the fear of magic that has seized the sophors of this village?"

I want to turn from her searching gaze, but find myself frozen in place beneath her scorching scrutiny. Even when she was alive, I could never escape my mother's interrogation. Now that she lives in the spirit world, her inquiries are even more intense and frightening. I can hide nothing from her.

My mouth is dry, filled with the vile taste of the truth that I must confess to her.

She leans forward, as if to study me more carefully. The words of denial die before reaching my lips.

I remember how I always tried to escape from my mother's judgment as a child, hiding in cupboards or running to the sanctuary of the woods near our home. I am now a grown woman, and I stand taller, throwing my shoulders back as I realize it is necessary to accept full responsibility for my actions.

"I escaped from the Witch Hunter by using magic. Doing so has cursed all of us. Once Lord Cranbourne fully recovers, my sisters shall be in danger because of my foolish actions."

Denial is pointless, for she knows these things as well as I do. Nothing escapes my mother's attention, even in this place.

She nods and I briefly hope she can change things, that my mistakes can somehow be reversed. She was a powerful witch on earth. Even here in the spirit world she might find a way to intervene.

"The Witch Hunter is a truly evil man who accuses innocent women and delights in their torture and execution." She paces across the worn stones of the garden path. "But there is another – a powerful dark lord who has been searching for you and your sisters. I sense danger, but I cannot discover who he is. I can only warn you to beware."

My heart skips a beat. Griffin Reynolds? Could he be the dangerous stranger who threatens my family?

She stops pacing and turns back to me. A gentle smile softens the curves of her face. "You must be brave my bychan cat, for it is up to you to discover the way and lead your sisters on a new path. It is no longer safe for our kind in Britain, for a great terror has seized the land. I have seen that your destiny shall lead you across the sea to the New World."

I nod, but how can find a way to travel across the great ocean that separates England from the new continent of America. And why I am given this mission instead of Aelwyd? As the eldest and most powerful witch in our family, shouldn't she be the one to find the path?

"I know we are not safe here, Mam, but how will I ever manage to find a way to the New World?"

My mother leans forward as if to touch my cheek gently with one delicate finger. "You must trust in the Goddess, Catlin. Pray to her, conduct the rituals, and watch for the signs from her. I cannot know all that will take place in the future, but I do know our family's destiny lies beyond the shores of Britain."

She drops her hand, but her gaze and her words hold me enthralled.

"You are the dreamer, Catlin, the one who can see beyond the boundaries of existence in the old world, a place that has grown to hate our kind. In the new land, there is opportunity and hope for a fresh beginning."

My mind tumbles with questions, but she steps away from me and into the shadows of the garden. My heart clenches and I ache with the familiar pangs of grief that make my chest tighten and my throat sore. Tears fill my eyes as I lose her once again. Each time we part is as painful and wrenching as the day I sat beside her, holding her hand as she slipped away from me to travel across the barrier of death and into the spirit world.

"Mam," I implore, "stay just a bit longer, please." Tears leak from my eyes and trail down my face. "I am so afraid."

She waves. "Trust in the Goddess, Catlin, and watch for the signs."

Then I am alone, and despite the beauty that surrounds me I want to be gone from this place. There is always suffering within the splendor — that is the painful lesson I've learned.

***

Catlin's body grew heavy as she returned from the Dream Time. She lay in a bed, covered by a rich, luxurious fabric. Opening her eyes she discovered Griffin Reynolds sleeping nearby. His hard-muscled, lean body seemed too large for the small wooden chair he was seated upon. The shadow of a beard darkened his cheeks and chin.

She wondered if he sat watch on her throughout the night. Then it occured to her that perhaps he was more guard than guardian. He'd witnessed her capture of the wind in order to complete her spell, and even though she was doing magical work to heal his friend, Griffin must be suspicious of her. He denied a belief in witchcraft, but that was before she healed Lord Cranbourne.

His eyes flickered open, and they were rimmed red and bloodshot. She felt a pang of guilt for keeping the man from his bed.

Catlin tried to swallow her fear. "Sir Reynolds, I bid you good morn."

Griffin smiled faintly at her words. "I bid you good day, Catlin, for you have slept through one day and into another."

He stood to stretch, and Catlin once again admired his long legs and the way the muscles of his chest pushed against the fabric of his doublet. He was a handsome man, and one who obviously possessed great physical prowess. He'd said he was a soldier, so the granite-like muscles she'd felt when he held her in his arms must be from long days in the saddle and the battles he'd fought against the King's enemies.

She blushed when she recalled their kiss before she slipped into Dream Time. He probably thought she was a woman of loose morals, and doubtless he hoped to continue the seduction she'd so artlessly interrupted.

"I humbly beg your forgiveness for sleeping overlong and keeping you from your own bed," Catlin said. "'Twas not necessary to stay by my side, for I could not have escaped even had I wanted to."

Griffin hovered closer, and for a brief, exciting moment, Catlin wondered if he were going to kiss her again. With such a virile man so close, she felt defenseless and seriously tempted, especially since she was still naked.

"I could not abandon you when I had no inkling if you were ill or simply exhausted from your—" He paused "—ministrations."

It was a safe word, and one that would not bring the condemnation of the household down upon her head nor lead her to the gallows.

Catlin attempted to sit up in the bed, but slid back down beneath the quilt when she discovered she might expose more of herself to Griffin Reynolds. "How is Lord Cranbourne? Has he regained consciousness?"

It was silly to try to hide her nakedness from the man, and she recalled the way his gaze had slid over her body last night, when she'd removed her gown to invoke the healing spell. It was a bit late to play the coy maiden. The heat on her cheeks made her want to slide completely beneath the covers.

The memory of his hands stroking her body created that glorious tingling in between her legs. Griffin Reynolds had somehow ignited a new hunger within her.

If Griffin noticed her discomfort, he didn't speak of it. Instead he walked to the window to open it a bit. Catlin leaned back into the down pillows and inhaled a deep breath of fresh air.

"If I hadn't seen him with my own eyes this morn, I would have called anyone who told me of his condition a bold liar." Griffin turned and smiled. "Lord Cranbourne appears to be hale and hearty. He has already consumed a meal that would challenge a starving hog, and now he's out walking." Griffin swallowed and bowed. "You have done a miraculous thing, my lady, and I shall never forget that you've given my friend back his life."

Catlin wanted to wave away his words, but the cost of demonstrating even this small amount of emotion shone in his eyes. He honored her with his praise.

"'Twas only what I am bound to do when help and healing is requested." She considered her next words carefully. "What did you tell him of the healing ritual?"

Griffin returned to her bedside and knelt, his face now level with her own. He took one of her hands in his and brought his lips to the knuckle. The gentle kiss made her skin prickle. "I told him a beautiful creature appeared as if by magic and promised me she would heal him. I described you as a young but wise woman, who knows the ways of potions and herbs. He knows nothing of what transpired last night, and I give you my word of honor, my lady. No one shall ever learn of it from me."

Catlin nodded as he rose from his knees and pulled himself up to his full height. She gave a deep sigh and leaned back into the pillows. She uttered a blessing to the Goddess that Griffin didn't plan to expose her to Lord Cranbourne.

"I had Cranbourne send for your eldest sister, for I know she must be concerned for your welfare." He waved toward a large oak wardrobe. "You'll find clothing that should fit you in there. I'll have hot water brought up to you for a bath, and I'm sure you would like something to eat." He grinned, and the deep dimples she'd admired the night before appeared at the corners of his exquisite mouth.

"If you are near as famished as I, then I offer you my deepest sympathy."

"My sister—"Panic seized her. "Will she be held prisoner here too?"

Griffin frowned and shook his head. "You are not held here against your will, Catlin. Lord Cranbourne has requested that you be his guest, in gratitude for your assistance."

"His guest? But for how long?"

"You are invited to stay here at Mabley Hall, as his guest, until you wish to leave, although I suppose it shall be with some caveats".

A tremor of fear whipped through her. "Caveats? Of what sort, might I be so bold to ask?"

Griffin shook his head and a deep crevasse appeared between his eyes as they clouded with a troubled look. "We need to protect you, my lady, and the other members of your family. There is already whispering in the parish about the way you disappeared from the gaol, and some people believe you used magic to escape."

"What of you, Sir Reynolds? How do you think I managed to escape?"

A slow, wicked grin lifted the corners of his mouth. "I have no doubt, Catlin, that you bewitched me with your beauty and convinced me you could help my friend. If it were truly magic that you used, I can only say I look forward to being put under your spell once again." He bowed elegantly.

Before she could ask any more questions, he disappeared out the door. Catlin nibbled upon her lower lip as his words tumbled about in her head. Few men would mention the word magic as a jest, so she did not know what to make of his remarks.

He was right about one thing, though. She and her family were in danger. Catlin needed to find a way to escape from Shrewsbury, and England. Her mother had urged her to watch for the signs.

Deep within her heart a small flame flared to life, and Catlin hoped Sir Griffin Reynolds might be one those signs. Yet as much as she wished he could be a part of some scheme to help her escape to the New World, she recalled the other part of her mother's conversation.

Somewhere, there was a man who represented a clear and terrifying danger to her family.

Catlin must discover what role Sir Griffin Reynolds might play as she searched for answers to this perplexing puzzle.

Chapter Five

Catlin bathed, enjoyed a hearty meal with some strong, bracing coffee and finally felt refreshed and better prepared to cope with her formal meeting with Lord Cranbourne.

A servant guided her down the huge stone staircase. Catlin had been too distracted by her need to attend to the young heir of the Earl of Shrewsbury the previous night to notice her surroundings. Now she took a moment to admire the beautiful architecture, tapestries, and paintings as she descended into the main entry of the house.

She recalled Aelwyd lecturing Catlin and her sisters about the local aristocrats. Mabley Hall had been the manor house since the time of the Crusades, when the first Earl of Shrewsbury had earned the gratitude of the King for his service against the infidels. The property he'd been awarded had been rich and the small stone keep of the original hall was enlarged through the years of successive Earls. Now the huge manor house spread across the land like a high-born and well-endowed lady stretched upon a luxurious chaise in her solarium. The structure was dignified, admirably situated and massively imposing.

A maid ushered Catlin into a large room paneled in oak and lined with walls of shelving filled with leather-bound books. A welcoming fire blazed in the corner fireplace, and both Sir Reynolds and Lord Cranbourne rose.

Instead of skin with a deathly white pallor, Lord Cranbourne possessed a warm and healthy glow. The nobleman moved with a controlled grace as he approached her. He bowed before her, and a sparkle of delight shone in his gentle brown eyes when he stood again.

Catlin had never seen such a transformation in any of the people her mother had healed. Could she have performed such a miracle?

"I understand you are the angel I must thank for bringing me back from the brink of death and restoring my health." Lord Cranbourne indicated a chair with a huge carved back. "Please be seated, for I wish to learn more about you."

Catlin sent a quizzical look in Griffin's direction. He stood by the fire watching her, his face fixed in an expression of cool detachment. He'd promised he wouldn't divulge her secret, yet could she truly trust him?

"I wish to introduce you to the Honourable Miss Catlin Glyndwr, my lord." Griffin said.

She curtsied and nervously smoothed the wrinkles from her borrowed dark blue gown before she sat down, aware of the careful scrutiny of both men. She licked her lips, hoping to prolong the moment before the interrogation she knew was forthcoming.

"May I offer you some coffee?" Lord Cranbourne stood next to a table that held a huge silver tray and a white porcelain coffee set decorated with a pattern of blue and white flowers.

"No, thank you," Catlin said. Silence ensued as Lord Cranbourne returned to his seat behind the huge desk separating them.

"I heard you were exhausted from your efforts to heal me the other night." Lord Cranbourne tapped his fingers on the desk nervously "I apologize for all that transpired before we ..." His voice stopped as he frowned. Finally he shrugged his shoulders. "I have no memory of what happened, other then I left for the Shrewsbury Gaol to interrogate a woman accused of witchcraft." He lowered his gaze to study his hands. "I knew I was ill, but I thought I would be finished quickly with that nasty piece of business and arrive home in time to meet Sir Reynolds."

Catlin twined her fingers together to stop them from trembling. She wandered into dangerous territory, but she needed to know this man's true feelings about her kind. "So, are you especially interested in the prosecution of witches?"

Lord Cranbourne's head snapped up and his mouth went hard as his eyes devoured her.

A tremor of forewarning coursed through her.

"I believe more accusations are made then can actually be proven." His scrutiny never wavered. "But I have a responsibility to ensure the parish is protected, and this particular witch was accused of malfeasance."

"And you allow the witch hunter, Bodwell, persuade you to condemn women accused of practicing witchcraft, even when the evidence is scant?"

Griffin Reynolds coughed, and Catlin wondered if he meant it as a warning. It didn't matter, because this was her only opportunity to ascertain how Lord Cranbourne would proceed should he discover her secret.

"I serve the law, and it is my duty to determine if a woman has committed blasphemy or done harm to another. If she is accused of magic, then it is my job to discover the source of her powers and protect the people of Shrewsbury." He looked away.

"Have any so accused ever been found innocent?" Her question hung in the air, like a bad odor that offended the noses of the perfumed gentry.

Lord Cranbourne shook his head. "I'm afraid that is the fatal flaw in our system, that no woman seems capable of proving her innocence once charged." He stood and moved next to Griffin near the fire. "To be honest, 'tis one of the most troubling aspects of this whole ugly business. I cannot know who is innocent and who is guilty." He shrugged. "That is out of my hands and for the Assizes to consider."

A surge of anger sizzled through Catlin. "And so the innocent must die, too? For if you cannot find proof to hang all the witches, you must at least condemn all the women accused of witchcraft?" A hard edge vibrated in her voice, but she didn't care. The injustice of the legal system infuriated her.

Griffin Reynolds shifted from his place near the fire, placed his hands on the desk, and leaned forward. The thick, heavy muscles of his arms bulged beneath his linen shirt, and familiar warmth swirled through her. Damn the man for making her react this way.

"This debate is for another time and place. Today we must decide upon your fate, Miss Glyndwr." Griffin said.

Her mouth went dry at his implication. Her fate? Were they planning to return her to the gaol? She shuddered at the memory of that dank, suffocating place filled with misery and misfortune. Sir Reynolds had made a vow to keep her use of magic a secret. Had that been merely a ploy to gain her cooperation?

"I wish to return to my sister's home." She rose shakily to her feet, close to losing control of her emotions as fear washed over her.

"I'm afraid that would not be safe." Lord Cranbourne said.

She shook her head. "But how can I. . ."

Before she could finish her protest, a knock sounded at the door.

"Yes!" Lord Cranbourne barked.

A maid opened the door and peeked in, she smiled weakly as she tiptoed into the room.

"The Honourable Missus Aelwyd ap Pryd is here to see you, milord." Her voice squeaked. When there was no response, the woman bobbed a curtsy in the gentlemen's direction before opening the door wider to disclose a woman standing on the threshold.

Relief swirled through Catlin at the sight of her eldest sister. Aelwyd was a powerful fire adept, who always seemed capable of handling even the most challenging situation. Catlin rushed forward to greet her sister.

"Aelwyd," she paused at the storm clouds raging in her sister's green eyes. "This is Lord Cranbourne and Sir Griffin Reynolds—".

"Gentlemen," Catlin pointed at her sister. "This is Aelwyd , my eldest sister.

The men stood transfixed for a moment, until Lord Cranbourne finally cleared his throat. "If I have died and face an ancient goddess, I can only hope she will be kind enough to forgive my paltry offerings in her honor." He made a spectacular bow in her direction.

When Aelwyd entered the room, a gentle golden light, spread out behind her and the soft scent of cinnamon filled the air. Catlin hid her grin as the two men succumbed to the simple glamour Aelwyd cast. It was clear her more powerful sister wielded her magic easily.

"I understand I need to express my gratitude to both of you for rescuing my sister and sheltering her from the storm last night."

While her voice was of a sweet, even timbre, anger flashed in her jade eyes. The gentlemen under her scrutiny squirmed.

"Of course, if it were not for her own foolishness she would never have been in such a predicament in the first place."

Catlin frowned at her older sister.

"But, I am most grateful to both of you for your assistance. A woman battling the elements on such a stormy night could have, well..." She batted her thick black eyelashes. "Things could have ended very badly for Catlin."

***

All of Griffin's senses reacted to the presence of the Glyndwr sisters. The pull of their exotic and enticing sensuality confused him. He rarely had a need, or a desire, to pursue a woman. He never had to because they eagerly pursued him.

Catlin turned and smiled. The red-haired beauty with dark green cat's eyes that tilted just a bit at the corners considered him for a moment, before glancing in Catlin's direction. Her lips pursed with an expression of concern. "How much time have you spent with my sister?"

Griffin shrugged with what he hoped was an air of nonchalance. "We only met again recently the other night, when she was —." He paused for a moment. "In need of some assistance." He glanced at Morgan.

"I watched her perform her tasks in order to heal my friend. After that she fell into an exhausted sleep."

Aelwyd ap Pryd narrowed her eyes at her sister before turning her attention back to him. "How long did she sleep?"

Griffin relaxed. Of course the older sister would be concerned about Catlin's health. After all, being arrested was a difficult experience for anyone, and even more so for a lady of quality.

"She slept for a full day and then a bit, Missus, but I sat with her through the entire time to keep watch."

Aelwyd's thin smile disappeared. "Did she seem overly disturbed in her sleep?"

Griffin pondered her question, for it seemed odd. Especially considering the strange and bewildering ritual he'd watched Catlin perform before she collapsed in his arms. And then there was that kiss. That sweet, beguiling kiss they'd exchanged that promised so much sensual heat in just the brief touching of their lips.

He recalled Catlin's nude body as she moved about the chamber performing her odd rituals to heal Morgan, and a shocking hunger seized him. He was not a man captivated by a woman, even a woman as beautiful and delightful as Catlin Glyndwr.

If he were a superstitious man, he'd imagine himself under some sort of spell. As a man who appreciated the nuances of sensuality, he ascribed his desire for the russet-haired beauty to his long sabbatical without satisfying his carnal needs. He needed to find himself a willing female to appease this hunger.

"She was uneasy," Griffin finally answered, "but the circumstances prior to coming to Mabley Hall were enough to keep even the strongest person troubled with nightmares for a fortnight." He turned apprehensively to Morgan, wondering if he recalled any of the events that took place at the Shrewsbury Gaol. "Your sister is a remarkable woman, I grant you that."

Aelwyd tilted her head before responding. "We are not like other women, Sir Reynolds, and that is both our allure and our curse."

She twisted away to whisper with Catlin.

Morgan watched the two women with a look of pure enchantment upon his face. "Have you ever seen such a thing, Griffin?"

Griffin watched the women from across the room. "Two beautiful ladies chirping gossip at each other like birds? 'Tis a most familiar sight at court." Irritation with Aelwyd ap Pryd and her secretive ways grew within him.

Morgan frowned at him. "Not that, you horse's arse, don't you see how unique these two women are?" Griffin frowned. This was an unusual reaction from a man who'd spent years avoiding the machinations of a father intent upon making a good marriage match. If he'd been asked any other day about his friend's interest in females, Griffin would have laughed.

Yet here stood Morgan gaping at two women like a besotted schoolboy. Especially when his soft gray eyes beheld the vivacious Aelwyd ap Pryd.

His friend's fascination with the women disturbed Griffin, and he vowed to watch these Glyndwr sisters very carefully.

Chapter Six

Catlin settled upon the window seat as Aelwyd poured several bowls of coffee for the small group gathered in Lord Cranbourne's study.

Frowning at her younger sister, she remained silent as she added several spoonfuls of sugar to Lord Cranbourne's coffee.

"I need to discuss the terms of my sister's release, Lord Cranbourne." She said.

Morgan paused. The cup stood frozen in the space between the table and his lips. "Release? I don't think you understand—"

"I'm aware Catlin's behavior has been reckless, but you must know she was falsely accused." Aelwyd indicated her sister with a nod of her head. "She was simply protecting herself from being ravished by that blackguard who calls himself a Witch Hunter." She sniffed. "Tit hunter is more of an apt description if you ask me."

Griffin nearly snorted as he watched Lord Cranbourne's head jerk up at her comment.

"I'm sure we can, well, what I mean to say is, um, without your sister's assistance last night my life would be. . . "

"I'm sure she was helpful in her own way." Aelwyd raised a delicately arched eyebrow.

Griffin grinned into his porcelain bowl as his friend attempted to maintain his composure. Few people were bold enough to interrupt the heir to Mabley Hall. Seeing these Glyndwr women behave in such an honest and forthright manner amused him, a welcome change from the court of Charles II, where he'd grown weary of all the lies, subterfuge, and treachery.

"Catlin tends to speak and act before she has completely thought through all of the consequences."

"Aelwyd! It's mean-spirited to talk about me as if I'm not in the room." Catlin's petticoats rustled as she crossed the room. "And if you'll stop flapping your tongue long enough to allow Lord Cranbourne to finish a sentence, perhaps you could avoid making the same mistake you ascribe to me."

Aelwyd rose a bit in her chair. She glowered at the two men, then appeared to reconsider and sat back down again. "Of course, how rude of me." She glared up at Catlin. "And how blessed I am to have a sister always eager to point out my shortcomings."

Morgan cleared his throat several times and his face shaded a tinge red. "Well, as I was saying, had it not been for Miss Glyndwr's offering her services as a healer, I believe this house would be in a state of mourning today."

Aelwyd's dark green eyes widened and her lips opened to form an O. She stood and leaned forward to whisper into her sister's ear again. Despite her effort at subterfuge, Griffin's highly trained ears picked up the conversation.

"Mam warned you," Aelwyd hissed. "You were never to perform another healing without all of us being present." She frowned, and the crease between her eyes grew deeper. "It was far too dangerous, and you could have, well, it might have . . ." She didn't finish the sentence, but the bleak look she threw in Morgan's direction belied the dire consequences.

"But everything turned out fine," Catlin assured her. "Lord Cranbourne is in excellent health today, despite all the doomsday predictions of what could have happened." She gave her sister a peeved look. "Quit fussing about all that and let's go home."

"That would be a dangerous mistake," Griffin interjected. The two women watched him, waiting for him to continue like sleek, shiny ravens perched upon a limb studying their quarry. Feeling their eyes upon him, the hair on the back of his neck prickled a warning. A shudder of alarm crept up his spine. Why did these women bestir him so much?

"Pray tell us why my sister would be in danger were she to return home with me?" Aelwyd asked.

Griffin stood up. "There is more to this tale then a healing."

He took a few steps to face Catlin. Her complexion had blanched. Did she think he intended to betray her to Morgan? Despite his vow to keep her actions a secret, he sensed she still didn't trust him.

He turned back to face Aelwyd. "There was a disturbance in the gaol last night. Doors were somehow opened and a powerful wind swept through the lower cells."

He watched Aelwyd's face carefully for a reaction and was surprised that she displayed only mild interest.

"The rushes and candles were doused, there was a terrible howling sound and it greatly disturbed the inmates." He added.

Morgan leaned forward. His friend had confided he had no memory of anything that happened before waking up feeling healthy and refreshed this morning. If Morgan had truly forgotten what had transpired at the gaol, perhaps it could be used in Catlin's favor.

Griffin motioned toward Morgan. "Lord Cranbourne has been suffering from an illness, and when the dust and filth was disturbed, he was overcome by an attack of lung fever."

"That's why I'm so grateful to Miss Glyndwr, because if not for her sudden appearance—" Morgan frowned. "Although I confess, I cannot seem to remember exactly how she happened to appear in the coach with us."

"I was waiting for Sir Griffin." Catlin moved to Griffin's side and entwined her arm with his.

The intimate gesture pushed the blood from his brain to his nether regions, and a rush of intense heat suffused his body.

"He intervened when that horrid man, Bodwell, attacked me." She looked up at Griffin, a blissful smile painted on her lips. "He chased my attacker away, and we discovered we had mutual acquaintances in London. He told me to wait in the carriage while he fetched you for dinner, and then he would take me home on the way to the Inn."

The easy way Catlin Glyndwr composed the tale astonished Griffin, yet he admired her quick thinking at the same time.

"It was most fortunate that when she observed your condition, she felt she could be of some assistance," Griffin added.

"Of course, and bloody right she was." Crimson color rose from Morgan's neck to turn his entire face red. "I apologize, ladies."

Aelwyd tapped her fingers on the table as she watched Catlin and Griffin.

"I'm pleased my sister could be of service to you, my lord, but now it's time she returned home to her family."

"No!" Catlin objected.

Griffin stared at Catlin, amazed at her outburst. While they shared the same sentiment, he wondered at her motives for suddenly protesting her release, especially since she'd been so concerned about being able to leave earlier in the day.

"You have been invited to stay here at Mabley Hall, but if you feel you must, you may leave." Morgan blushed deeper as Aelwyd stood and put her hands on her hips.

Before she could speak, Morgan held up one hand to silence her. "I would like to extend my hospitality to all of your family members, in gratitude for Miss Glyndwr's assistance last night."

Aelwyd appeared to relax, and a beneficent smile graced her face. "That is most kind of you Lord Cranbourne, but we could not possibly—"

"Offend you by refusing," Catlin interjected. "I think I should stay here for a few days, just to make sure you are fully recovered."

The heat of the glare from her older sister could have blistered skin with its intensity. "Perhaps we need to discuss this privately, Catlin."

Catlin still had her arm linked with Griffin's. When she attempted to pull away from him he put his hand over hers. She smiled at him.

His reaction was quick and unmistakable, as his blood heated and his cock grew hard. He tried to shift his attention away from his carnal needs "I think that's a sensible suggestion." He allowed his grasp upon her arm to relax, hoping he might be able to step away from her before she became aware of his state of arousal.

"And my dear—" He gazed down at her with what he hoped was a rapt expression "It will allow me to become better acquainted with your family."

His words hung in the air. Catlin's sister surveyed him with an expression that transformed from suspicion, to annoyance, to outright curiosity. He'd intrigued her, and that was certainly his purpose. He'd do anything to gain a few more hours with the delectable Catlin. But he slid a few inches from the enticing warmth of her skin and the fragrant scent of her hair. At the moment, she was too much of a temptation.

After what seemed like an eternity, Aelwyd nodded. "I believe I will remain here for a day or so, Sir Reynolds, and rest assured, I'm extremely curious about your relationship with my sister."

He winced. A clear image of a moth dancing around a dangerous flame popped into his head. It was clear that Aelwyd ap Pryd intended to guard and protect her younger sister.

Griffin had no doubt the woman could be a relentless and unforgiving enemy if provoked.

Catlin needed to steal away from her sister and find Griffin, yet she couldn't seem to get even a moment of peace and quiet solitude, much less privacy. The beautiful suite of rooms they were lead to couldn't even fully distract Aelwyd.

While her sister marveled at the rich ruby colored silk and velvet fabrics draped at the windows and surrounding the bed, she also watched Catlin carefully. Catlin trembled, waiting for the questions she knew were coming and wishing she could avoid the inevitable angry confrontation.

"Just how well acquainted are you with Sir Griffin Reynolds?"

Catlin's cheeks heated.

"We met the night I was arrested, when I was being questioned in the gaol." She took a deep breath. "I wasn't waiting for him in the coach, as you well know." She spoke slowly, pausing dramatically to buy some additional time. "I was facing serious charges and when he came to speak with Lord Cranbourne, he seemed . . . sympathetic."

Aelwyd snorted. "I imagine he was especially so after you cast a glamour to entice him."

Catlin shook her head vehemently. "I couldn't, at least not when we were at the gaol. I tried, but it was much later, when we were in the carriage with Lord Cranbourne." She twisted her hands as she paced across the room. "I discovered he's unusually strong and resistant to spells."

Aelwyd laughed harshly, but the sound clearly held no mirth. "Resistant? By the Goddess, I find he is just as easy to fool as all *sophor* men."

Jealousy flashed through Catlin. Of course, as a fire adept, Aelwyd's magic was so intense when focused that few *sophors* could resist her. In fact, she was one of the strongest practitioners of the arcane arts in the land. Few Mages possessed the ability to resist her will when she chose to impose it.

Catlin had only been initiated as an air adept for three years, and the weakness of her powers compared to those of her older sister incensed her.

"So if he resists you so strongly, how did you make him agree to corroborate your lies?" Aelwyd's voice dripped with incredulity, like wax from a sputtering candle.

Catlin shook her head. "I'm not sure why he didn't tell Lord Cranbourne the truth today." She licked her lips. "But he was in the room last night when I cast the spell to heal his friend."

Her sister stared at her, an expression of shock and horror widened Aelwyd's eyes and silenced her for several long minutes.

"You let him watch you?" Aelwyd spat at her like a furious house cat. "What kind of silly dunderhead are you?"

Catlin couldn't find the words to defend her actions. To allow a *sophor* to witness a magical rite was one of the most serious offenses a witch could commit.

"Why didn't you use a sleeping spell upon him?" Aelwyd marched back and forth across the smooth wood floor, stumbling upon the edge of one of the Persian carpets.

"I told you, he resisted the spell I tried to put upon him, and I had already asked the *sylphs* for their assistance to escape from the gaol."

To remind her sister of what had transpired in the confines of the jail was a mistake. Aelwyd's wrath spun out to the far corners of the room. "Can I assume that you called upon your elemental spirits to help you perform your escape?"

When Catlin nodded, Aelwyd bowed her head.

"We shall all be strung up at the gallows for practicing witchcraft!" The doom in her sister's voice made Catlin shiver.

'Twas Catlin's greatest fear, yet she trusted Griffin Reynolds more then any man she'd ever known despite their brief acquaintance.

"Sir Reynolds gave me his word not to divulge my secret, and so far he has kept that promise."

"The word of a Cavalier," Aelwyd spat as she rolled her eyes. "You've hardly chosen the most trustworthy of allies. The King sets a standard for his men with a lewd and debauched court that values the ways of a libertine more than that of chivalry." She paused, one long fingernail tapping her temple. "Yet he lied for you, and to someone who appears to be an old and treasured friend." She folded her arms across her chest. "Are you sure you didn't cast even a tiny spell upon him?"

Catlin shifted uncomfortably. Should she divulge her loveliest secret?

"Well, there was the kiss." She tried to mask the words with an innocent smile. "It was just a little one."

Aelwyd stared at her, and after a few moments, laughed. "My dear *bychan* cat, you have no idea whatsoever what you have done, do you?"

Catlin resented being referred to as a little cat, even if it was a family endearment. She shook her head. The kiss had excited her in ways she wished she could discuss with her older sister, but now was not an appropriate time to query her about men and carnality.

And why was Aelwyd laughing at her?

Chapter Seven

griffin leaned back in his chair and took a large gulp of claret. He'd discarded coffee in favor of stronger spirits once the Glyndwr sisters were escorted to their suite of rooms.

Morgan joined him, taking a hefty swig from his own goblet. "Extraordinary," he said.

"They are unique creatures, I vow." Griffin took another drink, draining the goblet. "'Tis a good thing they're not in London, for the King would be wooing both ladies to his bed. And likely at the same time."

Morgan laughed, and the sound delighted Griffin. Seeing the Viscount returned to full and robust health had been worth any price, even if magic had been involved. Although in the light of day, Griffin would not credit it. Spells, witchcraft and demons were ancient wives' tales, and in this modern day, when even the King accepted the validity of the natural sciences, it was not an acceptable explanation for what had happened last night.

Yet, Griffin could not discount what he'd seen with his own eyes. He'd watched in awe as Catlin Glyndwr did something to Morgan. And this morning, the miraculous recovery of his best friend convinced him that at the very least, she was a gifted and talented healer. In fact, perhaps the herbs she'd used to help Morgan breathe easier had also had some effect upon Griffin's own interpretation of the events that had taken place.

The one thing not lost to him was the image of Catlin when she'd dropped her gown to the floor. She'd been too distracted to see the evidence of his intense arousal, for which he was grateful, because the memory made his cock grow harder even now.

"I believe you have an eye for the dark-haired beauty with eyes like the summer sky." Morgan grinned as he stood to refill his goblet. He appeared to waver for a moment, and Griffin jumped to his feet quickly to offer additional support.

Morgan waved his arm away and laughed. "These strong spirits are affecting me overmuch, and I must remember that despite my rather astonishing recovery, I have been a man closer to the grave then I should like to recall."

Griffin nodded. "I think you should rest." He added with a hint of mischief, "I vow you shall require all your strength to contend with those beguiling sisters this evening."

Morgan straightened his shoulders and pulled on his heavily embroidered doublet. "I cannot decide which one of them is the more captivating." He shot a mischievous grin at Griffin. "The stunning and tumultuous Catlin or the fiery, outspoken Aelwyd?"

Griffin laughed at his friend's predicament. "And Catlin tells me there are two younger sisters at home."

Morgan winked. "Perhaps I should have them escorted here, so we can bask in their beauty, too. If they are even near as lovely as their older sisters, it would make for a most enjoyable evening."

Griffin shook his head. "Perhaps you should give yourself another few days to rest before you decide to accumulate a harem."

Morgan nodded, "I find I must agree with you, Griffin. If I am to be a suitable host to these lovelies, I shall need to get some rest today."

The two men proceeded out of the study and down the hall to the staircase. "I believe I shall retire to my own chamber, Cranbourne. I slept poorly in the chair next to Catlin's bed last night."

Morgan gave his friend a poke. "At least you were with her. I envy you that my friend."

Griffin's memory flashed back to the sight of a naked Catlin sleeping inches away from him. An uncomfortable rush of blood tightened his groin.

They climbed the stairs, each teasing the other as to his appearance, reputation, and sexual exploits. Their high good humor was evident, and the upstairs maids giggled as the two men passed by them, the bolder woman offering a ribald remark.

"Ye gents need a bit o' help with gettin' yer breeches off?"

Morgan gave a deep sigh. "There are so many lusty delights to savor, Griffin. How shall I ever be able to choose?"

Sir Griffin Reynolds stood at his own chamber door and grinned. "A starving man is always overwhelmed at his first sight of the banquet table, Cranbourne. You must first learn to enjoy the variety of tastes and refrain from gorging yourself."

Morgan gave a resigned sigh. His gaze flickered over the maid with the full, round bosom. She tossed her hair.

With obvious reluctance, he proceeded into his chamber, but before closing his door, he bowed in Griffin's direction and grinned "I'm most grateful to Miss Glyndwr, for I am discovering that life is good, my friend. Very good indeed!"

***

Griffin lurked in the dark shadows of the upstairs gallery, his senses as alert as if he were out on the hunt stalking his prey. Which, in a manner of speaking, was true.

The door he so carefully watched opened and a footman exited carrying an empty copper pail. A giggling maid followed the man, and the door slammed shut.

He'd wait as long as need be, for he would not be deterred from his quest to seek Catlin Glyndwr out, corner her, and get some answers to the multitude of questions tossing about in his head.

She finally marched out the door. Her mouth was twisted into a peeved expression as she brushed a lock of hair from her face. "I'll arrange for some of your things to be brought from the house as soon as possible, stop making such a fuss." She said.

As a torrent of intense objections erupted from Aelwyd, Catlin slammed the door. She leaned against it and rubbed a hand across her forehead. "God's tears but she can be a *daminol* woman when she wants her own way," she muttered.

Griffin smiled at Catlin's sour tone. She stepped away from the door to head down the murky, candlelit hallway towards him. There were few windows in this part of the house, where the oldest section of the original stone keep connected to the newer construction, and the shadowy darkness hid him well.

As Catlin scurried toward the staircase, he snaked out an arm to capture her about the waist. His other hand quickly covered her mouth to silence a scream as he pulled her behind a wall of heavy tapestries and into a small hidden alcove. "I beg your pardon, milady, but I felt we needed to speak in private," he whispered.

Her blue eyes took on a dark, stormy hue, and her body stiffened against him. Still, he was enjoying the sensation of her soft breasts snuggled against him too much to release her.

Griffin removed the hand covering her mouth.

"I will not attempt to escape from you, Sir Reynolds, so you can release me." Her voice contained an icy primness that made him laugh quietly.

"We have no need to stand on formalities, Catlin, for I believe we are well acquainted after the experiences we shared last night." He inhaled the womanly scent that rose from her warm, soft skin, and the familiar wave of desire for her washed through him. "Please call me Griffin."

Fear flickered in her eyes as she looked up at him. Was she afraid he'd expose her to Cranbourne? "I'm your friend, Catlin, and you need not be concerned that I shall divulge your secret to anyone." He gently stroked an ebony curl that had escaped her attempts to confine it. The glossy length wrapped itself around his finger.

She was all silk and softness and a lightning flash of desire reminded him of the many weeks he'd gone without female companionship. He prided himself on his ability to control his carnal appetites.

Being in service to King Charles offered ample opportunities to indulge in the sensual activities of a lascivious court. Until recently, he'd always been most happy to do so. But he'd tired of the games the women played, of the lies and social climbing. He was realizing he wanted something more. Yet he didn't exactly understand what it was he craved.

Catlin licked her lips as she stared up at him, igniting a flame that burned hot and slow within him. His cock ached to plunder the treasure between her soft, shapely thighs.

The urge to kiss her again overwhelmed him. He finally released her to take a deep breath, step away, and regain some control.

"I do not think Lord Cranbourne realizes I'm the same woman who was accused of witchcraft, arrested, and thrown into the gaol." She looked away from him, nibbling on her lower lip.

Griffin took another small step away from her to escape her intoxicating scent of herbs and flowers. Magic wasn't such a far-fetched notion when one was in the presence of Catlin Glyndwr. She certainly seemed to be bewitching him.

"Does that sort of confusion usually happen, after, well, you know . . . ?"

Catlin shook her head. "I'm not sure, because I've never cast a healing spell by myself, and I have certainly never done so in the presence of a *sophor*."

"What, pray tell, is a *sophor*?" He inquired.

A rosy blush flowed down her cheeks to the plush expanse of her full bosom, deepening from pink to scarlet as it traveled.

"It's just a word we use, to describe, well. . ." She blinked and gave him a tiny smile. "Some kinds of people."

The word struck Griffin as more humorous then insulting. "Do you mean those who have no imagination?"

Catlin brightened. "Yes, that's it." Her gaze dropped to the floor. "I mean those who are not like us."

"Witches?"

She looked up at him, and her eyes were wide, the pupils dilated to expose little of the white space surrounding the irises. "You know the penalty for that accusation and it is doubtful I could escape again if I'm imprisoned."

Griffin raised his hands to reassure her. "Have no fear, my lady. I swore to protect you and I would never break a sacred promise made to a friend."

She nodded and her shoulders relaxed as she shot him a tremulous smile. "I must trust you with my life, Sir Reynolds, because you witnessed my spell casting last night." Her voice softened. "I believe I have the ability to judge an honest person, and if I might be so bold, you appear to be a trustworthy man."

Griffin had no intention of betraying the trust Catlin Glyndwr placed in him. "You needn't worry, Catlin, your secret is safe with me." He took a step closer. "You offered to heal my friend, and I certainly cannot argue with the results, whatever means you used to achieve it."

She touched his arm gently, but her soft blue eyes still reflected her anxiety. "If he recalls what transpired before we brought him here last night, I fear he'll return me to the prison."

Heat surged through Griffin at her touch, as if he'd suddenly been settled before a blazing fire. Her scent filled his nostrils, and he marveled at the intense arousal he experienced whenever she was near. If this truly was magic, it should be desired and explored, not feared.

Catlin put her hands upon his chest and lifted her gaze to meet his, a tiny, mischievous smile playing upon her lips. "What shall I be expected to offer in payment for your silence, Sir Griffin?"

Griffin wrapped his arms around her, bringing their bodies closer together. He was now fully aroused. Could she feel the evidence of his desire through her gown and petticoats?

"I believe the same price you demanded from me last night will suffice."

Catlin started to protest and tried to pull from his embrace. Griffin leaned his head down, his mouth covering hers in a gentle trace of a kiss that soon deepened. His lips and tongue teased her mouth lightly, and she quickly responded. He grew bolder, pushing his tongue between her lips to explore the tender, secret delights within her mouth.

A light chirping sound echoed in the tiny space and Griffin opened his eyes, half expecting to see a bird in the room with them. Catlin moaned softly. He closed his eyes again, relishing the way she tasted of sweetness and spice. Her hands gripped the thin linen of his shirt. Fire sizzled in his veins and through his body as desire sharpened to become an overwhelming, passionate hunger. This was more than a simple reaction to a beautiful and desirable woman. There was alchemy between them. It baffled and intrigued him at the same time.

Finally, he forced himself to lift his lips from hers for a moment. "I don't believe you are a witch, Catlin Glyndwr, but it occurs to me you could be an enchantress."

Before she could answer him, the tapestries were ripped aside and Griffin faced a livid Aelwyd ap Pryd. Her expression was hard as glass and her green eyes flashed with bright gold flecks as she grabbed Catlin to pull her from Griffin's arms.

"I should have known," she sputtered at Catlin. "Telling you kissing Sir Reynolds was forbidden was probably the surest way to entice you to seek him out again."

She yanked on Catlin's arm. It was obvious she intended to drag her to back to their suite of rooms.

"Forbidden pleasure?" Griffin's voice reflected his amusement. "You make kissing sound like a most perilous endeavor, Missus ap Pryd." He shrugged. "I've never been seriously injured by kissing a beautiful woman, although in the aftermath, I confess I have been forced to fight several duels in defense of a lady's reputation. Shall you be challenging me at dawn?"

Aelwyd pushed her sister in the direction of their rooms before turning. "If you do anything to dishonor her, Sir Reynolds, you shall certainly wish you were given the opportunity to fight a duel with me."

The threat wasn't filled with venom or malice. To the contrary, she spoke softly, which only added to the rebuke. The hackles on the back of his neck rose.

Griffin bowed to Aelwyd in deference. "I assure you, Missus, I have only the utmost respect for your sister. I would never do anything to harm her or her reputation."

She frowned back at him. "It is not her reputation that worries me overmuch, Sir Reynolds, it is her heart. She is young and vulnerable, which means she could easily be misled by the likes of you." She folded her arms over her bosom, her lips thinned into a look of disdain.

Griffin inclined his head slightly. "I give my word of honor that I have taken no liberties with your sister."

Aelwyd's mouth formed a sour expression as she scrutinized him. "I believe I just witnessed what appears to be at least one liberty, Sir Reynolds."

He cringed at the truth of her words. "I assure you, my intentions towards Catlin are most honorable."

She sighed deeply. "I believe you do have the best of intentions, Sir Reynolds, but as we all know, the road to hell is paved with such."

The eldest Glyndwr sister turned and swept from the small alcove before he could compose a response, leaving the spicy scent of cinnamon in her wake.

He pulled on his doublet to remove the wrinkles left on the garment when he held Catlin within his arms. Despite the warning he'd received from Aelwyd, he had no intention of giving up on his pursuit of Catlin Glyndwr. He found her irresistible, and he wanted to get to know her better, despite threats from the vixen who guarded her virtue like a harpy.

Catlin was a mystery that Griffin intended to explore fully, thoroughly and completely.

Chapter Eight

"I really don't understand why you're making such a fuss over an innocent little kiss." Catlin flopped down upon the heavily embroidered silk coverlet of the bed. She traced the intricate pattern of peacocks, palm trees and golden sunsets. "I think he must have an immense talent for kissing, because I enjoyed it very much."

Aelwyd snorted. "And how would you know such a thing, since I cannot believe you've had enough experience at the task to compare one man's skill against another?" She stood at the end of the bed with her arms folded across her bosom and she gave a mocking laugh.

Catlin stuck her tongue out at her sister. "At least I didn't marry an old man who could not have been good for much of anything, most especially kissing."

Aelwyd's face paled and her lips thinned.

Catlin immediately regretted the bluntness of her remark. She sat up. "I'm sorry, Aelwyd, that was a cruel and thoughtless thing to say."

Aelwyd's emerald green eyes snapped and she fisted her hands at her waist. "It is especially mean since you know William was not my choice for a husband, but that of our father. My marriage was arranged to protect all of us."

Catlin climbed down from the high four-poster bed. She was contrite as she offered her apology. "I know," she confessed, "but I do so enjoy kissing Sir Reynolds, that being told I cannot do so is like telling me I shall never have plum pudding again. It seems most unfair."

Aelwyd gave a deep sigh and finally smiled at Catlin's mournful plea.

"So, his kiss is as sweet as plum pudding," Aelwyd cajoled,

"then I'd say 'tis most sweet indeed! Perhaps I shall try kissing him, just to see if you are correct." She tossed her head. "You know, I do have a great fondness for plum pudding."

A surge of jealousy flashed through Catlin, even though she knew her sister was teasing. "I vow, since I'm forbidden from kissing the man, if I catch you doing so, I'll make it rain in your bed." She paused. "I shall douse your fire dragons!"

Aelwyd sighed. "Neither of us shall be indulging in kissing, or any sort of antics, with any gentleman. At least not until I sort out the image I saw in my scrying mirror. Is that understood?"

Catlin nodded, although she did so with great reluctance. She shivered at Aelwyd's reminder of the vision she'd seen in her smoky mirror that might reflect images of the future.

A dark and dangerous stranger had appeared, and Aelwyd had experienced a feeling of extreme peril while gazing into the mirror. Most frightening was the sense that they were all in danger. The menace Catlin felt when the Witch Hunter attacked her combined with the warning Catlin received from her mother while in Dream Time forced her to agree with Aelwyd's precautions.

Aelwyd held up a hand. "Enough has been said." She waved a hand to indicate the space around them. "Sometimes these old houses have ears in the most interesting places."

Catlin understood the warning. Too much said about magic or witchcraft with a servant eavesdropping behind a chamber door or secret panel could send them both to the gallows.

"We have an opportunity to take advantage of the young earl's gratitude. His father, Lord Shrewsbury, is an important man who has the King's ear. Perhaps we can prevail upon Lord Cranbourne to take up our cause and intercede upon our behalf. It is even possible he might convince his father to carry our petition to His Majesty."

"But Mam said our destiny does not lie within Cymru or Britain. She told me it lies beyond the sea in the New World."

"You spoke with Mam?" Aelwyd paused in her stalking across the floor, frozen to a spot in the middle of the carpet.

Catlin squirmed uncomfortably for a few moments before puffing out her chest with pride. "Yes, during the Dream Time. She told me I must find a way to travel to the colony of Virginia because our future depends upon it."

"Those were her exact words?" Aelwyd crept across the carpet like a cat stalking its prey. "*You* must go to Virginia?" Her voice was just above a whisper.

Catlin fidgeted for a few moments longer. "Well, I believe that was truly what she meant. She said our destiny lies across the sea in the New World."

"It's a very big place, across the sea to the New World." Aelwyd said.

"Mam wasn't specific regarding the exact place, geographically speaking." Catlin raised her eyes to stare at the ceiling. "But I'm sure Virginia is what she meant."

"Geographically speaking, that's an interesting conjecture," offered Aelwyd. "And most opportune since I heard Sir Reynolds is planning to sail there soon."

"Perhaps that is what she meant about destiny." Catlin smiled sweetly. "It cannot be simple coincidence that he happened to arrive at the gaol just when I needed him."

Her sister tapped her fingers on the foot of the carved wooden bedstead. She lifted her head and her gaze speared her younger sister. "Do not delude yourself with dreams about this man, Catlin. He cannot be trusted."

Catlin tossed her head and narrowed her eyes. "You're wrong, Aelwyd. I would trust my life to Sir Reynolds, and you can, too."

Aelwyd shoved back away from the bed, shook her head and the fiery red-gold waves of her hair tumbled down her back. Small flames lit her jade eyes with amber highlights.

"I shall never again be foolish enough to trust any man with such a treasure." She pointed at Catlin. "'Twould be wise for you to learn the same lesson without as much heartache as I have borne." Aelwyd opened the door and stormed out of the chamber, leaving her sister sitting in bewilderment, confused by her angry outburst.

***

Catlin dressed with exquisite care, for she rarely had the opportunity to be in the company of young men, much less handsome gentlemen. Since arriving in Shrewsbury, she and her younger sisters had remained isolated within the confines of Aelwyd's house and shop, venturing out only for short errands.

Catlin shook out the folds of the pale blue satin gown and admired the intricate lace that trimmed the scooped neckline and full sleeves. She had begged Aelwyd to design a dress with pieces of lace insert, but the trim was all her sister would allow. Lace was a dear luxury unnecessary for the wardrobe of a country lass.

Still, when the maid who had been loaned to them finished fastening the ribbons of the heavily embroidered bodice over the dress, Catlin was pleased.

Aelwyd had insisted on returning home with several footmen to bring back a trunk packed with a suitable wardrobe for their visit to Mabley Manor.

Sir Reynolds couldn't help but notice her tonight, for she had taken pains to brush her hair to a glossy sheen before the maid arranged the unruly curls upon her head. The silver bodkins inserted in her coiffure should hold the arrangement in place for the evening.

The maid fastened her most precious piece of jewelry about her neck. The sapphire and diamond necklace reflected the color of her eyes, and she smiled again as she added the matching earbobs.

Catlin stood to turn in several directions to gauge the effect of her multiple petticoats. She had no intention of heeding her sister's advice to avoid Sir Reynolds tonight.

She tilted her head to see her reflection in the hand mirror, only to catch Aelwyd's expression as she crept up behind her.

"I shall most certainly be forced to guard your virtue this evening, for it seems you have put a small price upon a very worthy prize."

Catlin grabbed her gloves, slowly pulled them onto her fingers, and adjusted their length upon her arms. "'Tis only flirting, sister. I am a young woman and yet can hardly dream of marrying a wealthy merchant and attending court, as you did. My dreams must be of marrying a much simpler man of more common background. It cannot hurt to enjoy one evening of pleasure in so handsome a company as Sir Reynolds and Lord Cranbourne."

Aelwyd heaved a great sigh. "You are right, my dear. Since coming to live with me you've all been forced to hide away like novices in one of the old nunneries." She grimaced. "It is not a circumstance I would have wished upon you, but there's little I can do in times such as these."

She turned, her dark black velvet gown sweeping the floor. Despite her mourning garb, the cut of her gown was exquisite and the fabric was of a soft and delicate weave. The emeralds that circled her neck and hung from her ears were a perfect hue to compliment her fiery tresses.

The two women exited the suite of rooms and proceeded down the hallway to the large oak stairway. They paused on the staircase when they discovered Lord Cranbourne and Sir Reynolds gazing up at them. Both men wore wide grins.

"Our Goddesses return, Griffin. Let us worship them with our most outrageous compliments, richest food, and a liberal share of spirits." Lord Cranbourne bowed to them as they descended.

When the two women reached the bottom, Lord Cranbourne extended his arm to Catlin. "Might I have the honor of escorting you to the dining room, Miss Glyndwr?"

Aelwyd frowned at the breach of etiquette, for as the eldest sister the host should have offered to be her escort. Sir Reynolds cleared his throat and then turned to Aelwyd.

"Goodness, Cranbourne, in your rush you've overlooked the crown jewel of this assemblage." He bowed to Aelwyd. "Missus ap Pryd, I would be most honored to escort you to the table."

Griffin gave Lord Cranbourne a dark glower.

Lord Cranbourne seemed momentarily baffled as he covered one of Catlin's hands with his own, and then shrugged. "I've been away from the niceties of court life too long and I forget the rules of gentlemanly conduct. Of course, I should be delighted to escort both of these beautiful ladies to the table."

He offered his other arm to Aelwyd, and they proceeded in the direction of the dining room, leaving Griffin standing alone at the foot of the staircase.

Catlin twisted her head slightly to look back at Griffin. He shot her a wide, devilish grin that displayed his perfect white teeth. She shivered at the voracious look he gave her, and then turned away to find her older sister studying the exchange between them.

Aelwyd's brow wrinkled and her expression hardened into a

cold mask. Catlin resisted the urge to stick out her tongue in defiance. Instead, she turned back to Lord Cranbourne to bestow what she hoped was her most gracious and dazzling smile upon him.

"I hope you are planning a long stay with us, Miss Glyndwr." Lord Cranbourne said.

Catlin shrugged and leaned toward him, letting her scent of sweet herbs and roses drift up to entice him even more. "We shall see how long you can endure our company, my Lord. Since you have only recently recovered your health, I hope we do not tire you overmuch."

Lord Cranbourne gently raised her gloved hand to his lips. "I cannot imagine any tonic more healing then two such lovely women in my home." He kissed her hand. When he lifted his head a bright smile slowly spread across his face. "In fact, you have not only restored my health, but the very presence of such charming ladies has lifted my dark spirits to make me giddy with the delight of your company.

"And after dinner, perhaps we can enjoy some games. It has been ages since I have played at cards." He called over his shoulder, "What say you, Sir Reynolds, are you willing to roll the dice and take your chances with our lovely guests this evening."

"You know I'm always willing to tempt the fates," Griffin said. "But you would be wise to guard your treasure well, for I'm inclined to steal it away from you."

Catlin turned to see a feral glow in his eyes that kindled a heated response and burned to her very core. She shivered again, enticed by the way his gaze slowly rolled down her body, then back to focus upon her mouth.

She licked her lips as his eyes grew darker and sultrier. She knew she played a dangerous game, yet the man tempted and captivated her like no other before him. As she swept toward the dining room, Catlin understood exactly how a wild rabbit felt when a great hawk swooped above it. Beautiful to behold, but deadly to encounter.

Was Sir Griffin Reynolds the dangerous stranger who meant to harm her and her sisters?

Catlin didn't want to stay away from Griffin. Despite her

sister's warning and Catlin's own promise, she had to figure out her mysterious attraction to the man. She most certainly couldn't do that by avoiding him.

Chapter Nine

The dinner was a boisterous and lively affair, with the small party seated at a round table set at one end of the large formal dining room.

Lord Cranbourne explained his decision to forgo the formal table for something more intimate.

Catlin nearly giggled at the nobleman's exuberance. What a delightful change from yesterday.

"I rarely have the opportunity to enjoy the pleasure of even one beautiful woman. I vow I shall not squander this chance to converse with two beauties by installing you at various ends of that monstrous mahogany table."

They all took their places, allowing the footmen to seat them.

"I'm afraid we won't be enjoying a large supper this evening, for my chef has been accustomed to creating thin soups and bland gruel for my palate." Lord Cranbourne shrugged. "I believe he shall do well enough though, for my father brought him all the way from France. My butler tells me he is most enthusiastic to learn we have company this evening."

Lord Cranbourne took great delight in naming all the rich, delicious food they were eating. The first course consisted of rich crayfish bisque garnished with crème fraiche. The soup had a sweet, delicate flavor.

Catlin enjoyed the rich food and lovely furnishings. She felt like a princess thrown into a fairy story.

"I've heard 'tis all the fashion now to have a supper served in the French mode, called a buffet, I believe," Aelwyd said to Griffin.

He nodded. "The King was most taken with the customs of his cousin's court while exiled there and has adopted many habits of the French."

"And were you in exile with his Majesty, Sir Reynolds?" Aelwyd asked.

Catlin sensed a probing scrutiny beneath her sister's simple inquiry.

"Yes, Missus. My father and older brother remained here to protect our estate from Cromwell's usurpation, but when I was old enough, I was sent to serve the King."

"It seems my loyalty ended up saving my family, as there were plans to bestow the lands upon another petitioner after the Restoration."

Catlin smiled at him. "I think you must have lived a life of adventure, traveling with his Majesty and seeing the world."

His smile disappeared at her words and a flicker of sadness tinged his eyes, but he recovered quickly. "Of course, everyone knows 'tis better to be a Cavalier and wander across Europe having adventures then to be tied to a burdensome estate."

Lord Cranbourne raised an eyebrow in his friend's direction, but didn't respond to the remark.

"I understand you have plans to leave England and travel to the New World," Aelwyd said.

Griffin nodded at his dinner companions around the table as the silver-plated soup dishes were removed to be replaced with a salad of pear, apple, and chicory garnished with slivers of ham. "I am a most fortunate man because my father's brother decided to leave England and travel to Virginia when Cromwell seized the government. He established a successful tobacco plantation there, and recently bequeathed it to me." He raised his knife. "I shall be trading my soldier's garb for that of a yeoman farmer."

"It sounds to me as if you are trading one adventure for another," Catlin said, "for the New World is filled with exciting and terrifying things. I've heard there are wild beasts there, and savages who will sneak up on you in the dark of night and shoot you full of arrows." She was breathless with excitement at the idea of actually meeting someone embarking on such a journey. "But I've also heard many fortunes are being made there."

Aelwyd inclined her head at her younger sister, a warning implied with the gesture. "I suspect Sir Reynolds goes to seek his fortune, not to fight savages nor hunt wild beasts."

Griffin gave them a boyish grin. "I hope to share in the excitement of helping to shape a new colony, and if I do discover my fortune in America, well, that is the promise, is it not?"

Aelwyd shrugged. "From what I've read, most of the people who have traveled to Virginia have found only hard work and pestilence awaiting them."

Catlin intervened. "I've read a great deal about the colonies in the Tidewater, and I understand there is a good society of people living there now. There are churches, a civil government, and many fine homes being built." She warmed to her topic, "In fact, I've developed a desire to see the colony myself someday."

Her pronouncement was followed by several moments of silence from the others at the table and a troubled frown from her sister.

"All young women dream of exciting places they cannot possibly travel to, just like dreams of knights upon white chargers." Aelwyd sent a dark glower in Griffin's direction. "'Tis the innocence of youth that deludes them."

Griffin shook his head. "I think it's a worthy goal, for the men who live in Virginia have complained of the lack of suitable wives in the colony." He shot a teasing smile in Catlin's direction. "A beauty such as Catlin could have her choice of wealthy and established gentlemen, if she were so inclined."

"Which she is not, despite her foolish daydreams," Aelwyd snapped, turning away from her sister, and bestowing her full attention on their host. "This champagne is delightful, Lord Cranbourne. I have only enjoyed the beverage once, when my husband and I were invited to dinner at court. 'Tis a most refreshing spirit."

They went on to discuss the many new fashions of the court of Charles II, the French influence, and the gossip about the new Queen, Catherine of Braganza. When they finished the main course of turkey stuffed with sage and onion, served with a side of red cabbage and chestnuts, Cranbourne suggested they retire to the small parlor for dessert and coffee. In the parlor, Aelwyd immediately challenged Lord Cranbourne to a game of Ticktack.

Catlin wandered across the room to gaze out the mullioned windows, even though darkness had fallen outside. Griffin joined her, both hands holding flutes of champagne.

She hesitated when he offered her a glass filled with the bubbly wine. She glanced uneasily toward her sister who was absorbed by the game she played. Aelwyd was a habitual gambler and could not resist the offer to play against the wealthy Lord.

Catlin accepted the glass and whispered her thanks. Griffin indicated a small settee near the fireplace, inviting her to sit with him.

"I'm interested in hearing more of your opinions regarding Virginia," he said as he settled upon the damask cushion next to her. "It appears you have undertaken a study of the subject which quite frankly surprises me. I don't find many women interested in reading, much less researching the settlements in the New World."

Catlin squirmed uncomfortably. She and her sisters had frequently been accused of being over-educated for their sex. Her mother had been adamant regarding the subject and had insisted tutors in all the classic subjects be hired to school her daughters. Was Griffin serious or jesting?

"When we lived at home, at *Llithfaen*, we had a great deal of time to read and study. Our parents encouraged us and the priest found us to be apt pupils in Latin and Greek." She peeked up at Aelwyd, who was engrossed in her game with Lord Cranbourne. "My sister is especially adept at mathematics, and my youngest sister has shown great promise in her study of the natural sciences."

"I tend to agree with your parents. To waste a woman's mind on embroidery and gossip is a crime. Please tell me more." He leaned back in the settee and took a sip of his champagne.

"My father was a baron. We grew up knowing little about the outside world except what we read in books." She laughed lightly, which earned her an angry scowl from across the room as Aelwyd was momentarily distracted from her card game.

Catlin tried to assume a more prim and proper demeanor as she continued her tale. Griffin seemed genuinely interested.

"Like your family, Father found it necessary to support the Parliamentarians when Cromwell seized power, and because we lived so far from all the turmoil of the Civil War, we thought we were safe." She paused as tears pricked at the backs of her eyes. "But in such times, no one is truly safe, are they?" she whispered, trying to gain control of her emotions as she recalled all that had been lost to her family.

"Were your lands forfeited because your father was a Royalist?"

Catlin leaned forward, warmed by his interest. "No, but after my mother died, my father lost interest in the world. He spent all of his time in his chambers conducting a study of alchemy." She took a deep breath and reminded herself to be careful about this explanation. It would be dangerous to divulge too much. "And then he died, unexpectedly. We discovered another man coveted our lands." She watched her sister. Aelwyd was absorbed in her game and oblivious to them.

"And so he offered to marry one of you in order to gain control of your lands, is that what happened?" Griffin asked.

Catlin nodded her head. "Not just one of us, but my youngest sister, Seren. In fact, he insisted that it must be her." She paused to consider how she could describe the baby of their family, the fragile and perceptive young woman who was destined to become an earth adept.

"But, she couldn't tolerate the presence of the man without becoming physically ill. Seren is very sensitive to the moods of others, and she told us Baron Endevean is a very evil man." She shot a look at her sister who was now laughing with Lord Cranbourne. She must be winning to be in such a jovial mood.

"In the past, Seren has been too accurate in her assessment of others for us to doubt the truth of her words."

Griffin nodded. "If all your sisters are as exceptional as you are, Catlin, then I believe you." He leaned closer to whisper in her ear. "And I certainly hope to become better acquainted with more of your special talents in the coming days."

Catlin warmed and jumped to her feet, spilling some of the champagne on the floor. The bodkins in her hair worked loose and her carefully arranged coiffure would soon tumble down around her shoulders if she weren't more careful with her movements.

"I shouldn't..." She gasped for air.

Before she could compose herself, the door banged open and a tall, elderly man stormed into the room.

"I heard you were upon your deathbed, Morgan, and I've been

bounced and flung about for days in that infernal coach to rush to your side." He gave a loud harrumph. "I was forced to leave your stepmother at court, and you know how dangerous that can be!" He stomped his feet and glared at everyone in the room. "Then I was nearly swept off the road in a storm that left the track muddy and treacherous, but what did I care, for I needed to deliver a marriage contract before you expired."

The man threw off his cloak and lunged toward the couple playing cards. "Imagine my surprise to arrive on what I believe are your last days upon this earth, only to discover you hosting a dinner party."

Lord Cranbourne jumped to his feet and faced the old man, his mouth formed a grim expression, but his eyes snapped with good humor. "I can well imagine it, milord."

"'Tis enough to send me into a fit of apoplexy and put me upon my own deathbed," the old man grumbled.

"I don't doubt it a bit, sir," offered Lord Cranbourne. "I apologize for being in such good health, and I shall endeavor to make myself ill again as soon as possible."

Catlin shielded her mouth with her fan to hide her grin.

Lord Cranbourne raised a hand to indicate the two women. "I will ask your forbearance, my Lord. Please allow me to enjoy the company of the lovely Glyndwr sisters for a few more days. One of them is responsible for my recent recovery, and I wish to bask in their beauty and companionship for a bit longer."

The old man paused for a few minutes to study the two women and a twinkle appeared in his own eyes. "I believe judging just by appearances, I am inclined to offer my agreement, for I've not seen such beauty even in the King's esteemed court."

Lord Cranbourne bowed in the direction of the women. "May I introduce my sire, Lord Robert Fitz-John, the Earl of Shrewsbury.

Catlin and Aelwyd rose and dipped to a formal curtsy.

"I hope you haven't taken an undue interest in either of these beauties, Cranbourne, because I have your marriage contract with me, and it awaits only your signature to seal the agreement." He patted his doublet.

Lord Cranbourne's smile morphed into a groan of pain. "How very fortunate for me, milord that I managed to survive the night."

Chapter Ten

Catlin shivered, despite the fact that the morning was unseasonably warm for March. She scurried out the back door and toward the kitchen gardens. She needed to hide from her sister for a while. One look at her and Aelwyd would know something was amiss.

She required a private place to think, for she'd been awake most of the night in an effort to develop a plan. Yet she still had absolutely no idea how she could convince Sir Griffin Reynolds to take her with him on his voyage to the New World.

Catlin wandered over the perfectly manicured gardens and toward the wild woods beyond the gate. She peeked over her shoulder once more, expecting at any moment Aelwyd might come running after her to prevent her escape. Keeping secrets from a fire adept was impossible. Aelwyd's fire dragons were everywhere, acting as her spies.

As she paused to take a deep breath, Catlin's own audacity shocked her. To think of making such a long and dangerous voyage in the company of a man she barely knew was sheer lunacy. Yet, she remembered her mother's words, and knew she must pay attention to the power of prophecy.

Her sisters wouldn't understand, because they had not heard the words from their mother's own lips. Her family's destiny lay far beyond the borders of Britain.

"'Tis a *damniol* plan, even for me," she whispered before venturing deeper into the dark woods. How could she convince Sir Griffin Reynolds, the most handsome and charming rascal she'd ever met, that he should serve as her conscientious and responsible escort on a long voyage across the ocean? Perhaps she could take up alchemy to turn lead into gold for her next feat!

Catlin paused at a small bluff to enjoy the beautiful scenery spread before her. The early spring day had warmed enough to make her woolen wrap unnecessary. She enjoyed the view over a low valley, with the buzzing of bees in the blossoms of a small apple orchard providing a symphony behind her. She closed her eyes and breathed in the brisk, clean air.

"Are you running away from your sister?"

Griffin's deep voice startled her and she jumped. He stood within a clump of hazel, hidden from her view. If she hadn't recognized his voice she would have thought the place inhabited by a *bwgan*, the wild ghosts her mother had told stories about when Catlin was a child to keep her and her sisters from exploring the dangerous places surrounding their stone keep back home.

Catlin's heart continued its staccato beat now that she knew Griffin was nearby. Somehow she had to pretend being near this man did not affect her—a most challenging acting job as she tried to keep her gaze on the horizon and pretend a nonchalance she didn't actually feel.

"I wished to take a walk and enjoy this lovely morning," she said.

Griffin slowly ambled from the copse toward her, the reins of his horse held loosely within his grasp. "So, did you put a sleeping spell upon your fierce guardian in order to slip out of Mabley Hall?"

Catlin gave him a scathing look. "As if I would ever do such a thing, Sir Reynolds." She tossed her head in agitation, and her thick curls obscured her vision for a moment. She pushed her hair back with an air of annoyance. "I hope I need not fear you'll reveal my secrets, now that the Earl has returned to the manor."

Griffin looped the reins around a small rowan tree to allow his horse to graze. His mouth was set firmly, and a small muscle at the edge of his chiseled jaw seemed to throb.

She hoped he did not intend to kiss her again. Or did she perhaps wish he would? She struggled with her emotions, trying to sort out why Griffin Reynolds confused her so much.

"I think the old gentleman is as besotted with the Glyndwr sisters as Lord Cranbourne and I." He smiled coolly, displaying even, white teeth. "But I have assured you more than once, Miss

Glyndwr, that since I have vowed to keep your secrets, I shall not break my word."

She nodded. "I imagine a man of the world such as you has a great deal of experience making promises to all sorts of women."

Griffin circled her, like a lion stalking his prey. "I would never compare you or your sister to other women, for I find you both to be quite unique creations, even though I recognize you are very different from each other."

Warmth rose to her cheeks. "We share the same desire to keep the members of our family safe."

Griffin paused in front of her to gently lift a curl. "Safety?" He made a clucking sound. "That sounds dreadfully tedious and not at all as interesting as casting spells and calling upon the wind to do your bidding."

Catlin's mouth went dry. Was he still seeking some sort of bargain? What would she need to offer this man to purchase his silence and protect her family?

"You aren't going to tell the Earl of Shrewsbury about what I did—the spell, the wind, the gaol?" Her voice rose an octave as fear rippled through her.

Griffin stared down at her, a frown marring the perfection of his handsome face. "I repeat, for what I hope is the final time. I gave my word to protect you, and you shall discover I am a man of my word."

He took a step closer, and she shivered, but not from the coolness of the morning.

"My only question is, what have you to offer in trade for my silence?"

The hot edge of Catlin's temper flared. "Aelwyd tried to warn me about the treacherous ways of men, and most especially that a Cavalier could never be trusted." She took a step away from him. "I'm disappointed to learn she was right."

Griffin adjusted the baldric that held his sword. "Your sister harbors a rather unflattering opinion of me, and I suspect all men. Who has managed to turn her against all members of my sex?"

Catlin shrugged. "Perhaps it was her husband, although he was ill most of their marriage." She narrowed her eyes to glare at Griffin. "But somehow she learned that men are not honorable creatures, and the lesson seems to have proven valid in regard to your character, Sir Reynolds."

Griffin winced before he offered her a humble bow. "I apologize for teasing you, Catlin. It was an ugly jest and not at all appropriate for the circumstances."

Catlin stared at him, her mouth stuck open in astonishment. "You really don't intend to demand some sort of payment for your silence?"

Griffin pulled at the leather gauntlets covering his hands. After removing them he gently took her hand in his own and leaned forward to touch his lips to her knuckle. "I swear I shall never make any unreasonable demands upon you, for you have proven to be a good and honorable lady worthy of my respect and protection."

Catlin stared down at the thick, tousled hair that concealed Griffin's handsome features. A tiny fluttering in her belly swiftly descended to her most tender female parts. Her heart beat faster. Griffin had only been teasing her. He was a man she could trust and he had once again repeated his vow to protect her.

When he finally lifted his gaze to her face, she smiled at him sweetly.

"You're a wicked man, Sir Reynolds, to toy with my affections so callously." She pretended to pout. "I think I shall be very angry with you."

Griffin bowed again. "'Tis only what I deserve, my lady. But being in your disfavor is a most unfortunate circumstance, because it appears this is my last day here at Mabley Hall."

His words shocked Catlin. "Your last day. But you said at supper last night your ship isn't going to sail for another fortnight." Panic rose within her as she gasped for air. "You cannot be leaving so soon!"

Griffin shook his head. "I had thought to have more time here, and it distresses me to be leaving my friend." He winked. "And the lovely Glyndwr sisters."

He strolled to the place his horse was tethered to pet the beautiful stallion. Catlin wrung her hands together and tried to think quickly. She feared he'd jump astride his horse and disappear forever. This couldn't be happening— not now, when she needed more time to put her plan into action. Although 'twould help if she had some inkling of what she could do to convince Griffin to act as her escort and take her with him to the New World.

A small breeze ruffled her skirts and lifted her petticoats. A dark band of storm clouds hovered on the far horizon, and a momentary surge of power coursed through her. She quickly drew a sigil in the air before closing her eyes and silently bringing the old words to mind. The singing of her *sylphs* filled her ears, and the breeze roared into a stiff wind.

She opened her eyes. She didn't want Griffin to turn around and discover what she was doing. He must not suspect she controlled the weather.

He turned back to her with a soft smile curving his lips and forming a deep dimple on the side of his mouth. "We should return to Mabley Hall, the weather has taken a turn for the worse." He indicated his horse. "I'll carry you back on Storm so you won't get drenched."

He untied the leather reins and climbed up into the saddle, adjusting his sword to the side. He held out one arm in her direction. "Give me your hand, and I'll swing you up here."

She grinned at him. "Should I trust my life to a creature named Storm?"

Griffin pulled her easily into the saddle in front of him, and she settled one leg around the pommel, arranging her skirt and petticoats carefully. One of his hands rested around her waist while the other held the reins. The horse turned and headed in the direction of the manor house.

Catlin leaned back against Griffin's heavily muscled chest. The strange heat that always suffused her body when he was near made the day seem warmer then before. Her emotions whirled. She was thrilled to be so close to Griffin, but afraid of what might take place between them now that they were alone together. His kisses had promised so many sensuous delights.

They'd traveled only a short distance when a bolt of lightening danced across the dark sky and the horse shied sideways. A huge clap of thunder boomed just above their heads. Moments later another flash of lightening slammed into a tree close by, and a branch snapped off onto the path in front of them. Storm reared back on his hind legs.

"Hang on to me," Griffin said, as he used both hands to maintain control of the horse. "We're in for a rough ride."

The horse turned away from the direction of the house and the instant all four of its hooves were once again on the ground. Then he shot forward. Griffin swore as she turned her face toward his chest.

She shivered, terrified by the image of the forest rushing by them.

The wind had turned into a blustering tempest now. It tore at the trees and twisted limbs in all directions. She swallowed hard, aware that once again she had underestimated her powers. Gauging wind strength when casting a spell was a difficult chore and a feat she'd yet to master.

Rain slashed at them, and within seconds they were thoroughly soaked.

Griffin's muscles tensed beneath his doublet and linen shirt as he continued to struggle to control the rampaging horse. She knew his work was made more difficult by his concern for her. A momentary flash of conscience tore through her for causing the storm in the first place.

Yet while she couldn't be sure of the way events might unfold this afternoon, she still hoped for an opportunity to speak with him privately. A small rain shower had seemed a perfect solution. She was not convinced of her wisdom now.

The horse slowed. They were deep within the woods now. When Catlin finally lifted her head to look about them, only trees and brush were visible, still obscured by the slashing rain.

"We need to find some shelter," Griffin said. "There's a hunting cabin up ahead. We can duck in there until this weather passes."

Catlin nodded, although she suspected he was only informing her of his intentions, not asking for her consent.

The horse rounded a bend, and there was indeed a small cottage made of wattle and daub, with a thatched roof and several tiny shuttered windows. A lean-to sat at the side as they rode up a rough path overgrown with weeds. At least the horse would have some shelter, too. Relief flickered through her. Leaving the poor creature in the pouring rain seemed cruel.

Griffin paused at the doorway to the cottage. "I'll set you down here so you can go inside and get out of this miserable tempest. There should be some dry wood within, and perhaps you can find some linen toweling or a wool blanket."

One strong arm circled her waist as he gently pulled her from the saddle to set her upon the ground. He handled her so easily, like a small child in his arms.

She shook out her skirts and felt the bodkins pulling loose from securing her hair as she tried to pat the rain from her head. Another clap of thunder sounded overhead, and Catlin winced.

This storm was a true riotous gale now, and she once again cursed her inability to control her powers. When she finally arrived back at Mabley Hall, her eldest sister would give her a severe lecture. An adept always recognized when another elemental witch used her powers in the vicinity.

Catlin sighed and let her eyes adjust to the murky light inside the small cottage. A rock fireplace lined one wall with a pallet nearby, as if someone had been sleeping there. A round table with a few chairs stood in the middle of the room, and a rough cupboard squatted along an expanse of wall.

She found some dry wood and kindling in a pile in one corner and quickly stacked it in the fireplace. She'd remembered to carry her small leather bag with her today, which held her stone and flint. A tiny curling glow quickly blazed into a cozy fire. She might not have the assistance of her more powerful sister's elemental fire dragons, but she could still work her own kind of magic. Once tinder touched dry wood, her *sylphs* made sure sufficient air existed to keep a blaze burning.

The storm continued to rage outside. Rain splattered upon the roof in angry torrents.

She found the cupboard stocked with candles, more flint and stone, a few pieces of pottery, and a jug. Removing the cork, she sniffed and recognized the scent of Rhenish wine. She grabbed two pottery mugs and the wine and placed them upon the table. There was no reason she and Griffin couldn't be comfortable while they waited out the storm.

Catlin sat down upon the pallet after using a broom she'd found in one corner to get rid of any rodent invaders who might have made a nest there. She removed her leather boots and woolen stockings. They, too, were soaked through, and she set them close to the fire to dry.

The wooden door squeaked open on its leather hinges, and Griffin paused in the entry. Did he suspect she used magic to cause the storm?

"Well, you've made yourself at home in here, haven't you?" He took several long steps and dropped his saddle to the floor. He moved to the fire and held out his hands to warm them. "That damned storm came upon us with no warning."

Catlin didn't answer, but pretended to be busy trying to dry her hair by twisting it repeatedly to drain off the water.

He knelt on one knee to draw closer to the fire before giving her a sinful smile. "At any rate, I've somehow contrived to find a way for us to be alone together."

Catlin swallowed. What in the Goddess's name did she think she could accomplish by bringing this charming and dangerous man to such a place? She endangered not only her reputation, but her very virtue.

She was no courtesan trained in the sensual arts to persuade and entice men. She understood there were techniques a woman could use to mold a man to her purpose. She'd heard enough common gossip about the many women who gained favors by plying their charms in the King's bedchambers. Yet she'd not been tutored in any of the requisite skills, and she cursed her lack of knowledge.

She stood and padded to the fire, pulling one of the chairs forward to sit down. She placed her bare feet upon the stone hearth before leaning back. "I fear you have somehow arranged this, Sir Reynolds." She gave him what she hoped was a coquettish look. "I shall need to be vigilant, lest my good reputation suffer irreparable harm."

He frowned. "I'm afraid I didn't consider that. Perhaps we should go now, despite the storm."

A tremor of alarm surged through Catlin, and she instantly formed a plan. If she could arrange a way to remain in the cottage with him, if only for a brief time, perhaps she could cast a spell upon him strong enough to bind him to her. Once she'd done that, convincing him to keep her by his side would be much easier.

Her conscience pricked her. Her mother had warned her many times not to cast love spells, for the results could be very unpredictable.

"I doubt this storm shall last long enough for us to be missed, and I have no interest in getting soaked to the bone again." She gave him a sweet smile. "Shall we wait a bit and see what happens?"

Griffin wiped the water from his brow. "Wait?"

Catlin focused her intent and closed her eyes for a moment. She repeated the ancient words to create a love charm in her head. Of course, she didn't have the requisite supplies, but for her purposes, she didn't need anything very strong.

Griffin stretched his long legs out to put his booted feet closer to the flames. He didn't seem to react to her spell at all, although since she'd never used such a thing before, she had no idea how long it took for the subject to be affected.

She shuddered at her own audacity. To attempt something she knew could cause trouble was imprudent enough, but to be alone—unchaperoned—with a man was absolute foolishness. She cringed at the thought of Aelwyd's reaction when she discovered what Catlin had been up to this afternoon.

"'Tis only a spring shower and 'twill be gone before we know it." She tried to keep her tone light, but knew her cheeks were rosy with warmth. She suddenly felt nervous and shy.

"Then it seems prudent to wait it out." Griffin picked up a stick to poke at the hot embers of the fire. They didn't speak for a few moments.

Catlin rose and went to the table. "I found some Rhenish in the cupboard and thought perhaps a mug might warm us while we wait out the storm." She poured them each a portion, handed him one of the mugs, and returned to her chair.

She took a sip, and a curl of heat trailed down her throat. She set the mug on the dirt floor and attempted to make amends to her appearance.

Pulling the bodkins from her hair, she shook it out then used her fingers comb through it, anxious to smooth any snarls. Finally she threw her head back in hope she might look more presentable.

She lifted her head to discover a strange expression upon Griffin's face. His mouth was open, the mug frozen in his hands and his eyes held a glazed look.

"Is there something amiss? Is your wine sour?"

Griffin shook his head and took a quick swallow of the wine. He blinked at her and took a deep breath. "No, 'tis nothing, just..." He set his cup on the hearth and stood up. He took two long steps, paused in front of her, then reached down to grasp her hands and pull her gently to her feet.

A shiver of alarm mixed with delight rippled through her. She should be afraid, and perhaps she was, just a bit. But more then that, she waited, eagerly anticipating his next move. She didn't have to wait long. Sir Griffin Reynolds drew her into his embrace and covered her mouth with his own, bending her backwards across his arm.

Catlin's will bent, too, as his mouth devoured hers, then drew back and teased her lips gently before once again begging—no demanding—her submission.

Lightening flashed, but not from the storm above. Rather, the storm within her caused the bolt. Lethargic weakness left her bones melting to puddle upon the dirt floor. She was grateful for the support Griffin's strong arm provided.

His tongue pushed forward, beyond her small front teeth, and she opened her mouth to welcome his plundering quest. She could muster no defense against this man, for every part of her body craved his touch.

Her head spun, and she felt like a girl twirling about on a summer's day until she fell onto the soft grass. She tasted him, the wine sweet upon his lips. The dampness of his hair and clothes mixed with the moisture on her own and this should have chilled her. Instead as the heat blazed between them, it only made her swelter as if they were standing in the sun on a mid-summer day.

His lips moved lower, diverted from pillaging her mouth to eagerly exploring the tenderness of her earlobe. He gently nibbled, as if she were a sweet morsel he sampled.

She shivered, but not from the cold. In her mind, cold did not exist, only a trailing, molten path that flowed across her skin wherever his mouth and fingers traveled. His lips moved lower yet, to the small indentation at her shoulder, and another tiny flame ignited within her. She should be pushing him away, but it was sweet torture to have him holding her. She couldn't form the words to stop this sensual play.

He grasped her hand, led her to the pallet, and pulled her down with him. Before she even realized what was happening, he hovered just inches above her. His dark eyes looked feverish, as if he were barely conscious of his actions.

"You are so full of sweetness, Catlin," he murmured, his voice rough with desire. "Silky skin and sweet kisses, that is how I shall always remember you." He pointed at the door of the cottage. "If you wish for me to leave, you must say the word now." His mouth hovered over hers. "In a few more moments it shall be too late."

Too late? Too late for what? Catlin's mind raced for a brief interlude before realization seized her. He intended to make love to her, and he was asking for her permission.

Catlin's heart was beating so loud, she was surprised he didn't comment upon it. Her virtue stood in jeopardy, and she must somehow muster the strength to refuse him and send him outside to wait out the storm. Yet her breasts ached with a heaviness she didn't recognize and her body floated, as if she were weightless. She didn't want him to go, she wanted more.

Instead of asking him to leave, she gently pulled his mouth down to hers, answering his question with her own sensuous, demanding kiss.

Griffin's hands explored the soft curves and gentle valleys of her body. When he cupped one of her breasts with a hesitant, tentative touch, she stretched toward his fingers. Her skin prickled with a molten heat everywhere Griffin touched her. She licked her lips, but her mouth felt as dry as a desert storm.

He quickly helped her unfasten the ribbons holding her bodice together, and she delighted in the sensation of his warm breath upon her bare flesh as he trailed tender kisses from her throat to the deep valley of her décolleté.

When he suckled the hard, pink tip of one breast, she arched her back again. The languorous warmth built to a blazing crescendo within her. A thousand colors swirled behind her eyelids, and a gentle pressure swirled from her lower belly to move slowly to the soft petals of her womanhood. She wanted his fingers, his lips, and more.

A solid, urgent thickness pushed against her inner thigh.

"Do you feel how eager I am for you, my lady Cat?" His voice was garbled, as though he'd imbibed too much wine. Catlin didn't know how to respond, so she kissed him with an eager tenderness that she hoped demonstrated she understood what he wanted from her.

Griffin stood to unfasten the laces of his breeches as Catlin prepared herself for her first sight of an aroused and naked man.

Suddenly, the fire turned into blazing tongues of flame that shot out of the fireplace, seeking Griffin out as if trying to singe the skin from his flesh.

"Bloody damn hell!" he roared as he launched across the room in an effort to escape the inferno.

Catlin thumped her fists upon the pallet. Her fever of desire dissolved in the face of this sudden intrusion by Aelwyd's elemental emissaries. "I hate those *damniol* fire dragons."

Griffin had twisted away from the flames and now stood at the other end of the room, staring at her as if he were emerging from a dense fog. She snatched her clothing back into place to cover herself.

"I beg your pardon, Catlin. I have no idea what came over me, I should never. . . would never, I mean. . ." He drew one hand through the dark, unruly locks of his hair and looked at her, his brow wrinkled in confusion.

Catlin didn't know what to say, for to excuse him and lay the blame upon herself might expose her plot to entice him to take her to Virginia. Her love charm had worked better than she'd ever expected. She should be congratulating herself for the success.

Unfortunately, at this moment, with her body screaming for a release she didn't understand and her sister's minions watching her she was only confused and ashamed.

"I think we need to return to Mabley Hall," she suggested.

Another flame rose hot and orange from the embers, and Griffin nodded. "Bloody damned right you are. It's been the strangest day. I cannot explain my behavior Catlin, but I offer my most humble apology for what has transpired between us." He took another step backwards, away from her. "Let us be grateful it went no further."

He fumbled with his clothing in an attempt to straighten it. She should offer some sort of explanation. If only she could come up with something that didn't sound like a nursery tale.

Please don't concern yourself, Sir Reynolds, for I cast a love spell upon you. But I didn't actually realize how powerful it could be, so it was my fault entirely. Magic spells can be so unpredictable, you know.

Catlin couldn't confess her part in the sudden appearance of the storm or their hasty lovemaking. To do so would certainly indict her as a witch, and while Griffin might allow her to cast a healing spell upon his friend, he would most certainly not be happy to hear she was using magic to bend him to her will.

Men didn't care for women who contrived to make them do things they did not think of first. Even as young and inexperienced as she was, she understood the male enjoyed the hunt and pursuit of the female. Turning the tables made them very angry. Or so she'd been told.

Catlin needed to be more careful dealing with Sir Reynolds. He was already suspicious about her use of magic. She still didn't know if he was the dark man who had appeared in her sister's scrying glass and her mother's dire prophecy.

She needed to fight her intense attraction to the man and remain alert. Her very life could depend upon it. If only he wasn't so *daminol* appealing.

Chapter Eleven

Catlin and Griffin arrived back at Mabley Hall as the storm moved across the marches and left a beautiful rainbow crowning the treetops behind them. The ride back to the manor house had been quiet, as Griffin seemed disturbed by the events at the cottage. His dark mood combined with the deep shadows edging his face revealed his sense of guilt.

When they dismounted at the stables, Lord Cranbourne was waiting for a horse to be saddled. He ran out to meet them, his abrupt manner signaling his distress.

"Miss Glyndwr, we've been concerned about your welfare." He flushed as he caught her hands in his own. "Your sister is near sick with worry, and even I have been anxious about your whereabouts." He frowned at Griffin who still held the reins of his horse. "Did Miss Glyndwr lose her mount while the two of you were out riding?"

Griffin tossed a guilty look in Catlin's direction, clearly waiting to see which one of them would offer an excuse for arriving at the manor house together. She decided to be the one responsible for creating the story. Her confession to Lord Cranbourne would prepare her for the far more difficult task of convincing her sister of the tale.

"I went out for a walk and strayed too far." She nodded in Griffin's direction. "I met Sir Reynolds, who was out riding. He offered to bring me back to the manor house, for we could see a storm was brewing."

She slid a sideways look at Griffin, and while his dark eyes studied her carefully, nothing in his manner alerted her that he disagreed with her version of events. "Before we knew it, the storm was upon us and the horse bolted when lightning hit a tree on the path." She kept the story simple and easy to corroborate.

Griffin stepped closer and joined in the recitation. "We managed to get soaked thoroughly within minutes of the deluge, so we took shelter in the hunting cottage for a short time. When the storm passed, we rode back here."

His tone was light and carefree, as if they had simply been sitting in front of the fire playing cards, instead of playing a sensual game while they waited for the rainstorm to subside.

Lord Cranbourne frowned at his friend. "It would have been better for Miss Glyndwr's reputation had you chanced taking a chill and returned immediately to the house."

Griffin bowed in her direction. "It was my initial thought to do so, but the horse became frightened. I couldn't further endanger this fine lady, could I?"

"I assure you, Lord Cranbourne," Catlin said, "it was my own fault. Had I stayed in the gardens instead of wandering off into the woods, I would have been safe."

Griffin's mouth twitched when she uttered the word safe. She entwined an arm with Lord Cranbourne's and gave him a sweet smile. "Would you mind escorting me back up to Mabley Hall, my lord?"

The Viscount appeared to have been suddenly frozen to the spot. Finally Griffin coughed—probably trying to cover a laugh, Catlin thought.

Lord Cranbourne blushed as he swallowed. "I shall be most honored, Miss Glyndwr."

As they strolled up the path towards the house, Catlin twisted to hazard a peek over her shoulder. Sir Griffin Reynolds stared after them, his mouth set firmly and his brow knitted into a frown. He was clearly concerned, but Catlin couldn't be sure if it was for her or Lord Cranbourne.

***

Aelwyd waited for her on the main staircase. From the sour expression upon her sister's face, perhaps it would have gone better if she'd been found seriously injured or ill.

Catlin considered pausing to confess her identity as the accused witch to Lord Cranbourne and seek the comparative safety of the gaol rather then the wrath of her sister. But despite her eldest sister's anger, Aelwyd wouldn't actually injure Catlin. At least, she never had before.

Perhaps this time would be different. Aelwyd's expression was as dark and foreboding as the storm clouds during the recent deluge. Still, she appeared relieved to see Catlin.

"I have been terribly worried about you, Catlin," Aelwyd said between clenched teeth. "You did not inform anyone you were leaving the manor house."

Aelwyd's cold and emotionless voice chilled Catlin's blood.

"Shall we go up to our chamber, for I would not want you to catch cold in those wet clothes, or did you somehow manage to dry them?" The caustic edge was a warning to Catlin of the consequences for her indiscretions this afternoon.

"I do need to change," Catlin whispered, climbing the stairs with apprehension. As she slid past her sister and continued up toward their suite of rooms, Aelwyd did not move.

She stared down at the entryway. Griffin had finally arrived back at the manor house. Aelwyd pointed an accusing finger toward him.

"I shall deal with you later, Sir Reynolds." She gathered up her dark skirts, turned on her heel, and followed Catlin.

When they finally closed the door to their chamber, Aelwyd released her anger and frustration.

"Alone with a man, a Cavalier no less! How could you ever agree to such a thing? Do you care so little about your reputation? Don't you understand what could have happened? Your virtue was in danger!" Aelwyd spat in disgust. "Have you no desire to make a good marriage?"

Catlin stripped off her wet clothing and found a large linen towel to rub herself dry. She ducked behind a screen to remove her shift as her sister droned on about her behavior.

"Come out from behind the screen, Catlin, for I shall rebuke you to your face."

Catlin quaked at the icy chill in Aelwyd's voice. She slid across the chamber and stood a few steps away from the fire. Although she wished to warm her toes, her sister's temper could still flash out of control.

"You created that storm for your own benefit, did you not?" Aelwyd's emerald green eyes flared with a touch of amber

"I wished to speak with Sir Reynolds alone. It was imperative."

"So you whistled down the wind for a second time in the presence of this, this *sophor*? Does he suspect you of using your powers again?"

"Aelwyd," Catlin said sternly, "you must guard your words and lower your voice."

Aelwyd blushed at what should have been an unnecessary reminder about speaking so freely about magic in a place that could have spies. Her voice shifted to a rough whisper. "He already knows too much about you, and from the image my fire dragons gave me, you could have been compromised in that cottage!"

Catlin's cheeks warmed. "I think perchance they might have misinterpreted, exactly, well, what they were seeing."

In an instant the fire roared, red and orange flames licking the top of the fireplace.

"They do not appear to think so, my dear sister." Aelwyd responded, slapping her hands on her waist.

Catlin tried to recall how Sir Reynolds had turned the conversation when they encountered Lord Cranbourne in the stables. A flicker of inspiration hit her.

"I needed to convince Sir Reynolds to take me with him to the New World, and I thought I might use my feminine wiles to manipulate him."

Aelwyd made a rude noise before laughing. "Feminine wiles? Why, as far as I know, you'd never even been kissed by a man before yesterday. It takes a great deal of expertise to exert the kind of influence you speak of upon a man." She thinned her mouth and her eyes became emerald slits. "Even a *sophor*!" She marched across the room. "Are you inclined to take up the guise of a whore in order to get your own way, Catlin?"

The ugly words hung in the air, and Catlin's body chilled even more as her sister's accusation slapped her. "I did, manage--events." Catlin knew her sister understood what she meant. "—in order to contrive a meeting alone with Sir Reynolds."

Aelwyd's face wore a hard mask of condemnation, her mouth a

thin line slashed across her face.

Catlin wrung her hands. "But, not for the purposes of the things you believe. I wanted passage to Virginia and for Sir Reynolds to act as my escort."

Her blurted confession did not have the effect she had wished for, as the expression on her sister's face grew even harsher. The amber highlights in Aelwyd's jade eyes grew darker.

"You believe you have influence with these men, and you asked for that instead of for his help in reclaiming our lands in Cymru?" The winter chill of Aelwyd's voice put ice in Catlin's veins.

It had been an impulsive and foolish idea, but upon hearing it put into words, even Catlin was horrified at what she'd attempted to do. She bowed her head. "I am sorry. I know it was imprudent of me to consider making such a request. I shall go directly to the Earl of Shrewsbury and ask for his assistance with all haste." Tears filled her eyes. "I confess, of late I have not been thinking clearly. I simply am trying to do as I was advised. Mam told me to find the way, because I'm the dreamer. She said it was up to me to discover a means to get us all to the New World." Catlin drew one hand across her eyes, wiping the tears that now trailed down her cheeks.

"But that cannot be true, because all I have done is to make a huge muddle of everything. I don't understand why I cannot make it right, but I've failed, and I was trying to watch for the signs, but I didn't know what to look for, then Sir Reynolds came along, and, and..."

Her babbling explanation dissolved into a fit of weeping as she sat down in a chair placed near the fire. What difference did it make if Aelwyd became angry enough to blister her skin or singe all the hair from her head? She was cold, tired, and defeated. She had failed her family quite miserably.

Catlin's sobbing filled the air for a few moments before she lifted her gaze to find Aelwyd studying her carefully.

"Mam said there would be a sign? Why have you failed to mention this before?"

Catlin sniffed. "I tried to tell you, but you kept insisting I was only creating this story because I was infatuated with Sir Reynolds."

Aelwyd tapped one toe of her slipper on the floor. "I'm still not convinced that isn't the truth of the matter, but the mention of a sign does change things."

Catlin shook her head, "No, it doesn't, for I haven't seen anything that could be interpreted as a sign. There hasn't been any indication of what I should do, and in truth, I doubt there ever shall be."

"Oh, stop gushing you silly goose. Did Mam ever explicitly say that you had to see the sign?"

Catlin blew her nose. "No, she said to watch for a sign, but I'm sure she meant I was the one who would see it."

Aelwyd folded her arms across her bosom and shook her head. "I do not think so, my *bychan* cat."

Catlin bristled at being once again referred to as a little cat in her own language, then realized what Aelwyd had said. She stared at her sister with anticipation.

"Did you see something?" she whispered. "Something strange and wonderful?"

Aelwyd maintained eye contact with Catlin. "When I was out searching for you, the storm came up suddenly and I was caught unaware in the garden. Just before the rain came, there was a flash of lightening."

Catlin nodded. "I know. I haven't yet learned adequate control of the storms."

With her lips thinned to a judgmental line, Aelwyd nodded. "You need to spend more time practicing your spells and less time practicing your feminine wiles."

Catlin was about to protest when Aelwyd held up a hand to silence her. "That's not the point, though. When the bolt hit I was still out of doors." She moved across the room to stand by a window that looked down on the garden. "In fact, it split a tree so close I thought it would shake me out of my slippers."

Catlin bit her lip. "I'm so sorry, Aelwyd, and I swear tomorrow I shall begin practicing the phasing so that the next time I can—"

Aelwyd wouldn't let her finish. "That is not the point!"

Catlin avoided interrupting again, as she watched her usually composed sister twist the velvet curtain.

"I did not truly know what to make of it, and then I realized you were lost out in the storm so I needed the assistance of my fire dragons to help find you." Her words tumbled over each other in her rush to get them out. "And well, with everything else happening so quickly, it simply slipped my mind."

"Sister, you're not making any sense," Catlin said, aware that this in itself was alarming. Of all the Glyndwr sisters, Aelwyd was the most sensible and composed. She was trustworthy, dependable, and decisive. Even though they all knew how hard she fought against her fiery, tempestuous nature to be all of those things for their family.

And yet, at this very moment, Catlin had no idea what she was talking about. Aelwyd stared out the window nibbling at her lower lip and looking totally bewildered.

"I saw the Phoenix in the tree where the lightening bolt hit. It must have been the sign we've been waiting for." She turned back to face Catlin. Her fingers touched her throat, and there was a tremor in her hand. "To find our new path?"

Catlin couldn't hide her astonishment as her mouth dropped open.

"The Phoenix? But, it's so rarely seen by any adept. How could you, I mean. . ."

"Exactly," Aelwyd said. "If the Goddess sent such a powerful sign, we must not ignore it!"

***

"I do not envy your meeting with that termagant." Morgan had his booted feet upon the desk and a glass of claret in one hand. "That woman fascinates and terrifies me, and I'm not too proud to admit it."

Griffin shifted in his chair and shook his head. "Missus ap Pryd has every reason to be angry with me, for I acted foolishly this afternoon." He took a sip of his drink from the pewter goblet in his hand. While he refused to agree with Morgan out loud, he did harbor some trepidation regarding an audience with the Widow ap Pryd. It was not her temper he feared as much her obvious right to demand that Griffin do the right thing in order to protect Catlin's reputation. He was hardly in any position to make an offer of marriage, not with the King's errand weighing heavily upon him.

In truth, he'd tarried overlong at Mabley Hall already. He stared down at the dark red wine in his goblet, realizing things had started to swirl out of his control. He did not relish being at the mercy of destiny.

"So, what really happened between you and the dazzling Catlin Glyndwr?" Morgan gave him a sly smile. "I know you are both hiding something."

Griffin drew his goblet to his lips and took a long drink. "You know I do not indulge in tales about women, Cranbourne. We have been friends long enough for you to understand that."

Morgan swore beneath his breath. "So, there is more story to tell, and you simply refuse to give me the salacious details."

Griffin picked up the crystal wine decanter and refilled his goblet before handing if off to Morgan. "There is nothing to tell that is scandalous enough for your tastes."

Morgan pulled his feet from the desk and slapped his hands upon his knees. "How I regret your bloody damned sense of chivalry, for it has robbed me of many a delicious tale."

Griffin stood up before giving his friend a smirk. "Cheer up, my friend, for now that your father has acquired a bride for you, I shall be regaled with stories of your vigor in the nuptial bed." He winked. "You shall need to work quickly, as your father is already bragging about the heir to be born next year."

Morgan spat out a stream of wine. "He's going to saddle me with some pasty-faced country lass who will do nothing but badger me and give birth to a bunch of loud, disruptive children." He wiped at his mouth. "Marriage is an institution created by women to torture us poor men."

It was fruitless to argue the point. As the third and most useless son in his family, Griffin need never worry about pressure to marry and have children.

And yet, there were times recently when he'd begun to imagine watching his own children grow up in Virginia, as proud and strong as the trees he heard grew there in profusion. It was only a far-fetched fancy. His King still required his services. Dreams of settling down with a wife were just that—wild, unobtainable dreams.

Chapter Twelve

"The Phoenix?" Catlin's voice was hushed, as if even speaking of such a wondrous thing was forbidden.

In her lifetime, no one had ever mentioned seeing the rare and beautiful firebird. It was thought to be a legend, even amongst elemental fire adepts.

Catlin could barely contain her excitement. If her sister truly had seen the immortal bird with feathers that could burn to ash, only to rise again, it could be the sign her mother had mentioned.

Aelwyd stomped back and forth across the room, stumbling several times. Finally, she pulled off her offending slippers and threw them across the room.

"It means that despite all of my warnings against Sir Reynolds and the fact that I cannot trust the man, nor you, sister, when you are with him, that I am forced to concede you are right."

Catlin couldn't determine what was making Aelwyd angrier—the idea of sending her off with Griffin Reynolds or being forced to admit she was wrong.

Catlin smiled. Aelwyd was full of pride, one of the deadly sins. It was too much to ask that she resist a moment to enjoy a small tumble from the pedestal her sister had placed herself upon since the death of their father.

"Well, I am relieved you finally believe me, and imagine, it only took the sight of a legendary immortal bird during a fearsome tempest to convince you." She rolled her eyes and giggled. "I hope it shall be as easy to convince Sir Reynolds to do my bidding."

Aelwyd stopped pacing. "I do not think it shall be you making the request, for I suspect he might need a bit of prodding in order to do as we wish."

Catlin stared at her most powerful sister. Aelwyd was the

protector of all elemental mysteries, a high priestess, invocator, and mage. For her to even suggest using her powers to control a *sophor* was forbidden. A simple glamour was one thing, but casting a spell to force a *sophor* to your will was dangerous.

"You shouldn't, Aelwyd," Catlin protested. "You're needed to initiate Meaghan and Seren." Her voice rose an octave. "If the watchtower guardians learn of it, they could strip you of your powers."

Aelwyd waved her hand with a languid air. "I have no intention of endangering my position as an elemental mage. But from what my fire dragons have shown me, Sir Reynolds has an intense attraction to you, Catlin. I can judge how best to use that knowledge and perhaps not exactly cast a spell, but invoke a small glamour."

Catlin shook her head. "He resisted the one I tried to cast upon him in the coach, so I doubt if it will work." She gave her sister a mocking smile. "He is very strong, you know."

Aelwyd ap Pryd gave a tiny, secret smile in return. "You have no experience in convincing men to do your bidding, while I had the most perfect of subjects on which to practice." Her expression transformed into a grim mask. "An uncooperative husband."

***

"I am near starved, Griffin." Morgan swirled the dark liquid in his goblet. "You missed dinner today, so I dare say you are as hungry as I am." He set his goblet down upon the scarred wood surface of the desk. "I instructed cook that I wanted oysters for supper this evening, and I'll ask Flanders to get me some now to ease our hunger pains."

Jumping up, he opened the door, catching himself before he bumped into Aelwyd ap Pryd.

He bowed in her direction. "Begging your pardon, Missus."

"My Lord," she responded with a deep curtsy.

"I am searching for Sir Reynolds; do you perchance know where I might find him?"

The corners of Morgan's mouth lifted into a smile. "I believe he has been most anxious to speak with you. Please come in, I'm sure he'll be delighted to see you."

"Thank you," she murmured, before striding into the room and snapping the door shut behind her. She blinked.

"Sir Reynolds," she called out in an authoritative voice.

Griffin rose quickly to his feet. "Missus ap Pryd," he said, his tongue heavy and thick in his dry mouth. He gulped as he came to a full stand. "May I help you?"

"I wish to speak with you regarding my sister."

A sliver of fear slipped down his spine. "Catlin?"

Aelwyd sat in a chair opposite the desk. Her expression was as dark as the sky during the storm earlier in the day. The storm that was the reason for their meeting.

"Of course, Catlin. I do not believe you have had the opportunity to have congress with my other sisters yet, have you?" she snapped.

Griffin fell back into the chair at the desk. "No, Missus, not yet. I mean, I would not, with any of them, have congress, I mean . . ." His voice trailed off as he seized a goblet sitting on the desk and took a large gulp.

Aelwyd pursed her lips and inhaled a deep breath. She frowned up at him as he took another long drink from the goblet.

"Liquid courage", she suggested. "But aren't you a seasoned soldier, accustomed to facing your enemy?"

Griffin leaned forward and stretched his hands out in supplication. "I don't want you to think of me as an enemy, and I wish to apologize for everything that happened this afternoon, Missus ap Pryd."

He stood and forced his body to relax his tense muscles. "I am well aware I demonstrated poor judgment in taking Catlin to the hunting lodge, and as for what transpired while we waited out the storm, she is blameless." He straightened his shoulders, prepared to accept her anger. "Please do not punish her for my actions."

"Then I should punish you, shouldn't I?"

Griffin's head jerked back. Now the bargaining would begin. What price would he be forced to pay for a brief interlude with Catlin?

"I was making a jest, Sir Reynolds." Aelwyd finally said.

He sat back down and drained the goblet before turning. He

grasped a crystal decanter and refilled his empty cup.

"Do not excuse her behavior so quickly, Sir Reynolds. She has confessed to me she is quite infatuated with you, and I suspect she had some influence upon the events that transpired between the two of you today."

"I could not blame a lady for the actions of a knave." he said.

"Are you truly a knave, sir? Are you the sort of man who seeks to deceive women and trick them into a seduction, only to break their heart and desert them when you grow tired of their charms?"

Sir Reynolds jumped to his feet. He clenched his hands into fists at his side. "If you were a man charging me with such trickery and slandering my good name, I would demand satisfaction from you."

Aelwyd remained composed with her hands folded primly in her lap. "You speak so casually of dueling that I think you must participate in such games frequently. Can I assume you often find yourself in need of defending your reputation, or do you have frequent need to stand in defense of someone else's honor?"

Fury clouded his vision with a haze of blood red. He smacked a fist upon the surface of the desk. "I have defended the innocent, who were the victims of unfounded gossip mongering and envy." He took a deep breath, trying to calm his temper. "In cases when I found it necessary to draw my sword, it has been to protect others or to defend my king and country."

She nodded. "Then I am satisfied you are no knave, sir. Please, let us try to be civil to each other, for I have no wish to offend you with my questions."

"I apologize, Missus. Perhaps this conversation could take place another time, when I am in more control of my passions."

Aelwyd shook her head. "I fear there isn't sufficient time for us to assume a more composed state to discuss the matters I find most pertinent. I understand you leave for Bristol tomorrow and sail to the New World before the month is out."

Griffin nodded, glad to be discussing a different topic. "You must be relieved to know I shall no longer pose a threat to the honor or reputation of your sister."

She drummed her fingers upon the desk and glanced around the room, as if studying the furnishings until finally her gaze settled back on Griffin. "On the contrary, I have actually come to make a proposal to you regarding my sister's welfare."

He could feel the muscle near the thin scar edging his face twitch, and his breath came faster and deeper. Now would come the demand he marry Catlin for the sake of propriety.

"I should think you'd consider it best for your sister if I left as soon as possible, especially since you have made it clear you possess no high regard for my character and know she has expressed a certain, ardor, towards me." He folded his arms across his chest and glared down at her.

His obvious displeasure had no effect upon the widow. She primly slid her hands down the black velvet of her gown to smooth the wrinkles. Finally she tilted her head up at him. "I wish for you to conduct Catlin safely across the ocean and to the colonies. I want you to protect her during the voyage and ensure she is settled once she arrives in Virginia."

Griffin laughed out loud and stared at her

"Have you become a smashing bloody damned lunatic?" he shouted, before draining his goblet in one gulp and slamming it down upon the desk.

"I cannot think of anything I would rather *not* do." He stomped across the room.

"Your sister is of a tempestuous nature, given to rather strange pronouncements, and uninhibited actions. She seems to be followed about by great drafts of wind and storms." He marched back to the desk and pointed towards Aelwyd. "I think she's lovely, but to be quite honest, I value my freedom."

Aelwyd laughed. "Do not be so foolish, Sir Reynolds. My sister simply requires an escort. She would be little trouble to you, and your intentions are to travel to the colonies anyway. I believe it is quite a convenient coincidence."

Griffin could not believe the confidence of this woman. And it confused him that although she was demanding he escort her sister, she hadn't mentioned marriage.

"Catlin requires a chaperone to Virginia and it happens that you are going there soon. I see that as a solution to a problem, not a vexation."

Griffin stared at her, still unable to comprehend what she was saying. "You would trust her to travel under my guardianship?" He plowed one hand through his hair, "I would suggest that is rather like setting the fox to guard the henhouse."

"Perhaps," Aelwyd said. "But I suspect you are a fox who at least has some trepidation about consuming the hen."

Griffin raised an arched brow. "But destined to consume nevertheless, because it is his nature."

"I do not doubt that," Aelwyd said. "The unknown element in this equation is the hen, because she can be as cunning and scheming as the fox."

He slid her a devilish grin. "Regardless of the game, I will win because I am the more seasoned player. Are you prepared to wager your sister's honor in exchange for safe passage to the colonies?"

Aelwyd stood and ambled slowly to the fire. She held out her hands as if to warm them in the glow. "A wager is safe when you know you will win."

She bent forward and put her hands directly into the dancing flames. Griffin scrambled across the room to grab a woolen throw tossed upon the back of a chair.

"God's blood but you are mad, woman. What have you done?" He snatched the throw intending to quickly wrap her hands.

Aelwyd took several quick steps in his direction and held out her hands.

Griffin stared down in astonishment as a tiny flame-licked creature, glowing with the red, blue and gold of the brightest fire, sat in the palm of her hand.

The changing colors of the fire dragon mesmerized him, and he couldn't look away. In a few moments he relaxed and his breathing slowed. A soothing warmth suffused him, surrounding him with a soft, golden glow that smelled like cinnamon.

"Very good, Sir Reynolds." Aelwyd still held the fire in her hands, which had assumed the form of a tiny dragon. "Take several large, deep breaths. Feel the air moving into your lungs and out again."

She waited for him to do as directed. "Keep your eyes on the colors of my fire dragon, do not look away, but listen carefully."

He silently did as she asked.

"You will take my sister, Catlin Glyndwr, with you tomorrow

when you leave for Bristol. You will guard her well, making sure she is comfortable and safe while she travels with you to Virginia."

She paused for a moment. "Take several longer, deeper breaths." She urged.

He did as she asked. He wanted to fight against her, release himself from her control, but he was weak as a newborn lamb. He couldn't resist her voice

"You will do everything you can to protect and care for Catlin."

He stared at the fire dragon shimmering in her hand.

"When I leave this room, you will not remember this conversation, just the agreement."

The golden light turned a bright red, then to orange. He was surrounded by flickers of fire that weren't hot, but cool and comforting.

She drew away from him, and with a small, swift movement tossed the fire dragon back into the flames crackling in the fireplace. A large sputter of sparks blazed and she uttered a few words he didn't understand.

Griffin snapped to attention and quickly rushed to her aid. He held out the woolen throw. "Be careful Missus ap Pryd, for you might catch your gown on fire."

Aelwyd touched his arm and whispered her gratitude. Griffin shook his head and looked around the room. He'd often sat here with Morgan, yet it seemed strange and changed.

"I thank you, Sir Reynolds, for your most generous offer. I am sure Catlin shall be relieved to learn you are going to serve as her escort to the ship and on the voyage to the colonies of Virginia."

Griffin was about to object, but he stared at her, turned to look at the fire, then returned his gaze back to the widow's lovely face. He wasn't going to refuse her request. In fact, he felt familiar and soothing warmth. He wanted to agree to escort Catlin to Virginia. In fact, he was almost sure he had suggested it.

"I, um. . . it is my pleasure to be of service to your family, Missus ap Pryd."

Aelwyd opened the door and nearly toppled Morgan, who was preparing to enter the library with a footman behind him carrying a huge platter of oysters.

"I beg your pardon, Missus." He bowed.

Aelwyd curtsied and fluttered her fan before her face. "My Lord, you must have some interesting plans this evening to need such a vast quantity of oysters. I am happy to see all your appetites have returned in good order."

With that she dashed down the hallway, leaving Morgan with his mouth open in astonishment.

"I just had the most amazing encounter with Missus ap Pryd."

Griffin stared into the fire. He couldn't recall anything that had happened since Morgan left the room to find his steward except his agreement to take Catlin to Virginia with him.

"Oddsfish, what has that woman done to you, Griffin?" There was a note of concern in Morgan's voice.

"She is not a woman, she's a devil. Somehow she made me accept a task that I never wished to accept and yet am anxious to undertake."

"What in hell's name did you agree to, Griffin?"

"It appears I shall be chaperoning Catlin Glyndwr to Bristol, and then across the ocean on a voyage of several months. I shall be forced to maintain a close, very personal relationship with her during that time." He gave his best friend a sly, wicked grin.

Morgan's mouth twisted into an expression of agony, but his eyes glowed with mirth. "Oh, the hell of it, my friend. That woman is most certainly a nagging slattern and you the most cursed of men!"

They burst into a round of loud, raucous laughter.

Chapter Thirteen

"Really, ladies, we must be going." Griffin tried to contain his irritation. It seemed as if their leave-taking had been going on for days instead of only a few hours. Aelwyd kept remembering tidbits of advice she must dispense to Catlin, who then dissolved into tears as the final farewell between the sisters approached.

Griffin had little tolerance for a woman's tears. Surrounded by two weeping females, he found his teeth on edge, pushed to the limits of his patience. He wanted to escape as quickly as possible from this flood of female sentimentality.

He pulled Catlin Glyndwr from her sister's embrace to deposit her in his coach. He was already regretting his impetuous decision to bring the woman along. Actually, he was only guessing it was impetuous, because he had no real memory of the exchange with Aelwyd ap Pryd. All he could remember was some kind of bargain to accompany Catlin to Virginia. Whenever he tried to recall their exact agreement, his head began to ache.

If he had to endure much more of this crying and lamenting he was going to be forced to break his own rule about imbibing spirits this early in the day.

Catlin hung out the coach window, stretching her hands out to her sister. "I shall keep you informed of my progress," she promised.

"Do not hesitate to let me know if you need any kind of assistance," Aelwyd said.

The exchange amused Griffin. They spoke as if they could send a courier from one town to the next. He shook his head. Obviously they didn't understand that a letter from the New World would take months to travel across the Atlantic Ocean. The Glyndwr sisters remaining in England could not hope to learn of Catlin's situation until fall, if even then.

"Let us get on the road," Griffin ordered Carter, and the coach took off in a swirl of dust. Catlin didn't move from the window until they turned a curve, obscuring the view of Mabley Hall. She finally leaned back upon her seat and blew her nose into a handkerchief. Her eyes were rimmed with dark circles, her nose was red from crying, and her cheeks held a bright rose color. Griffin had never beheld such an appealing sight.

Since he had no idea how to offer her any comfort, he feigned interest in the passing landscape. Once she had composed herself, he would engage her in conversation.

She blew her nose again. "I suppose you think all that was just a loud, bawling muddle of overwrought women."

"You shall be separated from your family, probably for a very long time." He nodded at her. "I understand that can be extremely difficult for someone as young and inexperienced as you."

"Do you?" she said, tears still trailing down her cheeks. "I can't imagine a man would truly understand."

Her temerity shocked him. "Do you believe me a cold, unfeeling brute?"

She shrugged. "I do not know you well enough to make any judgments regarding your character."

He frowned at her. "And yet you sought the opportunity to travel as my ward on a long and arduous voyage to the New World." He tapped his fingers on his knee. "A most unusual condition to find yourself in with someone you know so little about."

Catlin lifted her pert little nose and sniffed. "I believe I'm a good judge of character, and the fact that you have kept my secrets up until now suggests you can be trusted."

Griffin crossed one leg over the other and leaned back against the seat. "Can you say the same of our interlude in the cottage the other day?"

She turned a bright pink. And Griffin found himself shifting in his seat as he recalled the way her body had responded to his, the way her lips had opened to invite him to taste the sweetness within her mouth. He didn't intend to embarrass her, but he needed to be honest regarding this issue.

"I would not expect a repeat of such behavior between us." She said, lifting her chin and pasting a patient smile on her plump lips.

Griffin gave a hearty laugh. "Catlin, we are going to be on board a ship, in dreadfully close quarters for several months. Do you actually believe we can fight this attraction we have for each other?"

The blush turned her cheeks scarlet before flowing down her neck and shading even the small décolleté visible at the edge of the ecru lace on her gown. He tried to look away, but she was like a luscious fruit that tempted him at every turn. They had been alone together for a less then a quarter hour and his self-control was already waning. Why in hell didn't he foresee this dilemma before agreeing to escort her?

Even as the thought occurred to him, he knew it would have changed nothing. He had probably agreed to Aelwyd's proposal because he wanted to be alone with Catlin Glyndwr. He found her innocence charming, her mind fascinating, and her sensuous curves attracted him like a butterfly to the sweet nectar of a rose. The fact he had imbibed too much of the good earl's claret that evening had given him the freedom to easily agree to something that appealed greatly to him anyway.

No, he could not blame anyone but himself for his current predicament. He had vowed to protect and defend Catlin, but he could end up being the biggest threat to her virtue.

"I know we share a certain, mutual attraction." She paused to wet her lips.

The movement of her small, pink tongue caused a quick, sharp hardening in the area of his groin. *God's teeth*, the woman could arouse him with no effort whatsoever. How in the hell was he going to resist her charms for months on end?

"We are adults, and so can recognize the need to manage our behavior. I trust you implicitly, Sir Reynolds. I believe you are a gentleman and would not take advantage of me."

Once again the image of the fox guarding the hen house entered his mind. The Glyndwr women had too little experience in the world to recognize a rogue when they encountered one.

But did he want to destroy her image of him as a fine and noble gentleman? For some reason, her innocent trust in him appealed to his sense of chivalry. Emotions he had long thought dead rose to bewilder him.

"Of course, I was not speaking as though my intentions were to pursue you, I simply wished to have a discussion before events transpired that we might both regret." A thin film of sweat coated his brow and he wiped it away with one gloved hand.

Catlin shifted in her seat and gave him a winsome smile. "Do not assume I would ever regret anything that transpired between us, Griffin."

The soft, sultry tone of her voice drove a hot explosion of desire through his blood. His ears hummed for a moment, and he shifted again in his seat to relieve the discomfort of his tightening breeches.

"Are you telling me you would welcome a seduction?"

Catlin lifted her dark eyes. "I said I would not regret it."

The blood in Griffin's veins began to sing.

***

Aelwyd had warned Catlin to guard herself around Griffin. Around all men. That once a man bedded her, he would have no interest in pursuing her as a wife.

But Catlin wanted to know if the things she felt when Griffin kissed her were common to kissing any man, or specific to kissing one she especially liked. She found it impossible to forget the way her body had responded to Griffin the day they were caught together in the rainstorm. When she spent time with him, she felt *dallu*, dazzled by rugged good looks that threatened to steal her breath away when they were together. Even sitting in the coach with him was a trial, for she wanted to move closer to him in order to enjoy the warmth of his body against her own. She had never felt such things before and she wanted to experience those sensations again. She could not imagine living in close quarters with Sir Griffin Reynolds and not feeling anything for the man.

Griffin turned from studying the landscape to look at her. "Despite what you've just said, you might regret your impetuous decision to travel to Virginia with me?"

Catlin bristled. "I've hardly had time to formulate any regrets. I suppose it is a long and arduous journey, so perhaps you are correct." She lifted her gaze to blink at him. "But I'm not a woman to whine and bemoan my fate. Once I've made a decison, I find a means to make the best of my situation."

He nodded. "I believe you. But, after the invitation you just issued, Miss Glyndwr, I cannot promise to hold to the vow I made to your sister to protect your virtue."

She shivered her own temerity. What had she been thinking to say such a thing to Griffin? She was no jade, accustomed to flirting with men. She lifted her chin to gaze out the window, attempting to ignore his teasing tone.

They were crossing the River Severn, and she knew the plan was to transfer their baggage to Lord Shrewsbury's barge to travel to Bristol and meet their ship. The excitement that was creating butterflies in her stomach spread up to make her heart beat faster. She was on her way to a grand adventure, and her hopes were high that she'd find a way to keep her family safe.

She changed the subject. "How long will it take for us to reach Bristol?

"If the weather holds as mild as it has been, perhaps only three days." He turned his gaze down to study a map he'd pulled from a case and spread across his lap. Catlin felt dismissed.

She wished she could think of some lively banter to trade with him, but she didn't have the advantage of a season at court. Her life had been lived in the confines of the family keep, with a cadre of loyal servants who had known her all her life. Now she felt like a rough country girl, lacking in all of the social graces.

"Is that a map of Virginia?" she asked.

Griffin lifted his head. "Yes, in fact it is the area surrounding Hawthorne Hundred, which is what the property—" he paused to give her a sheepish grin. "My property is called." He pointed a large, well-shaped finger to a spot on the map. "The main house is here."

"Main house," she echoed. "Is your plantation that large then?"

He shook his head. "I have no inkling as to the size of the house, but the lands surrounding it consist of over six hundred acres. With the indentured servants I'm bringing on the ship, I shall add another three hundred to that parcel."

"And are the woods still inhabited by the naturals?" She shivered. A terrible massacre of colonists by the natives only a few years before had decimated the colony.

"My uncle said in his letters to me that most of the tribes have moved on, or have suffered a great loss of members due to disease." His gaze flickered over her. "You have little to fear, Catlin, for within the confines of Jamestown, you should be safe."

Catlin had no real plan for what she would do once she arrived at Jamestown. She could probably marry quickly after arriving. Even widows were not allowed a natural mourning period in the colonies, for a single woman was a rare commodity and many men were in search of a wife.

She stared down at the map. "Is your plantation close to Jamestown?"

Griffin shook his head. "I do not believe so, for my uncle said it was fortunate to have such deep draft on the James River so the ships can be loaded with tobacco right at Hawthorne Hundred."

"It sounds like a lonely and desolate place." A sudden tremor of fear surged through her at the thought of being abandoned at Jamestown without Griffin's supervision, guidance, and companionship.

"His letters were filled with visits from neighbors and friends, even stories of parties and balls. I think the planters must have their own society and find congregating with each other to be most cordial. He never spoke of loneliness."

"Did he never marry?" she asked, wondering about this strange man who could abandon his native land for a dangerous life in the New World.

"No, he never married. He hated Cromwell and fought for the King. When Charles the first was beheaded, my uncle told my father he had no use for a country that didn't respect the monarchy, and he would leave England forever."

"So much pain and sadness, and he was in exile just like our own King Charles." She gave a deep sigh.

Griffin patted her hand gently. "Do not pity my Uncle Henry too much, for he lived a good and prosperous life. He wrote that he made a better life as a farmer in Virginia then he ever would as a gentleman in England."

"It sounds as if he were content enough." How did one achieve contentment? Her parents had seemed happy enough together, but had they truly experienced a deep and profound love for each other?

Was her own yearning for a love that transcended the usual business arrangement of marriage as foolish and impractical a dream as Aelwyd had always insisted?

She regarded Sir Griffin Reynolds, for lately her thoughts had strayed to fantasies of this man. The thought of taking him as a husband was enticing. Yet he'd never made any reference to the need to acquire a wife. She wondered of his opinion regarding the state of matrimony.

"Will you someday take a wife, Sir Reynolds, in order to have heirs?"

Griffin's brow creased into a frown. "A wife is a heavy burden to assume, so I believe it will be many years before I can marry. 'Tis just as well, for I am not a man inclined to be ruled by the desires of another."

A small lick of temper flared in Catlin. "So, you believe marriage to be a burden, then?"

Griffin laughed. "I have a preference to play the unencumbered rogue, Miss Glyndwr."

Catlin was shocked into silence. Any games of seduction she played with Sir Griffin Reynolds would be perilous. He was very clear about his intentions, and she should heed the warning.

If only she could somehow conquer the impetuous slave to sensation that lurked within her. For that was a part of her nature she sensed could lead her directly into Griffin's arms, and potential disaster if it remained unchecked.

Chapter Fourteen

The *Lady Bountiful* sat at the quay. The masts stood tall in the dull shadows of the late afternoon, and the poor light did nothing to inspire confidence in the aged ship. It was plain looking, with little paint and no ornate carving. With a high forecastle on one end and a raised poopdeck on the other, the middle of the ship was a buzz of activity. Crew members moved up and down the gangplank rolling barrels and carrying wooden boxes of various sizes.

"'Tis smaller then I expected." she said to Griffin.

"There are many ships leaving port for the Chesapeake this spring, but the Master of this ship is known to me, so I chose passage with a man I can trust."

She continued to stare at the ship, but grasped his sentiment. "An honest man is a rare commodity, so I have been told."

"We'll stay at an inn I know until we can board the ship. The winds must be satisfactory to set sail."

A small flicker of light appeared at the very edge of her sight, and she understood the signal. "What day did you hope to sail, sir?"

Griffin grinned, and she felt her heart skip a beat as his gaze seemed to stroke her. "'Twould be most fortunate if we can sail before Easter, for the fair winds are rumored to carry one quickly to the Azores in the early season."

"I expect you are eager to leave, to gain access to your fortune and estate?"

He grinned. "Since I now have you by my side, my fair Catlin, there is naught holding me within the borders of England."

She warmed, and a flicker of excitement spiraled down to her toes. "I have been warned, even by you Sir Griffin, to resist your honeyed words and subtle flirtations."

He leaned back in his seat and brushed a fleck of dust from his breeches. "I warn all ladies to avoid congress with rogues and scoundrels, but alas, few are willing to take my sound advice."

Catlin laughed at him, enjoying this opportunity to relax in his company and practice flirting. "I believe you offer such advice to confound us, Sir. For if you are warning us away from you, does that not increase the attraction?"

Griffin rolled the brim of his felt hat in one gloved hand. Sparkling good humor reflected in the dark chocolate hue of his eyes. "I certainly am counting upon it in your case, Catlin, for temptation is the very heart of seduction, is it not?"

Catlin tossed her head, several curls unraveled from the bondage of the bodkins holding her coiffure in place. "Perhaps, Sir Griffin, but are we not always advised to resist temptation? I believe to succumb to our carnal appetites will put our very souls in jeopardy."

Griffin tapped the roof of the coach and ordered the driver to continue on to the inn. "I can only offer our Lord's continuing pledge of forgiveness as my defense." He grinned. "Besides, isn't the verse 'tis better to rule in hell then to serve in heaven?"

Catlin eyed the profile of the handsome man sitting next to her. She faced a long and arduous battle between her conscience and her desire —a battle that could change her destiny if fought true and well.

Or cost her everything if she made a foolish and impetuous choice.

***

A light tap on the door startled Catlin. She spun around, patted her hair in place, and smoothed the wrinkles from her dark gray silk traveling gown.

A young girl not more then eleven or twelve years old stood on the threshold with eyes downcast. Her hair was a muddled brown beneath a dirty cap. Her worn linsey-woolsey dress was covered by an apron of the same dingy color. Beggin' your pardon, Mistress," she muttered to the floor while executing an awkward curtsy. "Sir Reynolds told me I was to be yer maid."

Catlin frowned. This sprite was very young and likely had no training in service. How useful could she be as a lady's maid?

The girl looked up and curtsied again. "I knows I ain't got the skills yer be needin', but it was the colonies for me or back to the gaol." She took a deep breath. "Sir Reynolds bought me bond and is givin' me passage. He says he thinks I'm right smart and could learn quick."

"Well, if he sent you then I'm sure he is quite right about your abilities." Catlin pointed at the girl's clothing. "But before you enter into my service, we need to get you cleaned up and into some decent clothing."

The girl lifted the edge of her soiled gown and and a tinge of rose colored her cheeks. "'Tis all I've got, Mistress, for before I was arrested I lived on the streets, makin' me way any way I could."

Catlin shuddered at the idea of this young girl forced to live in the shadows and find a way to survive on the dangerous streets of the port city.

"Come in," Catlin said, "and let me have a good look at you."

The girl scuttled into the room to stand near the fire, her small hands stretching out in an effort to warm herself.

She wasn't even five feet tall, and so thin. She obviously hadn't eaten a decent meal in months. Yet, underneath the crust of dirt, clear skin glowed. Her bright eyes and compliant disposition could make her a decent servant.

"What is your name, child?"

"Elizabeth O'Brien is me baptized name, but me Mam always called me Bitsy, 'cause she said I always goin' to be just a little bit of a thing."

Catlin laughed. "Perhaps she is right about that, Bitsy. But, where is your mother now?"

A dark shadow seemed to pass over the girl's face. "Mam died right after Twelfth night, of lung fever. I ain't got no more relations here in Bristol, for me Da died when I was only five."

"And how old are you now, Bitsy?"

The girl looked down at her worn shoes peeking out from beneath the frayed hem of her gown. "I got but thirteen summers, but I ain't afraid of workin' hard, Mistress." When she lifted her gaze, tears edged her brown eyes. Catlin was reminded of her youngest sister, Seren, and sympathy for the girl jolted through her.

"Sir Reynolds, he's givin' me a chance, and I want to show him I can earn me keep," the girl said.

Catlin gave a sigh. How could she refuse to take this poor urchin under her wing? "We shall have to get you cleaned up, Bitsy, for I cannot abide filth of any kind." Catlin circled the girl. "Once we find you some suitable clothing, you will need a bath."

The girl took a step back, a look of alarm crossed her face. "Mam always said too much bathin' causes sickness."

Catlin shook her head. "I believe the reason we have so much sickness and pestilence is because of the fear of a good hot wash with soap. Now let me speak with Sir Reynolds regarding your clothing. Do you know where he is?"

"In the taproom, Mistress. You want I should fetch him?" Bitsy rushed to the door.

"That won't be necessary, I'll go down and find him."

Bitsy's brown cow eyes went wide. "T'ain't proper, Mistress, for you to go down there by yerself."

Catlin flipped a curl over her shoulder and gave the girl a patient smile. "But, when I find Sir Reynolds, I shan't be alone now, shall I?" She tossed her dark blue velvet cloak with the rabbit fur lining over her gown and swept out the door before Bitsy could offer any more objections.

She needed to thank Griffin for being so considerate of her comfort on the voyage. It would have been difficult to fasten her bodices and get into her gowns without assistance. And she certainly did not wish to invite him into her cabin to assist her in undressing. Although the image of his strong fingers slowly untying the ribbons to her bodice and helping her out of her petticoats was enticing.

Too enticing. Catlin sighed deeply. She must gain control of these silly fantasies about the handsome and charming man. It was indecent. Unseemly. Perhaps even lewd!

And so delicious, a small voice chirped. We like him very much. We like the kiss. We want more kissing.

Catlin shook her head to clear it. As if her own imaginings

about the man were not troublesome enough, now her *sylphs* had designs upon the man.

At least she could console herself that she wasn't the only one tempted by the good looking and charming Cavalier. But her elemental spirits could be mischievous and might interfere.

That could ultimately have disastrous results.

Chapter Fifteen

Catlin entered the large taproom of the Boar's Head Inn and paused to allow her eyes to adjust to the smoky haze. Men were seated at rough wooden tables all around the room, but when she entered their voices died down. The proprietor rushed to assist her. "Miss Glyndwr, might I be of service?"

Catlin scanned the many faces. "I was told Sir Griffin Reynolds was here and I wish to speak with him."

"Aye, he was, Miss. But I believe he's gone to his warehouses."

He had warehouses? There was so much about him she needed to learn.

"I thank you." She remembered the dirty young woman waiting back in her room. "Could you send up some hot water for a bath? And a dinner plate too?"

The proprietor nodded and scuttled off.

Catlin pulled her hood up and turned to leave the room.

"Are you Miss Catlin Glyndwr by chance?" a deep male voice said.

Catlin blinked. She had not been introduced to anyone except the Innkeeper since arriving with Griffin last night.

She turned to find a tall, broad-shouldered man with long, dark hair staring at her. He was handsome and had the slick polished manner of the born aristocrat. His lips formed a smile, but there was iciness in his eyes.

"I do not believe we have been formally introduced." She backed away from him. Something about him alarmed her. A ripple of fear slowly swirled up her spine, while tiny pricks of alarm raised the hairs on the back of her neck.

"I apologize for being so bold as to introduce myself, Miss." He made a small bow, but his tone mocked her

"Sir Reynolds mentioned you would be traveling to Virginia on the *Lady Bountiful* when we met this morning. Because of the way he described you, I was sure when you walked into the taproom you were the beauty he spoke so eloquently about."

His pale green eyes glowed with an unnatural light that frightened her. "I am Ioan Purdy, the Earl of Sheffield, and will also be traveling to Virginia on the same ship."

He held out his ungloved hand.. She didn't want to touch him, but to ignore a peer of the realm would be most discourteous. She tentatively stretched out one hand, and regretted that in her rush to come downstairs she'd forgotten her own gloves. When their fingertips touched a jolt of pain arched into her hand and made her wince. She closed her eyes.

When she opened them, a purple and black glow surrounded Lord Sheffield. She yanked her hand away from his as inexplicable dread filled her.

Lord Sheffield stepped closer and sneered. "Don't be afraid," he whispered, "for I know all your secrets and I intend for us to become good friends. Powerful friends, because our kind should stick together, don't you think?"

Catlin whirled away from Lord Sheffield. Clearly, this man meant her harm.

Evil, whispered her *sylphs* in warning, but Catlin didn't need their counsel. The dark circle of black and purple told her everything she needed to know.

The Earl of Sheffield was a magician who practiced the dark arts, and the fact that he could perceive her own abilities made him even more dangerous.

She jerked her arm free and scrambled up the stairs, terrified Lord Sheffield might pursue her, yet too anxious to reach the safety of her chamber to look over her shoulder. She stumbled as she reached the top step.

Strong arms stretched out to catch her before she tumbled backwards. Catlin was so terrified that she struggled against the man who had captured her within his embrace.

"Catlin, what's wrong?"

Sturdy fingers grasped her chin and when she lifted her face, she found Griffin's dark eyes studying her with concern. "What's happened? Are you injured?"

Catlin collapsed against him, grateful for the familiar safety of his strong, muscular body. "There was a man--he approached me in the taproom." She trembled as the wave of terror washed over her again. "I was so afraid," she whispered, hot tears sliding down her cheeks. Her body was shaking and her throat felt dry. Her heart was thumping in her chest.

Griffin took a quick look down the stairs before gently giving her a tug and leading her into a nearby chamber. He kicked the door closed, led her to the bed, and sat down. Then he carefully settled her upon his lap. His fingers traced the outline of her cheek as he made soft, soothing sounds to calm her.

"It will be all right, *cariad*. I would never allow anyone to hurt you."

She leaned her head against his shoulder, comforted by the way he called her darling in her own language.

"I'm sorry, Griffin. It seems such a foolish thing, but there was something strange about the man. He was so evil, that it terrified me."

Griffin stroked her back gently. "You should not have gone down there by yourself, you know. Why didn't you send that girl I hired to be your maid, the little bit of a thing?"

Catlin had forgotten all about Bitsy, who was probably still standing in the middle of her chamber waiting for her to return. She stood, reluctant to leave the safety of Griffin's arms, but aware the close proximity of their bodies made her think about long, lingering kisses.

"That is exactly what I was coming down to speak with you about, but then you weren't there, and so this man, he said he knew you, and then. . ." Her voice trailed off. She blinked back tears as she recalled the image of the tall, dark man who had terrifed her with just a touch of his hand. The same horrible, retching fear consumed her again.

Griffin stood up and wrapped his arms around her. "Catlin, I don't understand, but please trust me. What is it about this man that terrifies you so?"

Catlin stared into his eyes. Could she trust him with one of her most precious secrets?

"It might sound ridiculous but this man had a strange light surrounding him, and it--" She took a step back away from him in order to better watch his expression.

"A light, coming from behind him?" Griffin said, a quizzical look on his face. He seemed to be struggling to understand her.

Catlin straightened her shoulders. "No, it comes from within a person. It's a way of judging his, or her, true purpose. And even more than that, my sisters and I can tell if a person is truly evil."

Griffin's brow wrinkled. "You can actually see such a thing?"

She nodded. "All the women in my family have the gift."

Griffin drew one hand through the long length of his hair." I don't wish to sound as if I doubt you, Catlin, but this thing you're describing, it's difficult to understand."

Catlin shook her head sorrowfully. "That's not the only problem, Griffin. This man--" She took a deep breath. "He's going to be on the ship with us."

Griffin stared down into her eyes. "I've promised on may occasions to protect you, Catlin, and I will honor that vow with my life, if necessary."

She swallowed hard at his statement. Her body relaxed against him, leaning into the strength of his courage and gallentry. She closed her eyes, inhaling the wonderful scent of sandalwood, tobacco, and unique male essence that always surrounded Griffin. A small flame of desire swirled within her and the sensitive tips of her breasts seemed suddenly too tender and painful against the fabric of her shift.

When she opened her eyes, Griffin stared at her, his eyes smoldering. Catlin wrapped her arms around his neck. All conscious thought flew from her mind, and she felt as if her very bones were melting into a puddle of hot, molten pewter. A sultry heat cascaded through her, making her skin warm and tender every place their bodies touched. His strong, thick fingers gently stroked her hair and the heavy curls tumbled down her back as the bodkins came loose and tumbled to the floor.

His mouth conquered hers in a kiss that was tender yet demanding. The joining of their lips progressed to an eager, hungry exploration. When his tongue gently flickered across her mouth, it was as if he patiently tested her willingness to give him more.

She was more then willing, as the spiral of desire that had started out as a tiny flame built to an uncontrollable inferno. His fingers moved from her hair to unfasten the clasp of her cloak, and the heavy velvet fabric fell from her shoulders and pooled at her feet.

"My sweet Cat, you are so soft and delicate, yet so filled with fire." He murmered.

His lips moved across her mouth again, tenderly exploring the sensitive interior of her mouth just beyond her teeth. When his tongue surged forward, she tasted rich coffee in his kiss. She wanted more of him, as every sensation her body experienced was heightened to the point of inflicting pain.

"I vowed to protect your innocence, yet at every touch I desire you more." His eyes pleaded with her. "How can I fight this urge to sweep you up, carry you to my bed and ravish you?"

She peered at him from beneath her lashes. The heat between them sizzled. The way he gently caressed her, making her feel treasured and protected, filled her with an intense desire to share herself with him--mind, body and soul.

"Why must you resist, sir?"

With a groan, Griffin swept her up into his arms and carried her across the room to lay her gently on the coverlet of the high, four-poster bed.

"Catlin, are you sure about this? I don't want you to regret this later."

Catlin drew put her arms around his neck and pulled him toward her for another sweet, sensuous kiss. "I am sure that I want you, Griffin Reynolds, and no other."

Chapter Sixteen

Griffin removed the baldric holding his sword. He pulled the tall, heavy leather boots from his feet, and tossed them aside with no regard for anything except that the voluptuous, delightful Catlin Glyndwr was inviting him to seduce her.

He was hard as stone, and the blood rushed through his veins like liquid fire. For a moment his conscience battled with his aching need, but his ravenous carnal hunger overcame his remorse at breaking his word to Aelwyd ap Pryd.

His fingers tangled in the ribbons of Catlin's bodice, and he had a brief impulse to use his dagger to quickly vanquish the pesky fastenings. His heart banged out a vigorous rhythm against his rib cage and his eagerness to taste the sweet fruit Catlin offered made him clumsy as an untried youth.

Catlin's beautiful, full lips formed into a smile as he made quick work of pulling the two pieces of silk fabric apart before yanking them above her head. Her gown quickly followed, for the tortoise-shell buttons fastening it posed no challenge for his impatient fingers.

When she was finally garbed only in her stockings and garters, she gave a pretty shiver, but the expression in her soft blue eyes didn't reflect fear. Griffin breathed a sigh of relief. He needed to calm himself, take his time and pleasure her with skill. His impatience to take her was making him awkward.

Griffin took his time enjoying the view of a naked and aroused Catlin. The pretty speech he'd planned to make withered in his throat, as mere words seemed too paltry a thing with which to worship this goddess.

"I dreamt of you like this so many times, yet the reality of your beauty robs me of my senses," he finally whispered.

Sweeping one palm down from her shoulder to slide across a pink-tipped breast, he paused to imprint her image upon his memory. If he only had this one night with her, he wanted it to last as long as possible. Likely on the morrow she would brand him a scheming rogue and demand he return her to her family. His finger circled the tender tip of the orb before he knelt and took it in his mouth and suckled.

As his lips moved to the other breast, she thrashed against the coverlet. Heat pulsed through him at every touch. Her skin was as soft and supple and he couldn't resist tracing the outline of her curves with each hand.

His cock throbbed as it pressed against his wool breeches. He thought he might burst before he could push himself into the soft, yielding heat of Catlin's body. Yet, he wanted to take this lovemaking slowly, to appreciate each precious moment with her.

Griffin stood to remove his breeches, and Catlin blinked as his cock sprang free. She tilted her head as she examined his body, and a slow smile stretched across her face. "You are far better endowed than the drawings of Greek statues I've seen. I doubt a fig leaf could cover that very well."

Griffin grinned as he yanked his shirt off, eager to return to the bed and Catlin. "Perhaps an oak leaf might suffice?"

She didn't shun his nakedness or respond with a maidenly shyness. Instead, her lips puckered with mirth. "Perhaps two oak leaves?"

He put one knee on each side of her body, then tucked one of his hands beneath her soft, round bottom. Her body shifted as he parted her legs, the fingers of his other hand gently kneaded the muscles at the top of her thigh. He enjoyed the velvet smoothness of her skin before dividing the dark curls at the apex of her womanhood to pull her tender lips apart. She gave a low gasp when he touched her there.

Catlin's eyes widened as Griffin leaned across her body, his mouth trailing hot, eager kisses down her flat stomach, to her thighs, and then even lower.

She moaned when his tongue replaced his finger at that most tender of pleasure spots. She leaned back upon the pillows, twisting beneath him as he savored the sweet woman's honey pouring from her. She desired him, for it was in the liquid heat he tasted with each stroke of his tongue against the satiny delights.

"I, never. . ." she moaned softly before gasping when his tongue flickered across the tender, sweet nubbin at the top of the opening.

He could fulfill her this way, but her sweet taste fired all of his senses, and he wanted to push himself deep within her, to feel the slick tightness of her body sheathed around him.

He left her heat, grasped one of her hands and guided her fingers to his rigid cock. He showed her how to touch him, and her gentleness against his flesh nearly brought him to rapture.

"Your touch could unman me this very instant," he said, his voice thick and husky with his desire.

She quickened the strokes, her mouth opened slightly. Her eyes glowed with a silver light as she gave him a saucy, delighted smile. He groaned with the exquisite pleasure she was giving him. Finally he was forced to push her hand away.

He gently moved her thighs apart and placed his swollen cock into the space between them. He paused and regarded her stretched beneath him, her lips red and swollen from the rough, demanding kisses of his lovemaking.

"I will ask you again, my *bychan* Cat, are you sure about this?"

He held his breath as he waited for her answer. If she refused him now, he'd need all of his self-control to climb off the bed and walk away from her. He couldn't be sure he had the fortitude to do it.

"I am sure of this, Griffin. If you don't finish this soon, I predict a nasty tantrum the likes of which you have never before seen in your life!"

He leaned down to kiss her and grinned. "'Tis a good thing too, *cariad*, because even though I asked, I cannot swear I could have stopped myself from ravishing you."

She touched his face gently, her fingers tracing along his jaw line. He'd called her his darling. Did she truly believe he'd meant it or did she suspect it might simply be an endearment uttered in the heat of passion? He again guided her hand to enclose his rigid flesh.

"'Twill be better your first time if you have some control, for it there will be some pain, if only for a few moments."

She nodded as she placed the sensitive tip of his cock at the edge of her moist, parted lower lips. Her hand trembled as she paused.

His own hand covered hers, and he thrust quickly to plunge into her silken depths.

Catlin gasped as her eyes flew wide-open. Griffin paused for a moment to give her time to adjust to having him within her. He swallowed at the sight of tears in her eyes.

He kissed her gently. "I'm sorry, *cariad*."

Her tight, hot, softness surrounded him. With the gentlest of movements, he pulled back before plunging once more into her steamy depths. It was heavenly torture, this pushing, only to withdraw and then push again. The rhythm of this dance was so natural, so primal that she tilted her hips up to meet him as he drove his cock down into her.

Her eyes closed, but she was breathing in short, eager pants. He put his hands beneath her bottom again, lifting her closer, plunging deeper.

Her eyes were glazed when she finally opened them to gaze up at him.

Griffin paused, fighting the urge to complete this coupling, forcing himself to go slowly for her sake.

"Are you in pain, Catlin?" he whispered.

She gave him a small, wicked smile. "I was, but now, there is so much pleasure and new sensation, I only wish to enjoy this as much as possible."

Griffin couldn't postpone his pleasure much longer. The slick tightness of her body brought him to the edge of completion with each thrust. But this was her first time, and he wanted Catlin to experience that moment of intense satisfaction he knew he could give her.

His strokes grew longer, harder and deeper. The rhythm intensified, until tension swelled within him. He'd soon be pushed over the edge.

Suddenly, her inner muscles tightened around him. Griffin," she gasped her voice rough and husky.

He closed his eyes as the room tilted sideways. A rainbow of colored lights flashed upon his lids, making him dizzy with a sensation of soaring through time and space.

A rush of air escaped Griffin's lips before he uttered a deep, satisfied moan. The hot pulse of his seed released into her.

With a few more thrusts, he stilled and rested upon his elbows on top of her, the expanse of their naked, sated bodies touching skin upon skin. She still held him deep within her.

Finally he regained his senses, opened his eyes, and leaned down to kiss her.

"I'm sorry if I hurt you, *cariad*."

Catlin's eyes slowly opened. "'Twas worth the cost of a pinprick to gain so much pleasure." She smiled provocatively. "I have a great desire to be tutored in the ways of lovemaking, and I believe I could be an apt pupil to a talented instructor such as you."

Griffin grinned down at her. "It will require long hours of tedious exercise, for I can be a most demanding teacher." One hand gently stroked her breast and the rosy nipple grew to a hard nubbin in his hand.

Catlin moaned. "I shall apply myself most diligently to my lessons, I assure you, Sir Reynolds."

His mouth moved to explore the hard tip of her round, full breast, and she squirmed beneath him.

"Well, schooling will likely resume in a short time, but for now we should enjoy a brief respite." He kissed her gently on the nose. "I have business to attend to, and you should put your new maid to some good use."

Catlin sat up abruptly. "God's teeth, but I forgot all about her!"

Struggling to bring her legs over the side of the bed, she gave a small flutter of protest when Griffin easily captured her. He pushed her back upon the pillows, with one hand enclosing both of hers to pin them above her head.

"Perhaps I should reconsider." He flicked his tongue across the tender skin beneath her ear. "I might not want to release so adept a pupil."

Catlin pouted. "But I left Bitsy waiting for me in my chamber, and I promised her a bath and some new clothes." She worried her lower lip. "That's the reason I went to the taproom in search of you, and somehow I became totally distracted and forgot the very reason I was pursuing you."

"Ah, but the important thing is that you caught me, *cariad*, and for that I am eternally grateful. It certainly makes me the most fortunate man in the kingdom today." His hand brushed against the pile of dark curls between her legs, and she squirmed before shaking her head and brushing his fingers away.

"We can continue our lessons at a later time, but I should see to the girl, for she's probably terrified."

Guilt flashed through Catlin for abandoning the girl to enjoy sensual play with Griffin. For years Aelwyd had warned Catlin she must learn to control her uninhibited nature, or it would lead to her downfall.

Griffin released her, and Catlin jumped from the bed to grab her petticoats. She yanked them over her thighs and turned to ask for his help in fastening them.

"I derive more pleasure from divesting you of your clothing then assisting you in donning it," he complained.

Catlin batted his straying hands away and picked her gown up from the floor. "We shall certainly have more then enough time to indulge in games of pleasure on board the ship. You said you have business to deal with today, and I must see to Bitsy."

Griffin grinned down at her. "I'm relieved you've accepted her services, for I couldn't abandon the poor waif upon the dock. She looked so lost and forlorn."

Catlin smiled at this proof of his gentle heart. While he might appear a cold and hardened soldier to some, he had demonstrated to her on several occasions that he possessed a kind spirit.

"I think you chose well, for it appears the child has had a miserable time of it these past few months. We shall make sure her circumstances improve."

Griffin stood and snatched his clothes from the messy pile where he'd discarded them. "I'm going to my warehouse, then I'll stop by and speak to the ships Master. I'll ask that the knave you told me about be removed from the ship's crew. Too bad you don't know his name. 'Twould make the task easier."

"But he told me his name, as if he were fully entitled to make my acquaintance without a proper introduction."

Griffin shook his head. "Imagine the impudence of the man, he should be drawn and quartered!"

Catlin frowned. The man had frightened her, and Griffin was jesting. "He is evil incarnate and should not be allowed on the ship to America. Who knows what kind of wicked intent he has for traveling to Jamestown?"

Griffin yanked his breeches up his legs and laced them. "I shall make sure he troubles you no more, my sweet Catlin. Simply give me the man's name and I'll see he's put off the ship!"

Catlin lifted on her tip toes to give him a grateful kiss. His hands grasped her waist and he pulled her closer. Their mouths slid against each other in a wicked tease.

"I can't tell you why he frightens me so, but 'twill be easier for me if I know he isn't stalking my steps each day."

Griffin touched one cheek gently. "Of course, now the lout's name, so I can make sure he never troubles you again."

"Lord Purdy, the Earl of Sheffield." Goosebumps rose on her skin at the name.

Griffin's body stiffened and he stared down at her with a shocked expression. His hands dropped suddenly to his sides.

"The Earl of Sheffield," he said in a hollow voice. "Are you sure?"

"Absolutely." She nodded. "He seemed quite proud of his title, and I think he tried to use it to impress me. He even thought I'd allow him the liberty of kissing my hand."

Griffin's silence troubled her, and she backed up to better see the expression on his face.

"What's wrong?"

"I cannot ask the Master to remove him from the ship." His voice was cool and detached.

Catlin felt a lump form in her throat. Griffin had assured her he'd get rid of the man who frightened her. What would make him change his mind so quickly?

"He's an evil man, Griffin. You must ask the Master to leave him here in Bristol. I cannot bear the thought of traveling on a ship for several months with such a man." She shuddered at the thought, her skin growing icy cold with goose bumps.

Griffin sat down on the bed. His eyes held a dark storm of emotion, and he held his hands out to her, as if begging for her forgiveness.

"It isn't because I don't wish to do as you ask, Catlin. It simply isn't possible."

His remorse failed to move her as she stamped her foot in protest. "You swore you believed me, Griffin. Was that merely a ploy to get me to share your bed?" Tears filled her eyes.

He stood up, anger transforming his face into a mask of fury. "I asked not once, but twice if you were sure you wished to surrender your virtue to me. Do not play these games with me. 'Tis too late for regrets."

She tossed her hair and her temper flared. "I believe it is you who are the more practiced at such sport, for I am a simple country lass with no worldly veneer from traveling the continent or visiting the lascivious court."

Griffin stood above her, his fists clenched as the muscle beneath the faint scar on his cheek twitched. "I have not teased your maidenhood from you nor played false with your emotions. I pledged my protection to you upon my honor, and would do as you ask if only 'twere possible."

"Pretty talk," she spat at him, "but I wonder if you are afraid of the prowess of this earl and think he might challenge you to a duel over his right to travel on the Lady Bountiful."

Gray clouds shadowed his eyes, and the twitch in his cheek grew to a pulsing throb. "Enough of these insults to my honor, for you know nothing of the ways of the world. You've just admitted that." He drew one hand through his hair. "It's not possible to put the man off the ship because in truth, he owns the damned thing. He's a powerful lord who has been appointed to a high post in the colonies." He crossed his arms across his chest. "I am neither rich enough nor influential enough to challenge the man, so I cannot do as you ask."

Catlin stared at Griffin and tried to absorb his words. "He owns the *Lady Bountiful*?" She stood in the center of the room, as if frozen to the spot by an icy wind swirling down from the North Country. "Then we shall be forced to seek passage on another ship, perhaps one that leaves next week." She tried to keep the quiver of fear from her voice. "It should not delay us too long, for ships sail every day from Bristol to the colonies."

Griffin crossed the floor and grasped her shoulders. "We

cannot wait for another ship, for I have paid passage on this one." He released her and and she felt like a great weight sat upon her chest.

"I'm not a rich man, Catlin, and I need every copper I have for improvements to the plantation." He walked to the window and opened the shutter.

He gestured out the window toward the water. "My future lies out there, across the sea. I will not give up my dream because you experienced some childish foreboding when you encountered a stranger."

Catlin's belly cramped as though she'd been struck, and she reeled in shock at his words.

"You must decide, Catlin, because I aim to leave on that ship on the morrow. You may come or you may stay. It is of no consequence to me." He stormed out the door and slammed it behind him, leaving his angry words hanging in the air.

Hot tears slid down Catlin's face. She recalled Aelwyd's warning.

Trust no man, for they all turn faithless in the end.

Chapter Seventeen

All her life, people had warned Catlin to beware of her impulsive notions, and yet time and again she'd been the victim of her own recklessness. Perhaps never more so then today, she mused, as she left Griffin's chamber and headed for her own.

Not that she regretted her sensual interlude with Griffin. She'd never felt so many wonderful, delightful things. But, she needed time to sit and sort out her experience with him. Griffin had given her several weak excuses for remaining on the *Lady Bountiful*. But, she knew he wasn't telling her the true reason.

Catlin need not have worried about Bitsy, who was sitting cross-legged on the floor in front of a blazing fire. She had a large trencher balanced on her lap and was finishing a hearty meal. Her eyes grew wider as Catlin entered the room, and she stumbled to perform an awkward curtsy.

"Beggin' yer pardon, Miss, but I was hungry, and the food smelled so good, I didn't mean to..." She indicated the empty platter. "I guess I didn't know me own belly."

"I ordered all the food for you, Bitsy. I can see you're much too thin and anyone working for me will need to be strong and hearty. Now finish up, and then you can have your bath."

Steam rose from a large wooden tub in front of the bed. Catlin bustled to her clothing chest to grab a bar of wrapped soap scented with lavender, a rough cloth, and one of her linen shifts.

She turned to Bitsy. "I want you to scrub yourself until every inch of you shines, do you understand?"

"Egad, Mistress," the girl protested. "Don't ye know too much scrubbin' is bound to give ye the smallpox? That's what me Mam always said." Bitsy stepped closer to the fire and away from the hot water in the tub.

"Nonsense," snapped Catlin. "I suspect you're full of vermin, and a good scrubbing will rid you of them." She straightened to her full height. "I cannot abide filth, so if you will not bathe I shall just have Sir Reynolds return you to the gaol."

A look of horror crossed the young girl's face. Catlin hadn't meant to terrify the child, but her mother had held that better bathing habits would save many a life if practiced by the more unfortunate members of society.

Catlin put the shift on the bed and pointed at Bitsy. "I haven't had time to purchase new clothing for you." Her cheeks warmed when she remembered exactly what she had found time to accomplish this morning.

"I can wear me own things after I wash."

Catlin put a finger on her mouth as she considered the girl's clothing, which was little more than tattered rags. "I'll give you a few things to wear, and once you are cleaned up and dressed we shall go out and buy you new shoes.

Bitsy squealed. "Egads, Mistress, I ain't never had me no new shoes."

She crossed the room and stripped off the torn and filthy clothing. "I swear, I'll scrub meself until my skin peels off."

Catlin turned her back as the girl splashed into the tub. Bitsy gave a surprised yelp and Catlin whirled quickly.

"Are you alright?"

Bitsy nodded. "I'll be fine, just the water was hotter than I s'pected. No worries, Mistress." She held the bar of scented soap to her nose. "Will I smell as good as this when I'm done?"

"Surely, and I'll even find a few ribbons for your hair if you allow me to comb out the snarls."

Catlin's promise elicited another squeal. "Ye and himself must be the best folks there ever was, for I'll be the envy of every girl on the ship with all me fine clothes and such."

Catlin sorted through her carved wooden chest and found a gown, apron, and stomacher for Bitsy. She kept wondering what compelled Griffin to hold to his decision that they sail on the *Lady Bountiful*. He'd always been honest with her before. But it was clear he harbored a secret. It was a mystery she was determined to solve.

***

Despite their argument, Catlin never wavered in her resolve to travel with Griffin to Virginia. Their dinner conversation that evening was stilted, with references to the mild weather, questions about Bitsy, and comments regarding the food.

As she watched him eat, she considered using a tiny spell to make him change his mind. It would be easy to convince him that they could wait a few days and sail upon another ship. Yet Aelwyd had used magic to convince him to bring her on the voyage in the first place. And there was the matter of the love spell she'd cast when they were stranded in the cottage.

Griffin was no fool, and he might grow suspicious if he once more agreed to something he didn't remember.

"Did you find the items you needed for your little maid?"

"She was absolutely delighted with everything I purchased for her. I've never seen anyone so happy about a new pair of shoes." Catlin smiled despite her annoyance at Griffin. "When I bought several very serviceable linsey-woolsey gowns for her, she acted as if I'd given her the finest velvet and brocade."

Griffin smiled back. "She's likely to be a mischievous imp, but I couldn't stand seeing her sent back to that cesspool of a prison." A dimple appeared at the corner of his mouth.

"I should warn you," Catlin said. "I believe she's quite besotted with you. She chatters on endlessly about how handsome, strong and noble you are. You've gained an ardent admirer."

He shot her an amorous look. "If only her mistress still held the same regard for me." Griffin's coffee-colored eyes sparkled with a sensual invitation.

Catlin grabbed her wine goblet and took a long drink. Gads, the *damniol* man was irresistible. When he looked at her like that, her blood nearly boiled. Details of their afternoon tumble sprang into her head, nearly making her choke.

"I possess a high regard for you, Sir Griffin." She took another sip of wine.

"Really, and yet I think you are perturbed with me at the moment because I would do your bidding today."

Catlin shrugged, suddenly aware that the room was too warm.

She pulled her woolen shawl from around her shoulders. "I was distraught because you said you believed me about the things I sensed regarding Lord Sheffield, yet you refuse to change your plans for sailing upon his vessel."

Griffin speared a slice of roast beef. "It is quite possible you sensed the man is evil, for I've heard enough tales about him to know he possesses a bad reputation. But that changes nothing."

Catlin wanted to object, to find out why he was being so pigheaded, yet she didn't want to argue with him again. She wasn't sure of the depth of the spell Aelwyd had cast upon him. If it wore off before they left Bristol, she might find herself stranded upon the shore.

"I won't deny many of the gentry have behaved in a most deplorable manner these past few years. I think 'tis a pity our king doesn't always demonstrate good judgment when considering who shall be rewarded for service to his majesty." He tore a bit of dark bread from the loaf.

Catlin toyed with the stem of her pewter goblet. "And yet you insist we sail with such a man, and I cannot fathom your reasoning."

Griffin gave her a dark glower. "I'm not a man accustomed to explaining myself to anyone, much less to a woman."

Catlin's heart thumped. The stern tone of his voice frightened her a bit.

Griffin sighed. "I beg your pardon, Catlin, for my foul mood, and for being such a poor supper companion." I have been forced to neglect the properties left to me for many months, to serve the king. I'm anxious to finally be off to take control of my plantation. If I seem too abrupt or gruff with you, 'tis simply my eagerness to become a man of means."

He returned to his meal. A ribbon of dark brown interwoven with dull red appeared, just barely visible, above his head.

Griffin Reynolds was lying.

***

Griffin hated deceiving Catlin, especially after she'd offered him the gift of her body and her trust, but if he divulged his true purpose for insisting they sail upon the *Lady Bountiful*, her life could be in jeopardy.

Damn the king and his constant demands. Such thoughts were treasonous, yet he couldn't help feeling constrained by the stipulations his majesty, Charles Stuart II, put upon anyone who declared their loyalty. First he'd faced the debacle in Ireland, now another dangerous mission to the New World.

Rumors that a group of Puritans conspired to assassinate the king had surfaced. Griffin had been dispatched to investigate. That he'd recently been named heir to a tidewater tobacco plantation was a convenient coincidence. Griffin had assumed a ruse, at first, pretending an eagerness to find a new life in the colonies. Later, the idea had seized him, and he began to dream that he might retire his commission and become a gentleman farmer.

Never before had the idea of exchanging his adventurous life as a member of the elite corps that spied for his majesty appealed to him. Lately, though, the thought of settling down, staying in one place for longer than a few weeks and gaining some peace had obsessed him.

The more time he spent with the bewitching Catlin Glyndwr, the more intense his longing became for that bucolic life in Virginia.

He watched Catlin surreptitiously as she sat across from him in the coach, engaged in earnest conversation with her little maid. Just as he had suspected the moment he spied the small, dirty urchin standing with the other prisoners offering indentured service to escape their sentences, the girl had stirred Catlin's nurturing sensibilities. He grinned at how the girl kept pushing her feet out from beneath her gown and petticoat to admire her new shoes.

The coach stopped at the quay and the door opened. Griffin descended and held out a hand to assist Catlin. She dazzled him, garbed in a gown of dark blue silk that mimicked the color of her eyes. Silver lace edged her generous bosom, and his eyes were drawn to the deep valley between her breasts. In a flash his desire made itself apparent, and he chastised himself for acting like a boy smitten with his first maid. She fired his blood with passion. When she was this close, her breath warming him with its sweetness, her womanly scent rising to entice him, he had to force his mind elsewhere to maintain his composure.

"I've been able to arrange a cabin for you, so you won't be forced to sleep t'ween decks." Griffin pointed at the Lady Bountiful bobbing at anchor. "It'll provide you with a bit more privacy."

He'd paid dearly for the cabin at this late date, bribing the Master to ensure Catlin was not put in the large communal living quarters that many passengers shared between decks. Privacy was especially important now, considering the events that had transpired between them yesterday. He fully intended to become her tutor in the many ways of carnal satisfaction, just as she'd suggested. She was too rich a temptation for him to resist.

Catlin frowned as they faced the ship. "'Tis still too small a craft for such an arduous journey, if you ask me."

Griffin put his hand on her back and steered her toward the gangplank stretched from the quay to the ship. "I assure you, this ship has made the journey many times, in addition to being sent to the East Indies for trade. It is a small ship, but sea-worthy."

The crew scrambled to stow barrels and large wooden crates below in the main hold. Griffin didn't miss noticing the many heads that turned when he strolled on deck with Catlin upon his arm. She was a beautiful woman, and he'd need to guard her well on the journey. They'd be many weeks at sea, even with a fair wind, and other men aboard would covet her.

As the Master's eyes dropped to feast upon the expanse of creamy bosom Catlin displayed, Griffin felt the urge to issue a warning to the man. He resisted, and then stepped forward to block the other man's view.

"Please allow me to introduce Miss Catlin Glyndwr." He flicked a hand in her direction but still blocked the Master's eyes from a full view. "I'll be escorting her to Virginia and have been given the privileged position of guarding and protecting her on the voyage."

"And who serves to protect her from you, Sir Reynolds?"

The smooth, cultured voice was familiar, and Catlin took a quick step closer to Griffin, bumping against him as another man stepped from the shadows.

Griffin bowed. "Sheffield, I didn't expect to see you on board so early."

Ioan Purdy, the Earl of Sheffield, crept closer, his cat-like green eyes never straying from Catlin. "I have much to look forward to on this voyage and was eager to be here when our most honored passengers came aboard."

Catlin's breathing quickened and her skin flushed. She trembled as Griffin turned to grasp her arm. She was visibly shaken by the sudden appearance of Sheffield.

"I beg your pardon, Sheffield, but I wish to settle Miss Glyndwr into her quarters. Please excuse us."

He started to turn in the other direction, but the Earl of Sheffield stopped him by stepping arrogantly in front of them.

"It is because I most ardently wish for an introduction to the lady that I came aboard early." He stepped closer to Catlin, hot desire flashing through his eyes. "I fear when I approached her yesterday at the Inn, my eagerness to make her acquaintance made me forget the standards of etiquette." He bowed to her. "I wish to make amends today."

Catlin took a small step backwards. Her mouth twisted into a tremulous grimace. He couldn't think of any way to avoid introducing her to Sheffield that wouldn't be a blatant insult to the nobleman.

He sighed and turned to a now pale and obviously upset Catlin. "May I introduce the Honourable Miss Catlin Glyndwr, daughter of the late Baron Glyndwr of *Llithfaen Keep* in Wales." He squeezed her arm gently for reassurance. "Catlin, this is the Earl of Sheffield, who has recently been appointed secretary to the Governor of Virginia?"

Lord Sheffield stepped forward, his gaze never wavering from performing a blistering appraisal of Catlin.

"I'm enchanted to meet you, Miss Glyndwr, and I hope we shall have ample time on this journey to become well-acquainted." He grasped her hand and touched his lips to her gloved fingers.

A chill traveled through Griffin as Catlin recoiled from Sheffield's touch. A predatory glow in the man's eyes signaled his desire for her more than words ever could.

Griffin steered Catlin away from the man. He glowered at Sheffield, offended by the man's supercilious behavior. Before he could utter a rebuke, Catlin stumbled and he put his arms around her for support.

Catlin turned to him, real terror stamped upon her face and reflected in her eyes. "I'm not feeling well, Griffin."

"I'll take care of you," he whispered as she melted into his embrace.

Her sky-blue eyes flickered, then closed as her body went limp and she collapsed in his arms.

It was clear to him that she had finally succumbed to the excitement of sailing to the New World. Or it was possible she suffered from an over tight stomacher. Bitsy was not a practiced ladies maid.

But, why had Catlin suddenly seemed so terrified?

Chapter Eighteen

darkness swirls around me, the air so thick it's as though the murky fog of a fall evening envelops me. There is a silence both strange and frightening. No small animal stirs in these gloomy shadows. No leaf rustles in the breeze. I'm suspended within a cocoon of mist and night. A malignant presence is here with me, and I shudder to imagine who or what is waiting beyond the inky darkness.

A dim figure stands at the edge of my consciousness, and I hope it is Griffin calling me back to his world. When the figure moves, something familiar yet frightening swirls within me. Instinct tells me it's not Griffin. Terror ripples through me, because even before his face becomes clear to me, I know who lurks in this preternatural gloom, waiting for me.

"You cannot be here," I whisper hoarsely, aware my voice signals my alarm.

The Earl of Sheffield moves with the casual elegance of one born into a life of privilege and status. His long legs carry him through the fog, until he stops within an arms breadth of me. I fight the urge to turn away and run. He cannot know how much he terrifies me. 'Twould be an advantage I have no intention of giving him.

"I brought you here so we could talk without your nuisance of a protector coming between us." He gives me a wicked grin. "He is most attentive for a man who claims the duty of chaperone was somehow foisted upon him."

Catlin clasped her hands into tight fists, ready to defend herself if necessary. "I do not see how my travel arrangements are of any import to you, milord." I lift my nose in the air and would wave my fan in his face, if I were actually holding a fan.

He grins, his teeth looking sharp as a wild beast in his wide mouth.

"I'm interested in every facet of your life, my bychan dewines."

I step back at the implied possession and endearing tone in his voice when he refers to me as his "little witch" in my own tongue. "How dare you call me that?" I protest. "I am not, nor shall I ever be, your anything." Venom fills my voice. "And while I won't refute the description you give me, I see the truth of who you are. I know you are a creature of the dark arts."

Lord Sheffield takes another step closer to grasp me around the waist. I'm shocked he can actually touch me in this shadow world. I'm truly horrified now, for I have no way of protecting myself from this assault. He jerks me closer, until his face looms over mine while his thickly muscled arms crush me to him.

"While others might be blind to the blackness within your soul, I know you for the wicked magician you are." I say.

Does this revelation affect him? His response is another sly grin. It infuriates me.

"And I know you are an elemental witch, Catlin Glyndwr. If I am wicked because I wish to possess you and help you learn to fully appreciate and use your powers, then I accept your assessment of my character."

His green eyes glow with a preternatural, searing, desire. I struggle against him, but his arms hold me as fast as if I am in a vise.

"Release me," I demand, trying to infuse my voice with more courage then I actually feel. Yet it still sounds more like a pathetic plea then an order. "I'm disgusted by your touch! You will never possess me nor use my magic."

His gaze scans my body, and I feel bile rising to my throat. I can't fathom where I am, for it couldn't be Dream Time. Horrible things like this have never happened here before. I close my eyes and make an attempt to summon my sylphs.

Sheffield quickly turns his face away from me and he frowns. While I don't know anything about this place, I sense if he can touch me, then I most certainly should be able to affect him. I take advantage of his momentary distraction to bring my knee up quickly, catching him fully in the stones. His face contorts in pain and his arms release me.

Within moments a cloud of small, bright lights fly at him. They attack him like an enraged swarm of bees. He falls to his knees.

"Don't imagine I can be so easily captured, Lord Sheffield. Your druid magic might be strong, but I have the blood of generations of Glyndwr witches flowing through my veins."

I take several steps away from him to summon more magic and take leave of this horrid place. His thick voice calls and I turn back to him.

"I shall have you," he vows. His eyes hold an angry, red fire that burns with hatred. "You will be mine, or I will destroy you. There can be no other way."

I swallow my fear, refusing to let this devil know I'm afraid, for all evil thrives on the fear of others.

"Heed me well, Dark One, if you touch me again, I shall use all the forces at my command to destroy you." I wave a hand in the air to draw my sylphs back to me.

"You cannot break the vow of protection." He sneers.

"That vow applies to sophors, not to mages, adepts, or magicians." I clap my hands three times for emphasis. "The vow I make now is that I shall use all of my powers to fight against you and your dark minions. You never should have come aboard if your intention was to seize control of me and make use of my magic."

My heart beats faster as the words tumble from my mouth. "Do not test me, for I am not the weakling you mistake me for. All Glyndwr witches grow slowly into their full powers, but no one challenges them once they become adepts."

I turn away from him, closing my eyes to better concentrate. Within the space of a few breaths I know the mystical between world has dissolved for I can hear Bitsy arguing with Griffin.

"She wouldn't eat naught for the mornin' meal and likes as not she's taken the vapors 'cause of it."

"I doubt missing one meal would make her faint from hunger." Griffin's voice was sharp. "Was she ill last night at bedtime?"

"She was right as rain," the maid said.

Heavy footfalls crossed the floor. Griffin was pacing. "I should have listened to her warning, but I couldn't fathom that Lord Sheffield would cause her such a fright. 'Tis my own fault for being so pig-headed."

"Well, I'm of a mind to agree about that," Catlin said, slowly opening her eyes to find herself reclining upon a small wooden bunk. The room was dim, but she was grateful the terrifying mist and shadows of the between world had disappeared, along with the nefarious Lord Sheffield.

Griffin knelt beside her and took one of her hands. "Are you feeling better, my *hudol* cat?

She smiled at the charming endearment offered in her native Welsh language. "Do you truly find me enchanting?"

Griffin touched her cheek. "Too much so, I fear. My courage

deserted me when you fainted away. I was ready to return to shore."

He gazed at her with an expression of adoration that made her slightly discomforted. How much of his affections were due to her sister's magic, and how much because he truly cared for her? It was a vexing problem one faced when mixing spell crafting with passion.

"You would do that for me?" She felt a surge of happiness.

A small dimple played at the corner of his mouth. "I'm finding it more and more difficult to think clearly when you're around, *cariad*." He leaned forward and kissed the tip of her nose. "I believe I am enchanted, for I find it easy to forget my obligations and vows when you fill my head."

He stood. "Now, I'm going to have your little maid get you something hot to drink. Rest here for a bit and once we set sail I'll come down and get you."

He gave them a reassuring nod. "Sometimes the first few days out of port can be rough. Both of you need to take the time to get your sea legs." He bowed to kiss Catlin's hand, then walked out the door.

"Egad, but ain't he a fine gentleman?" Bitsy burbled, as she watched Griffin leave.

Catlin leaned back upon her pillows to close her eyes again. He was indeed a very fine gentleman, dedicated to protecting her with all his warrior's skills.

But she knew it would take more then a sharp sword and a strong arm to defeat Lord Sheffield. He'd cast a powerful spell and managed to capture her today, and she knew that the next time, it wouldn't be so easy for her to escape from him.

***

Catlin must have dozed off, for while it seemed only moments since she'd sipped at a cup of peppermint tea, Bitsy informed her several hours had passed.

The ship sailed with a regular pattern of rising and dipping in the water. Creaking and splashing echoed through the cabin. Bitsy sat on a thick pallet positioned on the floor, her complexion an off color of green.

"I don't like all these upsies and downsies," she mumbled.

Catlin took a deep breath. She didn't feel any sea sickness so far, but she was still lying down.

Catlin slowly brought her feet down on the rough plank flooring of the cabin. A momentary wave of dizziness engulfed her, but once she closed her eyes and took another deep breath, it passed.

"Sir Reynolds tapped on the door a bit ago, and said if ye was awake he'd take ye up topside." The girl put her hand to her mouth. "Don't know why a body would want to do such a thing. 'Tis hard enough to hold me stomach down here."

"Don't bother yourself about it, Bitsy." Catlin said as she smoothed out the wrinkles of her gown. "If you can muster enough strength to help me fix my hair, I'll let you nap down here while Sir Griffin shows me around the ship."

Bitsy struggled to her feet and appeared almost ready to topple over again before grabbing the edge of the bunk for support. "Upsies and downsies," she grumbled. But when Catlin handed her the boar's hair brush, the girl became all business. "Ye put the fear in all of us this mornin', Mistress. I thought ye might be taken with the plague. Like to scare me outta another year's growth."

Catlin smiled. "I apologize for that, Bitsy, for you cannot spare the loss of any more height."

Bitsy plucked the brass bodkin from Catlin's hair and let the dark mass of curls tumble below her shoulders. As she pulled the brush through the thick locks, she kept up a steady chatter.

"I believe he's right smitten with ye, Mistress."

The child's astute observation made Catlin smile. "I believe you might be correct in that assumption. I must admit, he's handsome, charming, and most captivating." Catlin warmed. Her words amounted to a confession of her own feelings for Sir Griffin Reynolds.

"He don't hold a candle to our Sir Reynolds, though."

Catlin frowned and turned to face Bitsy. She grabbed the brush to halt Bitsy's ministrations. "I thought we were talking about Sir Griffin."

The maid shook her head. "I were talkin' 'bout his Lordship, that Earl of Sheffield. He was pacin' outside this very door when ye took ill. Right worried about ye, he was."

Catlin turned away from the girl and waved for her to continue to fix her hair. She tried to make her voice nonchalant. "Did you happen to see him during that time?"

"Aye," the girl gushed. "He was prayin' for ye, 'cause when I went out to get a pitcher of water to bath yer face, I seen 'em with his eyes closed, lookin' all troubled and such." Bitsy made a few final pats to Catlin's hair. "I believe ye could have yer choice of gentlemen wooin' ye Mistress. And mebbe even become a Countess."

A wave of nausea slammed through Catlin. "That's not very likely."

"I ken he's most taken with ye."

Catlin shuddered at Bitsy's words. She rose, grabbed her shawl, and fastened a wide-brimmed straw hat over her curls. "I doubt I need trouble myself about the Earl of Sheffield. He certainly has more important things to consider then wooing a simple country maiden such as me."

A light tap at the door sent a wave of fear rolling through Catlin. She imagined somehow Lord Sheffield knew she was talking about him.

"Catlin, are you well?"

She rushed to open the cabin door. Griffin leaned against the solid door frame. His brow furrowed as he examined her closely, then a playful glint appeared in his eyes and he grinned.

"Ah, I see you've recovered." He stepped into the cabin and offered her his arm. "I've come to escort you topside, for we've pulled out into the channel and we'll be passing the Isle of Wright." He paused for a moment.

"That is, if you are feeling well enough."

"I'm feeling much better," she said and looped her arm through his.

He put a hand protectively over hers. "I could speak to Sheffield, if his presence terrorizes you so much. I'll ask him to keep a goodly distance from you."

"Please do not trouble yourself about that man, for it was a childish whim, just as you said." She leaned against his arm. "I feel safe within your protection, and while I must confess I would not wish to become friendly with the man, I can learn to ignore him."

"The Master tells me he hopes for strong, steady winds to fill our sails and make our journey swift." Griffin stood at the bottom of the ladder leading up to the next deck and took her hand.

"Oh, I believe we can count on the blessing of a friendly wind, Sir Griffin. In fact, I'd wager this could be one of the fastest and easiest crossings this tiny ship has ever made."

"Let us hope from your lips to God's ear," he said.

Or Goddesses's ear, she silently added.

Chapter Nineteen

The *Lady Bountiful* sliced through the waves, tossing salt spray and showering the edges of the deck with a fine mist. The sun beat down upon them, and the blue sky held only a few thin wisps of clouds high above.

Catlin sheltered her eyes with one hand as several of the seamen climbed the rigging to adjust the sails. She held her breath, for the journey up the ropes crisscrossing above them looked perilous. Yet the agile crew seemed unfazed with their dangerous duties.

"'Tis a fine day, is it not?"

Catlin turned to find a woman near her own age standing next to her. "Yes indeed, a fine day," Catlin said politely. She'd been introduced to this woman--Dorothie Colebank was her name, she recalled.

"We've been most blessed with such good weather, I'm told."

Catlin nodded. "A quick and uneventful crossing is what the Master predicted yesterday."

Dorothie stared off in the distance. "'Tis a good start to a new life, I'm thinking."

Catlin lifted her face to enjoy the breeze dancing across her skin. Dorothie was traveling with her younger sister. They'd recently been orphaned and would join relatives in the Tidewater colony. Watching them together made her lonely for her own sisters.

Rather than pine for her family, though, Catlin had taken advantage of the time available to her while on board ship. She'd spent the last several weeks studying her grimoire, practicing spells, and considering ways to protect herself against Lord Sheffield's dark magic.

Not that he'd presented any direct threat to her. When passing each other in the hallway below or on deck, the earl bowed to her as is he were a courtier paying homage to a lady of the court. She wove a strong protection spell around herself, and for good measure cast one for Griffin and Bitsy, too.

Despite the lull, Catlin remembered his vow in the twilight world. He was biding his time, waiting for an opportunity to spring some sort of trap. The next time he would not catch her unaware.

Dorothie lifted her chin, looking above Catlin's shoulder, and a blush crept up her throat to color her cheeks. Catlin turned to find Griffin standing behind her.

God's teeth, but the Cavalier collected admiring women like some men amassed wealth. It seemed every female, he met, regardless of age, became totally besotted with him.

He bowed. "Miss Colebank, you are looking lovely as usual."

The woman looked disheveled and grimy. Not that Catlin's own appearance could be much better. Since they'd been enjoying such good weather on this voyage, rain water for washing was now carefully rationed.

Catlin blinked at the high clouds and pondered giving them a push. A small squall would provide some much needed replenishment of their water supply.

"I've heard of your plantation, sir," Dorothie said to Griffin. She shot an inquiring look in Catlin's direction. "Will you be residing at Hawthorne Hundred too, Miss Glyndwr?"

Before Catlin could inform the inquisitive Dorothie Colebank that where she resided was none of her affair, Griffin spoke.

"I've been charged with protecting Miss Glyndwr, so of course she'll be staying on the plantation once we arrive in the colony."

Catlin gaped at him open-mouthed. If she were to live on his plantation, it was news to her. She silently fumed.

"My cousin also has a tobacco plantation on the James River," Dorothie said, "so I hope once we are all settled to see more of you, Sir Reynolds."

Catlin seriously doubted if Miss Colebank cared to see any more of her. It was obvious she was interested in pursuing Griffin. And she could see he was intentionally flirting with Dorothie in a obvious effort to make her jealous. Well, she could play at this teasing game too.

"I'm sure Sir Reynolds will have plenty of time to call upon your family." Catlin gave him a sly look. "He tells me he is most eager to find a wife once he settles down upon his plantation."

Griffin frowned. Dorothie blushed an even deeper rose and stuttered a few words. Within a few moments she excused herself.

"That was a bit cruel, don't you think?" Griffin said.

Catlin shrugged. "The woman was obviously fawning over you, so why not give her maiden heart some hope you might wish to woo her?"

He twisted his mouth sourly. "You know quite well I shall not be wooing any other woman."

Catlin turned to stroll upon the deck. "Really, and how would I know this?"

Griffin took her arm and pulled her gently to the rail. "Because we have an understanding."

Catlin tilted her head to gaze up at him in confusion. "Do we, sir?"

Griffin narrowed his eyes. "Are you toying with me, Catlin?"

She brushed one hand across the thick muscles apparent even through the sleeves of his coat. "Would it give you pleasure if I did so, sir?"

A silver glow shaded the darkness of his eyes. "Do you tease me, *cariad*?"

She smiled at his pet name for her. "Perhaps, but I think you need encouragement, not teasing."

He moved closer to her. "Your little maid sleeps in your cabin, so you have been well-protected from my advances."

Catlin glanced up at him coquettishly from beneath her lashes. "She does not sleep in your cabin, does she?"

She took several steps before Griffin caught up with her.

"Are you proposing an assignation?" His gaze roamed over her figure. "It is daylight."

"Aye," she said, and gave him a cheeky grin.

His eyes burned with hot lust, and he grasped her elbow to steer her toward the steps leading to the lower deck.

She gave him a flirtatious pat. "I don't think we should be seen leaving the half-deck together, for that would arouse suspicion, don't you think?"

Griffin released her arm and nodded. "I suppose you're right."

Officers, crew members and passengers milled about, taking advantage of the lovely warm weather and enjoying the freedom and fresh air.

"If you'll excuse me, sir, I'm feeling overcome by the heat and sun." She curtsied to him. "I believe I shall go to *your* cabin to rest."

Griffin gave her a devilish grin. He raised an eyebrow in her direction. "I believe that's an excellent idea, for you do appear most fatigued."

He escorted Catlin toward the ladder leading to the lower decks. "Enjoy your rest," he said, winking at her.

Catlin paused at the bottom of the narrow stairway to adjust her skirts. A shadow fell on her and she gave an inadvertant shudder.

She turned to find herself face to face with Lord Sheffield. She swallowed her fear and forced herself to maintain a pretense of composure, despite the fact that she was terrified by his sudden appearance

"Get out of my way," she snarled.

He spread his arms to prevent her from slipping around him, and sneered down at her. "I wish to speak with you, witch." His voice held a tone of disdain.

She raised a hand and spread her fingers to snap a warding spell at him, but he quickly grabbed her wrist. She twisted against his hold and raised her other hand to grasp her sapphire amulet. She prepared to gather her power.

But before she could touch the amulet or even organize the words of the protection spell in her head, a foul-smelling cloth covered her face and she dissolved into a pool of darkness.

When she came to her senses again, she was stretched across a bunk with her hands bound in front of her.

Lord Sheffield sat at the foot of the bunk. When she tried to scream, no sound emerged.

"I've made sure we will not be interrupted, witch."

He traced a finger up her ankle and she shuddered.

"I've been searching for you for a very long time and now that you are finally be mine, I intend to prolong the pleasure of taking you for as long as possible."

He yanked the fabric of her gown above her knees. His lascivious expression chilled Catlin to the bone.

"I knew you would use magic to keep me away, so I prepared a mixture that would render you defenseless long enough for me to break your protection spell." His raised the hem of her skirt to expose more of her legs. "You have challenged my skills in alchemy and magic, and while I should be most annoyed with you, I find your refusal to come willingly to me very arousing."

His hand rubbed the inside of her upper thigh and Catlin gagged. She ached to struggle against him, to scream her hatred for the man. She could only watch helplessly as he fondled her. His hand brushed against the triangle of curls at the apex of her thighs. Bile churned in her stomach and then rose to her throat. Her heart hammered beneath her breast and her skin crawled with revulsion at the man's touch. Catlin wished she had a dagger to slash the man's throat and remove his bowels.

Sheffield rose and began to disrobe. When he stood clad in his white linen shirt, breeches and boots, he glared down at her. His eyes held a glazed, fiendish fire.

He sat and lazily traced one finger across her breasts, dipping into the valley separating them before squeezing each mound until she ached from the abuse.

Sheffield and his kind wouldn't stop with her. She realized if he knew about her family that he could use her to manipulate her sisters. He'd hold her captive and demand they share the secrets of their magic. Secrets they'd fought to protect for centuries from men like him.

"You will learn to enjoy the pain and then to crave it," he whispered, his voice harsh with cruelty. He leaned on her and his rough lips captured her mouth in a voracious kiss. He pushed his tongue into her mouth with an angry force that was ruthless.

A silent scream of protest roared through her head. She wanted to squirm away from him, rear back and attack him with her fists. Instead all she could do was silently beg for him to stop.

His kiss was sloppy and his breath reeked of brandy. When he finally lifted his face from hers, he stretched his mouth into a sneer. "You can't scream for your precious protector and I'll enjoy you for as long as I wish. You have no way to resist me now, witch."

Her stomach heaved and she fought against the terror that engulfed her. She was frozen, unable to move or fight against this cruel abuse. Tears filled her eyes. She would gut this man when she was finally free.

Tears of humiliation dripped to trace a path down her cheeks. Sheffield's eyes glowed with a strange preternatural fire.

She realized fear and anger would be of no assistance to her now. So she tried to concentrate on a spell to break his power over her.

She nearly fainted as he parted the tender lips between her legs and thrust one finger deeply into her with a hard, vicious stab. Darkness began to engulf her but she fought against it. She couldn't succumb to the pain in his touch because she needed to find a way to fight this evil druid.

He raised his head and glared at her as he withdrew his hand. His mouth went hard as stone.

"The bastard deflowered you, didn't he?" He pulled himself off her and stood. His face was contorted into a mask of rage. His eyes as icy as the depths of the ocean beneath them. "I wanted to be the first, but you've acted his whore and robbed me of the opportunity." He backed away from her, an expression of disgust painted across his features.

Catlin tried to gather her wits. Her fear was drowning any ability to develop a plan to fight him and she needed formulate a plan. She had to escape but she didn't know what he'd used to drug her. She did know he also used powerful magic to keep her quiet and subdued. If she could find a way to break his spell, she could fight him.

She would need to be cunning in order to discover a way to escape. She had no intention of allowing the earl to rape her.

Sheffield returned to the bunk. "He likely left one petal untouched, and I shall capture that for myself."

The earl flipped her to her stomach, facing her to the wall and pulling her legs to the floor. His brutal hands lifted her skirts again.

With a deep sigh, he slowly outlined the cheeks of her bottom with his palms. "'Tis better you learn my preferences from the start, anyway."

Catlin raged against this new offense, sickened by his foul intention. 'Twas a sin punishable by death and even more proof of the man's evil nature. Gutting him wouldn't be good enough, she'd see him burned until the flesh melted from his bones.

With her last ounce of courage, Catlin called out to the world of elemental spirits, the guardians, and the Goddess. Power swirled up from her toes to the tips of her fingers.

The ship rocked as if a giant hand suddenly pushed at it, and then rolled as if riding down a powerful wave. Sheffield stumbled backwards. Catlin rose and whirled to face him.

"Bitch of a whore, I'll have you now, and when I'm finished you'll understand the power of your master!" His face contorted as he fumbled with the laces of his breeches.

The ship rocked again and Catlin leaned back against the edge of the bunk and braced herself to remain upright. The motion threw the Earl of Sheffield sideways, and he hit the wall of the cabin with a loud whack.

The flame in the lantern fastened to the wall above him flared high before it exploded into a thousand dripping sparks. The shower of fire plummeted upon him and ignited the sleeve of his shirt. Sheffield howled.

It broke his grip on her. The binding holding her hands transformed into a thick black snake, which released the hold upon her wrists. When the snake fell to the floor, she faced the earl, ready to do battle. Her terror had coalesced into a thick, dark fury. Her stampeding heart slowed to a steady, constant drumbeat. She traced a sigil in the air and drew in the power of her elemental spirits.

A wind whipped through the cabin and the flames threatened to engulf Sheffield. He was thrown back to land roughly against the bunk, and he screamed with pain and frustration.

Catlin scrambled to the door and wrenched it open.

"I warned you--you bastard! I hope you burn like a Samhain bonfire."

She stumbled out into the hallway scrambling to the doorway of Griffin's cabin. She pushed her way into his room, slammed the door behind her, and leaned back upon it, finally releasing the breath she hadn't realized she'd been holding.

She fell to her knees and struggled against the nausea that

threatened to overwhelm her. As she finally let the tears cleanse their way down her face, her disgust and loathing for the earl's behavior forged a hard core of fury deep within her.

She was tempted to tell Griffin about the attack, but she knew he'd confront the Earl of Sheffield and challenge him to a duel. That could put his life in danger. Lord Sheffield, she felt like spitting to get rid of the foul taste of him from her mouth, might summon magical assistance in a battle with Griffin. This was her quest and she must face it without Griffin forfeiting his life.

Her body shook with the residual effects of the attack. She sat on the floor and finally succumbed to tears. Her eyes leaked and her nose grew sore from wiping it as she let the terror that still shrouded her have free reign. Her shoulders shook with great, wrenching sobs.

Her stomach finally threw up the sour bile that had twisted her belly. She managed to inch to the slop bucket and not retch on the floor.

She heard a scuffle in the hallway outside the door, and the angry bellowing of Lord Sheffield as he screamed for help.

She frantically searched the room for a weapon. If he attacked her again, she'd kill him. She grabbed Griffin's sword from the baldric hanging from a peg and backed into the farthest corner of his bunk.

More voices joined the melee, as someone called for a bucket of water. She hoped flames consumed Sheffield before they could douse him. The bastard deserved to be flung into the pits of hell!

She knew somehow Aelwyd had sent her fire dragons to answer her call. The transformation of the leather binding into a snake was surely a sign from the Goddess. The snake was a symbol of her ever regenerating life force. Catlin swore an oath that she'd never again be caught in the snare of the druid. She'd kill him the next time he laid a hand on her.

Chapter Twenty

Griffin slipped into his cabin and stood staring at Catlin, his eyes displaying his shock as he gazed down at her. She knew her appearance must be alarming. Her gown was wrinkled and although she'd tried to adjust the bodice to cover the ripped lace edging the neckline, she was still disheveled. She couldn't stop the trembling that made her teeth chatter.

"Catlin, are you all right? He pointed at his sword, still clutched in one of her hands. "What in hell happened?"

He took several long strides toward her. His brow was twisted in confusion, but his eyes held a warm glow of sympathy.

"It appears Lord Sheffield experienced some sort of mishap this afternoon." Her voice was a harsh whisper, roughened by her crying.

"Could have set the entire ship on fire, from what I'm told." Griffin's voice was calm, and he reached for the sword. She reflexively yanked it back away from him. She wasn't ready to surrender the weapon, even to him.

"How fortunate for everyone aboard that he failed," she said. "I hate the man, so 'tis no matter to me if he manages to set himself ablaze. Tis only what he deserves."

Griffin stepped back away from her. "Did he approach you again? Try to talk to you?"

Catlin twisted her mouth into a cruel smile. "Yes, he spoke to me."

She watched his face as anger contorted Griffin's features. She needed to be careful. If he decided he needed to protect her, it could mean danger or even his death.

"He stopped me when I came down below." She lowered the sword, took a deep breath and turned it to hand it hilt first to

Griffin.

"I believe it's time I took action to make the man leave you alone." Griffin took the sword, returned it to the baldric and then took it down to fasten across his chest. "He obviously needs convincing I was serious about the warning to stay away from you."

Catlin jumped from the bunk and slid across the room. Her heart was beating a staccato rhythm and her mouth was dry as the desert in a sandstorm. "You don't have to warn him, because I already did."

His gaze rested on her for a few heartbeats. "I don't think that will be. . . " He blinked in confusion. "Did you have anything to do with. . . ?"

She straightened her shoulders. She had to think quickly.

"He tried to grab me, and I stumbled into the lantern. It fell on him, setting his clothing on fire." She shrugged. "It was an accident, but when he was trying to stomp out the flames scorching his cape, I warned him you would disembowel him the next time he dared touch me."

"Bloody right I will!" Griffin vowed. He touched one of her cheeks gently. "I'm sorry. I know how he affects you."

Griffin's arms circled her waist, and he pulled her gently against his body before lowering his head to capture her lips. His kiss was soft and tender as he carefully brushed his lips against hers.

She needed his touch and his kiss, to wash away the filth of being man-handled by Lord Sheffield. Only Griffin could make her feel so warm, safe and protected. She wanted to wipe away the horrid memory of being held captive by the disgusting Lord Sheffield.

Griffin finally released her and turned her gently toward the door.

"You've had a fright today and I know any encounter with Lord Sheffield upsets you." He leaned forward to kiss the top of her head. "We'll meet another day, *cariad*."

She didn't want to leave the protection of Griffin's cabin, but she couldn't share an afternoon of lovemaking with him after Lord Sheffield's violent attack.

She wished she could submerge herself in a tub of blistering hot water to wash away the filthy memory of Sheffield's touch. But, she'd have to settle for a tepid sponge bath.

She stretched out one hand to trace the faint scar edging Griffin's face. She tendered him a soft smile.

"Thank you for understanding."

He turned her hand to kiss her palm before lifting his gaze to lock onto hers. "I swear Catlin. If Sheffield ever touches you again, I'll skewer him."

She nodded. "I'm counting on it."

***

"From the look on your face, I'd hazard you're a man in love."

Griffin blinked his eyes, tearing his gaze from the view of Catlin and Bitsy scrubbing clothes in a large wooden washtub. He turned to the ship's Master.

"She's a beautiful woman, and I've been charged with protecting her. If I find I must look upon her to discharge my duties—" Griffin shrugged his shoulders. "I shall not complain."

Master Williams stared at the two women. "I admit to being jealous. She's a handsome lady." He leaned forward to roll the ball toward the dozen wooden pins set opposite them. "You're a lucky man, if she returns the sentiment."

Griffin remained silent, pretending to concentrate on his own turn at toppling the skittles arranged across the deck. Truthfully, he didn't know her true feelings for him. Of course she'd given herself to him, but Griffin knew there was a difference between lust and love.

"'Tis a good thing you kept her from Old Rowley's eyes, for she is exactly the type of woman he favors— voluptuous, and possessing an innocent yet sensual charm."

Griffin frowned at the Master. "Shall we concentrate upon the game? I'd regret having to challenge the most interesting man on board this ship to cross swords in a duel over a lady."

Griffin watched the two women hanging linen sheets upon an improvised clothes line. "I admire her as much for her spirit and wit as for her beauty."

"As I said—" the Master arched a gray eyebrow in his direction and smirked. "You appear to be a man in love." He took another shot, knocking down several pins.

After taking his shot, Griffin watched the women completing their domestic tasks across the deck. He marveled at the way Catlin turned an unpleasant job into an amusing diversion. She and Bitsy were splashing water at each other. Many of the men on deck paused to watch the females frolicking.

He couldn't resist the allure of Catlin in her simple blue linsey-woolsey gown covered with an apron. Her russet curls were touched by strands of copper as they shone in the sunlight. They were constrained by a ribbon, yet still managed to tumble down her back enticingly. He recalled how silky smooth her hair felt between his fingers. Her cheeks blushed pink from the steam rising from the tub and reminded him of the way her complexion colored in the midst of making love.

He strolled across the deck, calling an apology over his shoulder to Master Williams. "I'd best make sure the ladies don't misbehave."

Catlin had her back to him, so she couldn't see him approach. Bitsy was wringing out a length of linen towel, but he put his finger to his lips to indicate his wish for her silent compliance. Bitsy smiled back at him.

Catlin spun quickly, put a hand in the tub, and splashed water at him. Griffin stared down at his now soaked doublet and breeches. Catlin shot him a coquettish smile.

"Why Sir Griffin, I didn't know you were there." she said, with mock innocence.

Griffin tried to grab her, but she was too quick for him and slid to the other side of the tub. She put her hands in the water and once again splashed him, then laughed. "I think you are in dire need of a bath, Sir Reynolds."

Griffin tried to round the tub, but she glided across the deck to duck beneath a large linen sheet. Many of the passengers and crew now watched the duel of wills between Catlin and Griffin. They urged her to run, and several of the men made ribald comments regarding a fitting punishment for the disrespectful wench once Griffin captured her.

His feet slipped in the soapy water and he slid across the deck.

Griffin felt his boots losing their grip, and he wondered if he'd be able to catch himself before he fell overboard. He needn't have worried.

Catlin grabbed the edge of his doublet and yanked him back, saving him from a fall from the ship but bringing him to a rather ungainly plop on his rear. She quickly released him to race off again.

She flashed a vivacious smile at him, and Griffin quickly pulled himself to his feet, once again enjoying the chase. The prize would be well worth the effort.

Catlin grasped one of the braces, yanking herself up a few feet off the deck. She paused when she was out of arm's reach and stared down at him.

"Sir Griffin, you've grown a bit slow and lazy during these long days of sailing. I think you need more exercise."

Griffin climbed up the rope, forcing her to move even higher. When he finally noticed how high they'd climbed, his irritation turned to concern.

"You've had a fine jest, Catlin. Now we should get down before you're injured."

Catlin answered him with a laugh. "Look." She pointed off the bow of the ship.

Griffin turned away from her to see a school of dolphins leaping from the water. For a few moments he thought he saw small figures riding upon their backs. He blinked. It must have been the sun shining in his eyes.

Catlin looked down at him, her smile full of confidence. "Shall we climb to the crow's nest and see if we can sight land?"

Griffin's heart plummeted. It was close to fifty feet to the top of the main mast, a dangerous climb even for the seasoned sailors on board ship.

"Catlin, don't be foolish. You've had your fun, now let's get down."

She looked up, the desire to explore clearly warring with her good sense.

"Please, Catlin, if something should happen and you fell, my honor would require that I fling myself off the rigging after you." He winked. "If you care nothing for your own skin, then come down in an effort to save mine!"

She laughed, but followed him down the ropes to join him on deck again a few moments later.

Griffin captured her in his arms. "You've been found guilty of ambushing an officer of his royal majesty's cavalry. I believe you need to be punished."

Catlin pretended to struggle against him. "Release me you rogue, for I was only protecting myself against an assault." Her eyes narrowed. "One made by sneaking up from behind me, I might add."

"Subterfuge," Griffin said.

"Trickery," she responded.

"Give her a smack lad," one of the crew members said. "'Twill show her who wears the breeches."

The women on deck responded with a jeer.

Catlin lifted a delicately arched eyebrow, and her lips curved into a teasing smile. "Sounds like a severe punishment for an innocent jibe."

"Perhaps I can find a more just punishment for my humiliation in front of all these people." He pulled her closer, leaned her back over one arm, and gave her a long, lingering kiss.

Her soft lips opened and invited him to explore the sweet secrets of her mouth. Desire washed over him, and he craved more of her mouth, more of her body, and all of the wild, wanton pleasure she could give him.

When he finally lifted his head, her eyes were ablaze with a look that sent even more heat to Griffin's groin. His cock stiffened.

He should have known better than to pretend a flirtation with this woman. Her passionate nature ignited a fire in his blood that could not be denied. He'd probably made a spectacle of himself in front of all these people.

Catlin stood and pushed him away from her. With both hands on her hips, she confronted him, feigning irritation. "One kiss is surely sufficient payment for an imagined insult, for as I said before, Sir, you are in dire need of a bath!"

She turned on her heel and marched away from him.

Griffin would have been stunned if she hadn't whispered one word before walking away that quelled his need for the moment.

One perfect, lovely, enthralling word.
"Later."

***

"Your teasing this morning was quite delightful play." Griffin's tongue explored the delicate skin edging her ear and she snuggled against him. Her quick response to his touch pleased him.

She couldn't speak because he slowly drew his tongue over her lower lip before pushing into her mouth. Her eager sigh told him she was enjoying the pleasure he elicited.

He plundered the sweet treasure of her mouth, sparring with her tongue. Finally, he reluctantly withdrew.

She shivered as his hands leisurely unfastened the ribbons holding her bodice together, eager to explore the soft curves of her body.

She moaned when his hands drew the fabric away from her heated skin and he cupped her full breasts, his fingers gently kneading the soft mounds.

Catlin leaned back against the wall of the cabin, her eyes closed in response to his manipulations and her breathing growing more ragged by the minute.

His own breath came faster, as his blood heated only to pool in the hardness between his legs. He ached to push into her, yet he wanted to savor their lovemaking, make it last.

He moved his mouth to minister to her other breast and pulled her petticoats and gown to her waist. He gently inserted one finger deep inside her. He discovered her woman's honey warm and slick between her legs.

"I want you," he said, fumbling eagerly with the laces of his breeches. "I can't wait much longer."

Catlin's sky blue eyes darkened. "Yes," she responded, "take me now."

It was all the encouragement Griffin needed. He was thick and heavy with his desire for her. Without another word he pushed her against the wall while he lifted her legs up to encircle his waist. With one eager plunge, he entered her. She was wet and tight. It was exquisite torture to keep from spilling into her with just the first thrust.

"Yes," she moaned, arching toward him.

Griffin moved his hips in a steady rhythm of entry and withdrawal. She locked her arms around his neck and held him captive within her embrace.

They rocked together, their bodies moving in a timeless measure in search of mutual pleasure and satisfaction. Griffin ached for release, each surge into the sensual heat of Catlin's body bringing him to the brink of satisfaction. Yet he refused to cheat Catlin of her fulfillment. Finally, she arched against him, crying out his name as her sheath pulsated with wave after wave of release. She collapsed against him, her head settling upon his shoulder.

Griffin plunged deeply into her several more times before crying out his own climax.

They trembled against each other. He kissed her lips gently, still cradling her against him, still deep inside of her.

Catlin traced one finger along the side of his face. He cringed when she touched the scar, but he didn't pull away.

He carried her to the bunk, setting her down upon the blanket as if she were a fragile glass figurine. He stretched out next to her. Their coupling had left him sated, but spent. He took several deep breaths and worked to calm the staccato beating of his heart.

Finally as Griffin leaned up on one elbow to stare down at Catlin. He admired the rosy hue of her skin and reveled in the soft, satisfied tone of her voice when she giggled up at him. He'd never known a woman so comfortable with her sensual appetites, and the more time he spent with Catlin Glyndwr, the more he craved these lusty interludes they shared too rarely.

"Why have you refused to come to my cabin? You've ignored my most unpleasant state of arousal." He played with the nipple still exposed to his view and it puckered beneath his fingers.

Concern shadowed her brow. "My family has practiced a means of preventing a woman from conceiving a child for many centuries."

Griffin was intrigued. "Is it truly possible to do such a thing?"

She nodded. "We keep a record of our courses, and because we are all so tied to the cycle of the moon, it is not difficult. But there are times when it is not possible for us to lie with a man, for to do so would make us quicken with child." She smiled. "I thought it best to avoid you at those times, because as I've confessed before, 'tis impossible for me to deny you."

Griffin's heart soared at her words. If she couldn't resist him, then she held strong feelings for him. Feelings aside from lust. She had to care some for him. Perhaps she didn't love him, at least not yet. But he hoped someday she would.

"I'm always astonished by you, *cariad*. Your family holds secrets I can't even imagine, and when we are more settled, I hope you'll share more of this strange knowledge with me."

Her mouth snapped shut and her eyes changed to a midnight blue hue. She shrugged her shoulders. "Many have wanted to learn the secrets we possess, and some have even killed in pursuit of that knowledge."

Her words shocked him. She was a capable herbalist and a gifted healer, but now he was beginning to realize her family possessed secrets that put their very lives in danger. No wonder Catlin had been so anxious to escape from England.

He sat up and pulled her into his arms. "I will protect you, Catlin. I make you this vow, while I live, no one shall threaten you or your family."

She put her head on his shoulder. "You can protect me with your sword, Griffin. I have no doubt of that, but there are forces in our world that require more than courage and strength. I can only hope I possess the power to protect you from such evil."

Her kiss silenced his protest. He'd never before heard a woman make a pledge to protect him.

Yet while she'd vowed to shield him from harm, she had never once told him she loved him.

Chapter Twenty-One

I *face a wild creature. A great giant maw of a mouth filled with sharp pointed teeth stretches beneath two bright eyes burning blood-red and orange with an angry fire. Flames burn at the foot of the apparition, and the creature is well over ten feet tall. Long sharp claws protrude where fingers should be on the ghost's hands A pale green aura surrounds the creature. The color of change.*

The ghost doesn't seem capable of speech, but stands at the edge of my consciousness. It turns and points to the west. Somehow, even without words, I understood. Danger. Something dark and threatening waits for me in that direction and the ghost is warning me.

But, I have no choice. I must face whatever dangers necessary to find a safe place for my family in the New World. It's too late to turn back, but I will heed this strange messenger and be more careful on this mysterious adventure to Virginia.

***

Catlin smiled as she recalled the all too brief interlude with Griffin in his cabin yesterday afternoon. She wondered if they might manage to steal another hour alone together today. Sir Griffin Reynolds had awakened an insatiable and unbridled appetite for sensuality within her. Passion was tantalizing to explore.

A moan snapped Catlin back to reality, and she sat up, aware that only Bitsy could have made the sound. Leaning over to look at the small figure curled up on the pallet next to her, she reached out to shake her maid, who moaned again.

Catlin pulled the covers back and slipped out of her bunk. The coldness of the rough floor shocked her, but not as much as the gray pallor of the girl lying on the pallet. Thick, green bile trickled from the corners of Bitsy's mouth.

Catlin found the pitcher of water, copper washing bowl, and a linen towel back with her. She knelt next to Bitsy and gently wiped the filth from the girl's face and hair.

"Don't worry, Bitsy, I'll take care of you." Catlin rinsed the cloth. "You've taken a fever, but I'll brew you some tea and you'll be feeling better in no time."

Catlin stood to throw her gown on over her shift and yanked the bodice closed as best she could. Without Bitsy's help, she couldn't fasten the ribbons tightly. To protect her modesty, Catlin pulled her velvet cloak around her shoulders.

"I'm going to get Sir Reynolds to help me, Bitsy." Catlin hated to leave the girl alone, for even a short time, but she needed someone to fetch hot water and alert the crew one of the passengers had taken ill.

Stepping from her cabin, a flash of fear shot through Catlin. Lord Sheffield stood just outside her door, almost as if he expected her to be leaving. He held a heavily bandaged arm with his other hand.

Catlin squeezed her fists closed, ready to fight the man should he attempt to seize her again. Even though she'd woven a powerful protection spell to guard against the evil lord, his dark powers terrified her. She swallowed. Her pulse was beating a thundering rhythm in her ears, but she needed to pretend a calm she didn't really feel.

"Experiencing difficulties this morning, Miss Glyndwr?" His voice was smooth and oily, the pretense of concern evident to her.

"Nothing you need worry yourself about, milord

As she turned toward Griffin's room, Lord Sheffield snapped out one arm in the small passageway to prevent her from moving.

Catlin's temper flared and she held out her hand, ready to use a repulse spell if he came any closer.

"I know you are too well protected to harm." His eyelids thinned to ugly slits. "Some spells work better on weaker creatures who do not possess magical powers. If you cannot be persuaded to come to me for yourself, perhaps you will do so to protect others."

Catlin's heartbeat echoed in her ears. Of course, she should have been prepared for this. The dark magician wouldn't abandon his quest to possess her, but he could change his tactics. He'd watched her and knew Bitsy was more than a servant. Catlin had grown very fond of her young maid. Now Lord Sheffield would use Catlin's affection for the girl against her.

"What have you done to her?" Catlin's voice shook and tears wet her eyes despite her attempt to control her emotions. "How dare you threaten a *sophor*? 'Tis against the creed, and you well know it."

Lord Sheffield offered her a malicious grin. "My kind does not subscribe to your precious creed. Such rules make you weak, and I have no time for those who are weak and helpless."

Catlin longed to summon her magic and punish this malevolent magician. His kind gave adepts a bad name, and were the reason witches were hunted and executed throughout Europe. Black magic had forced Catlin and her family from their ancestral home.

A dark, angry power slammed through her. A red haze glowed just beyond her vision, and the desire to destroy Lord Sheffield became a hot, wild force within her. Her raised hand warmed, as if growing ready to hurl a painful curse in his direction.

A tiny bright light sparkled before her. *Do not*, a small voice chirped at her. *Evil tempts you to do evil.*

Catlin let her hand fall to her side. "I will not use your tactics to fight this battle, Lord Sheffield." Power tensed within her, then she twisted her head, and the man was smashed against the wall. "But I warn you again, the protection we offer to sophors does not include your kind." She eased her way to the large oaken door to Griffin's cabin.

"Your powers have grown even stronger." Lord Sheffield rubbed one shoulder. "Or perhaps it is your hatred of me that feeds your power. Have you ever considered that?"

Catlin's temper flared, and the lanterns lighting the hallway flashed too, as if an invisible wind fanned the flame. "You should avoid tempting me to test that theory, Lord Sheffield, for your own life could be at stake."

He barked an unpleasant laugh. "'Twould be a most exciting contest, my *Bychan Dewines*."

Her angry retort to remind him she would never be his Little

Witch dissolved before she could form the words, for he quickly climbed the ladder to the upper deck.

Catlin paused before tapping on Griffin's door. She dearly wished she could cast one good cursing spell on the earl. Despite the fact that it would come back upon her three times, the cost might be worth it if she could finally be rid of the loathsome Lord Sheffield and the threat of his dark, ugly magic.

Griffin answered her knock, his white linen shirt open at the neck to expose the smooth muscles of his chest.

"I need your help, Griffin."

His expression immediately turned to one of concern. His brows knotted and his lips went thin.

"What's happened, Catlin?" He started out into the narrow passageway. "Is it Sheffield again?"

She touched his thickly muscled arm, seeking reassurance and shook her head.

"Bitsy has taken ill, and I need some hot water to make a tea and some cool, clean water to wash her and bring down the fever."

Griffin frowned. "Do you think it could be the plague?"

The Black Death had swept through Europe, dragging thousands to a quick, painful demise. If the disease was on the ship, it could quickly decimate both crew members and passengers.

"I don't know, she was fine last evening, chattering as usual before bed. Mayhap she ate something that didn't agree with her."

"Everything we eat of late is so disagreeable," he said. "I suspect that to be the case."

Catlin nodded. "You'll bring what I need then?"

He gently kissed the top of her head. "I told you before, *cariad*, I shall always be your must humble servant. You have but to ask it of me and it shall be done."

"Thank you," she whispered. The tears she'd held back finally leaked from the corners of her eyes.

Griffin pulled her into his strong arms, wrapping her in the familiar cocoon of safety and warmth. She leaned against his broad chest and listened to his heart beat. It was a strong, steady rhythm that reassured her.

"You are a gifted healer, Catlin. I'm sure Bitsy will recover with your help." Griffin released her.

"Go take care of the girl and rest assured I'll bring the things you need to your cabin."

"Thank you, Griffin." She slid out the door and ducked back into her own cabin, to find Bitsy on the edge of consciousness and shivering. Catlin hung her cloak upon the peg near the doorway and pulled her counterpane from the bunk. She covered Bitsy and knelt on the floor next to the girl's pallet.

Bitsy was still feverish and her eyes fluttered open.

"Mam," she whispered her voice thick with pain. "It hurts, me belly, Mam. It hurts so bad."

"I'm going to help you, Bitsy." Catlin kept the tone of her voice as calm and soothing as possible. "Just close your eyes and try to sleep."

Griffin and a young boy returned with the supplies.

"Set the kettle of hot water on the charcoal brazier over there." Griffin pointed across the small space. "And put some of the cool water in that basin."

The boy complied, then bowed in Catlin's direction. "If ye need naught else, I'll be leavin'."

"Thank you," Catlin uttered, already dismissing him. She wrung a linen rag in the water and gently wiped at Bitsy's face. The girl moaned.

When the cabin door shut, Griffin squatted next to Catlin. His mouth formed a hard line and a deep furrow of concern wrinkled his brow. "There are three other cases of sickness this morning. The Colebank sisters have taken ill, and a servant to the Whitman family. All young women. Is it possible they ate something to cause this ailment?"

Catlin shook her head as she wrung the cloth out again.

"'Tis hard to say, as the victuals we're given to eat are so disgusting it surprises me all of us have not taken ill."

Griffin nodded. "Still, it baffles me that of all those who ate yesterday, only four young women are ill. Can you think of another cause for the sudden sickness?"

Catlin stood and opened the carved wooden trunk at the end of her bunk. "Many things that can make one sick on board ship—contagion, bad food or water, filth and vermin. It's all made worse because of the close quarters we live in."

She pulled some small paper packets from a collection at the top of the trunk. "Still, I'd expect more people to be sick if it's the food or water. 'Tis most strange that only these few have taken ill."

Catlin sprinkled the contents of several packets into a small crockery pot, then added hot water. The brisk scent of mint diffused through the small space.

"I'll brew some herbs that should settle the stomach and get rid of the bile. I'll give you some to carry to the other sick women, and I hope you can encourage them to drink it."

"Will you need to call upon the wind spirits to assist you in this healing?" he asked.

His tone held curiosity, not condemnation. Should she tell him her suspicion that Lord Sheffield was using dark magic to inflict this illness upon the women?

She longed to share her concern, yet something held her back—a lack of trust she needed to overcome, and fear. Fear was a heavy burden, difficult to purge once it seized hold.

"I don't think so, but I need to wait and see if this brew can bring down the fever and soothe the stomach." She stirred the concoction with a wooden spoon. "Does the idea of my power to call upon the wind frighten you?"

The light of the lantern shadowed Griffin with an ethereal, golden glow, as though he were an avenging angel dedicated to fighting pain and evil. The vision comforted her.

"You inspire, delight, and entice me, *cariad*, but frighten?" He crossed the room and touched her shoulder. "I cannot believe there is ever anything you could do to frighten me."

Catlin looked into his ebony eyes, her heart beating faster. "I wish I could believe that Griffin, but I fear a time will come when you turn away from me. That what I truly am shall sicken and disgust you."

He took her into his arms. "I know other men have failed you, Catlin. I cannot repair the damage they've done." He stroked her hair. "I can only keep repeating my promise to protect you. It's a vow I shall never break."

Catlin leaned into his embrace, enjoying the comforting scent of sandalwood and tobacco she'd come to associate with him.

"Vows between lovers are made to be broken, Griffin. 'Tis the nature of desire."

He touched his lips to her forehead. "I love you, *cariad*, and those are words I do not utter lightly. I have sworn an oath to protect you, and now I swear one to stand by your side. If there ever comes a time when I deny you, use my sword to pierce my heart. Death is the only fit punishment I can imagine for ever hurting you."

He took one step away from her, the sleeve of his shirt brushing against the bodice of her gown. His gaze flickered down and his expression grew warm. "I love you as a man loves a woman, and that includes everything you are—sweet, mysterious, and sinfully decadent when you are in my bed. Can this not be enough for us?"

Catlin sighed. Could it be enough? Especially when Griffin learned her powers made her more than a talented healer? What would his words mean when he discovered she was a powerful witch in control of storms and tempests?

She stepped back into his arms, promising herself she would enjoy every precious moment of her time with him. They would share long hours of coupling and rich moments of joy and pleasure. She knew in her heart this time would eventually come to an end, and she shuddered at the thought of the day he'd back away from her in denial. It would happen, for she knew no *sophor* was capable of understanding the demands placed upon her by the blood running through her veins. Someday Griffin would see what she truly was.

This fear kept her from saying the words in her heart. He would turn from her, for there was as much curse as gift when a *sophor* loved a Glyndwr witch.

Chapter Twenty-Two

"There is no sign of improvement in the other women." Griffin drew his hand through his dark curling locks of hair. "Yet no others have taken ill, a fact I find most disturbing."

He folded his arms across his chest, vexation showing in the deep furrow between his eyes and the thinning of his lips. "Is there anything more you can do for them?"

She hesitated. There was more, but to confess the truth could jeopardize everything that had passed between them. He had proclaimed his love for her with honesty and expected the same kind of candid truth from her.

She enjoyed the way they'd worked together these past few days, moving all of the sick women into her cabin. He remained by her side as she nursed them, making cups of herbal tea, wiping down their fevered brows, and helping bathe them in a mixture of water, white vinegar, and rosemary. They were both exhausted, but few others on board volunteered to help. Everyone was too afraid this illness could be the killer plague.

It wasn't the Black Death. While the women did not improve, neither did they grow more feverish or develop the ugly bubo, the plague sore that was a clear signal of the disease. They thrashed about, whimpered in pain, but got no better or worse. Catlin had seen bewitching. This was a spell, not a contagion.

How could she explain to Griffin without sounding like a dunderhead? He knew she was capable of great healing, but did he suspect she was also capable of immense magic? She had to explain it in a way he could not only understand, but accept.

"I could try the means I used on Lord Cranbourne, calling upon my healing powers."

He raised an eyebrow in her direction. "Do you think it could work?"

She shrugged. "I would not offer unless I thought it could bring them out of their stupor. But I cannot say for sure it will heal them."

Griffin assessed the women stretched upon pallets spread across the floor of her cabin. "But we must be careful. If others thought you were using—" He paused "—unusual means to heal, it could create rumors and gossip."

She nodded. "The crew poses a serious problem, for seamen are the most fearful and superstitious lot I've ever encountered."

Griffin folded his thickly muscled arms in front of him and leaned back against the door. With the cramped quarters in her tiny cabin, scarce a place existed to sit.

"What do you need?" He asked without a moment's pause.

Relief swept through Catlin. She'd thought this morning that the only help she could provide would be a concoction to make the afflicted women sleep more soundly. With Griffin's help, she'd release them from the spell Lord Sheffield had cast upon them.

***

Catlin stood as close to the center of the cabin as possible. She held her sapphire pendant at arm's length, circling the room while chanting the ancient spell for uncrossing black magic. The old language rolled off her tongue, and speaking the words out loud energized her.

Candles flared at the cardinal points, each inscribed with the sigil for healing.

Catlin finished circling the room and held her hands above her head to begin the invocation to call her *sylphs*.

She called to her elemental spirits, asking for assistance. Several miniature glowing lights appeared above her head.

The bargain? The chirping voices of the *sylphs* argued amongst themselves.

We want you to send the man to Dream Time, for we should like to play with him.

I will not, Catlin answered indignantly, and you all know better than to ask such a thing!

More twittering and chirping ensued, and finally one voice rose above all the others, silencing the cacophony.

A cone of sugar, two silver spoons, a bag of goose down, and a piece of red velvet fabric. Catlin sniffed at the high cost, but she knew the *sylphs* could demand even more payment for helping her fight the ugly darkness cast upon the women lying in the cabin. She was in no position to argue

She nodded and clapped her hands three times to seal the bargain.

Catlin picked up her willow wand and touched each sick woman before stooping to place a small purple amethyst stone on each of their chests. Next, she stepped to the center of the cabin where she'd cleared a space and placed her altar. She'd drawn a pentagram on the floor. Her copper washing bowl filled with water, a saucer of salt, a few peacock feathers, a stem of dried lavender, and a large amethyst geode that glowed in the candlelight sat in significant positions.

The twinkling lights of her *sylphs* glimmered purple, generating the healing energy to repulse the evil bewitchment.

"When I give you the signal," she said to Griffin, "open the door quickly."

She sprinkled salt in the water, then picked up one of the peacock feathers. She dipped it into the liquid and showered the women. Each of them had been moved to a cardinal point.

"With this gift from the sea, I wash evil from your flesh, from your heart, and from your spirit."

She returned to the altar and picked up the geode and scooped a handful of a fine powder of burned nettles and pine from a bowl.

"With this gift from the earth, I cleanse evil from your flesh, from your heart, and from your spirit."

She shook some of the powder from her fist to dust each woman's face lightly.

Bending forward, she picked up one of the candles. With a sweeping movement she drew the candle from head to toe of each woman, careful not to drip wax upon them.

"With this gift from the sun, I cleanse evil from your flesh, from your heart and from your spirit."

After repeating this sequence three times to invoke the guardian spirits, she paused to take a deep breath. Finally she bent to the altar to gather the sprig of lavender. She held the dry branch to the candle, and within moments it flamed, filling the room with its purifying scent.

Catlin held the glowing herb above each woman.

"With this gift from the sky, I cleanse evil from your flesh, from your heart and from your spirit."

Without bending down, she tossed the smoldering herb into the copper pot, and quickly turned in a circle three times before stopping to clap her hands.

Griffin pulled the scarred oak door open to a slit. Within moments a sharp, whistling wind snaked down the ladder leading to the upper deck and circled the room.

The flames of the candles danced as the wind shrieked. The curtains hanging on the side of the bunk fluttered, clinging to the bars above like a sailor clinging to the rail in a stormy sea.

The purple glow from the elemental *sylphs* grew brighter, and before long the cabin seemed bathed in an ethereal light reflected in every corner.

As Catlin started the ancient chant to counter the evil enchantment, each one of the victims grew restless, mumbling and tossing about on their pallets, begging her to stop.

Catlin ignored their pitiful cries, for it was the black magic begging her to stop, not the afflicted women.

The wind howled as Catlin closed her eyes, raised her arms straight up, and called upon her element to come to her aid for help and healing.

"Capture the evil from these innocent victims. Carry it upon your wings of mercy, and drown it in the depths of the sea."

Lowering her arms, she once again turned in a circle and ended her invocation with three more quick claps.

"As I have said, so shall it be."

Scuffling sounded at the door, but Catlin ignored it and took a deep cleansing breath. She prepared to assist the women scattered about the room as they regained consciousness.

Instead, when she opened her eyes she found Griffin pinned to the floor by one of the sailors.

"I told you the woman was a witch, and here you have your proof." Lord Sheffield pushed his way into the room behind the seaman.

"See, there is black magic here. She curses these women and makes them sick for her own evil purposes."

Catlin's temper flared to life. It took all of her self-control not to fling a spell at the man and watch him burn like a cinder in the hearth. The man was as much a criminal as any highwayman riding the roads or murderer stalking the streets of London. It made her blood boil to hear him spewing lies.

"I was trying to help these women, not harm them." She clenched her fists.

Griffin struggled against the man holding him down. "I'm witness to her actions, and I assure you Miss Glyndwr would never hurt anyone."

Lord Sheffield laughed, the sound breaking brittle and harsh in the air. "Oh, I'm sure you are willing to serve as her witness, for 'tis well known you swive the wench whenever given the chance."

The crewman laughed at the crude remark, his dark eyes almost disappearing in the fat ugliness of his face.

Griffin punched the man and knocked him off balance momentarily. He lunged toward Lord Sheffield, but the crewman knocked him to the floor again with a kick.

Another crewman joined the fracas, and before long, blood covered Griffin's face where their fists had pummeled him into submission.

A dark rage stormed through Catlin. Griffin was suffering a beating to protect her. She would punish these men, most especially Lord Sheffield for this outrage.

The fat ugly crewman pulled out a short knife and held it to Griffin's chest. "If ya move again, matey, I'll carve ye up like the Christmas goose."

"Leave him alone." Catlin's command came out as a scratchy whisper. The blood flowing from Griffin's wounds terrified her. Her hands were shaking, but she needed to maintain control if she was going to help the man she loved.

"Grab her and tie her hands, for she will use a spell upon you if you leave her free," Lord Sheffield warned.

The other crewman lunged toward her, and the metallic taste of fear swirled upon Catlin's tongue. If they bound her hands and threw her into the brig, she'd never see Griffin again.

She held up one hand and drew a protective sigil in air. The symbol sizzled in an outline of flame, and the crewman backed away from her. His face was white and his eyes as wide and round as the full moon.

"Take her, I order you!" Lord Sheffield screamed.

"Why does he command you to seize me and not do so himself?" Catlin kept her voice low and melodic. "Is it because he knows the full extent of my powers and wishes to protect his own life while putting yours in peril?"

"Hear her confession." Lord Sheffield pounced upon her words. "I dare not touch her because she has already tried to ensnare me with her wicked magic. She came to my room and attempted to place an enchantment upon me."

The wind had died to a thin keening sound. Catlin's circle of power was still in full force. She raised her arms and uttered a phrase in the ancient language. Immediately the ship rose up in the water, as if pushed by a giant hand. The sound of the wind grew louder, rising from a squall to a howling tempest.

The first Mate peered over Lord Sheffield's shoulder at her, his terror obvious.

"I have called down the wind for protection, and if you continue to threaten me, I shall sink this ship to the depths of the sea."

Lord Sheffield screamed a string of obscenities.

"You will not sacrifice all these innocent lives." He sneered. "Your precious creed would never allow it!"

The ship twisted to the side, and the men grabbed the door to remain standing. The tempest hurled the ship from one giant wave to another. Men on the upper decks shouted as they tried to pull down the canvas sails.

"I will not be delivered into your hands, Dark Magician, you can count on that. I prefer death to being a part of your foul design." Her *sylphs* danced around her, their light now pulsing with an angry red.

The first Mate turned and started down the hallway. "Leave be, we need all hands on deck to bring the sheets down."

The two crewmen released Griffin, and he slumped to the floor.

Catlin wanted to rush to his side, but Lord Sheffield still held his ground at the door.

The crewmen rushed by him, ignoring demands that they stay in the cabin and lash Catlin's hands. The nobleman's face was a blazing scarlet mask.

The ship was tossed again and the earl lost his footing, skittering backwards across the hallway. He hit the wall with an angry smack.

Catlin put up both hands, grasped at the deep power rising from within her, and pushed. The huge wooden door slammed shut. Lord Sheffield wailed in furious protest on the other side.

She closed her eyes, spoke a repulse spell, and sealed the door with magic. She had no intention of opening it again until she could be sure they were all safe from the machinations of the evil dark druid.

Catlin rushed to Griffin's side. Her heart clenched painfully within her chest when she discovered the large gash in his shoulder. The crewman must have used his knife, and now blood poured from the wound.

She lifted her skirt and tore off a large piece of the petticoat to attempt to staunch the flow of blood from the knife wound. She made small reassuring sounds to him, but more to soothe herself then to encourage Griffin. He had lost consciousness.

Hot, angry tears rolled down her cheeks. Griffin suffered because of her. She'd known Lord Sheffield wouldn't stop until he possessed her, and yet she hadn't trusted Griffin enough to divulge her fears.

Now the man she loved poured his blood out upon this pocked and scarred floor, thousands of miles from his home. He could die without ever knowing she loved him with all her heart

The ship climbed a wave, twisted, and then plummeted down a deep valley of water. Passengers screamed, and Catlin realized she must call back the furious elemental spirits she'd unleashed.

Her heart felt shattered into a million cold, hard pieces of ice. Why should she care for the *sophors* on this ship? Likely they'd have joined the crew in condemning her for practicing witchcraft. A pure, unrelenting hatred for these mere mortals suffused her, and her thirst for revenge momentarily blinded her.

A soft moan brought her back. She turned to find Bitsy sitting up.

"Mistress Catlin—" Her voice was raspy and hoarse. "Might I have a drink of water? I'm most fearfully parched."

The girl's gaze settled upon Griffin, and horror lit her features. "Bloody hell, Mistress, what's happened to Sir Reynolds?"

The other women stirred on their pallets, and Catlin realized she hadn't opened the circle and released the magic. If there was one final hope for Griffin, she had to take a chance and seize it.

Standing up, Catlin closed her eyes and opened the bargaining again with her *sylphs*.

You've asked for this man and so I shall offer you this—three days and an hour within your realm, and then you shall release him back to me.

A bright fluttering of excitement surrounded her.

We shall decide when to release those in our dominion, for you do not command us.

They were right, but since elemental spirits had no real concept of illness or injury, they possessed no advantage in this bargaining.

Then he can stay here, she responded silently. For I would never send a *sophor* to the Dream Time without a way out. As you well know, they cannot ask for release on their own. Nor would they.

That was the secret no mortal knew—that to be captured within the magical kingdoms was an eternal sentence. A human would never ask to return to the pain and suffering of the world once he'd experienced the never-ending pleasures of the Dream Time.

Catlin shuddered at the idea of saving Griffin's life only to sacrifice him to the elemental spirits. If they insisted on their stipulation to control his time in their world, she would refuse.

Finally, after much chattering, the *sylphs* silenced.

We are in agreement. Three days and an hour shall this man dwell with us, and then you may call him back. If he chooses to return to you, so shall it be.

Catlin understood this as a final offer. She nodded wearily and clapped her hands three times. Within moments, Griffin's body stiffened, his eyes fluttered open, and his body shimmered with a silver and white glow. As she watched, his breathing settled to a regular rhythm and the flowing blood became a trickle, then a gentle oozing until finally it ceased.

"Toss me the counterpane from the bunk, Bitsy. Sir Reynolds has lost a great deal of blood, and I need to try to keep him warm."

Bitsy tossed the blanket to Catlin. Muttering her thanks, Catlin spread it over Griffin's body. She wanted to lie beside him to offer her warmth, but the tossing and dipping of the ship reminded her she must deal with the storm raging outside.

The other women remained unconscious, but their color had returned and they no longer moaned or thrashed about in a stupor.

"Will Sir Reynolds be all right?" Bitsy asked Catlin.

Catlin gently touched Griffin's face and traced the thin line of the scar that ended near his chin. "He needs rest to regain his strength."

Catlin tried to make her voice reassuring so Bitsy wouldn't sense her fear. What if, when Catlin called Griffin to return to her from the magical Dream Time, he refused to hear her voice? She might have sentenced the man she loved to an eternity in the between world that hovered at the edge of life and death.

Chapter Twenty-Three

I *open my eyes and blink several times. I'm not in Catlin's cabin on the ship as I expected. I'm stretched upon a large, soft bed with a mattress stuffed with the finest goose down feathers Tapestries filled with unicorns, elves, fairies, and other assorted magical folk cover the walls of the room. The threads shimmer and pulse, making the scene almost come alive.*

The hangings draping the bed are made of fine silk and velvet, and when I reach out to touch the coverlet thrown over me, I discover it's a supple, thick fur. When I lift the covering I discover I'm naked.

A sweet aroma scents the air. It's the herbal fragrance that serves as Catlin's signature perfume. I inhale deeply. She must be in this room someplace. There are no windows, yet a warm golden glow of light illuminates the shadows. If I'm in a prison, it's the most luxurious cell I've ever imagined. If Catlin is here, I might never wish to be released.

I see someone from the corner of my eye. The figure of a woman emerges from a dense fog at the edge of the room.

As she comes closer, the womanly curves and voluptuousness of her figure appear. I swallow. The playful sway of her hips and her long hair flowing down past her shoulders mesmerize me.

My mouth goes dry when she pauses next to the bed to gaze down at me. It's Catlin, and she's utterly beautiful in an ethereal way I've never perceived before. Her soft blue eyes hold a sensuous promise, and I lick my parched lips in heady anticipation.

"Catlin, where are we?"

She smiles, a soft secret expression crossing her face. With one quick movement she removes a silver pin from near her shoulder to release the thin gown covering her. The silky fabric comes apart as it swishes to the floor, revealing her naked beauty.

My gaze settles upon the full, round globes of her breasts. The hard pink tips glow in the strange light, beckoning me to take each nipple in my mouth, to savor the delightful feel of her, to taste the silky nectar of her skin.

My cock grows hard. She stands just beyond my reach, and I want to leap from the bed and pull her down with me. I ache to push into her hot, tight sheath, and the depth of my desire, this carnal hunger for her, astonishes me.

I'm not an untested boy experiencing his first swiving. I don't understand this burning, unquenchable need I have for Catlin. It unsettles me.

As the blood rushes through my body, it pools in my groin, making it ache with a desperate craving to join our bodies together.

"Dream Time," she whispers. Her voice is breathy. It makes sense, for the real world could never be this sweet. She gives me another mysterious smile and slips into the bed to join me.

Pushing me back against the plump feather pillows, she straddles my body. Having her soft, round bottom settle across my thighs arouses me even more. This position is pleasantly surprising, for it allows me to take both breasts into my hands while watching her eyes darken with passion.

With a gentle kneading, I cradle each orb as if it is a rare and valued treasure. When I try to shift her body to place her beneath me, she places a hand gently upon my chest to halt the movement.

"You are my prisoner," she declares, her voice more musical and lilting then usual.

I relax and spread my arms wide. I wonder if she might produce a length of silk to fasten my hands to the bedstead, and the thought thrills me. Again, I'm astonished at the wickedness of my thoughts in this dream.

She leans forward, offering me a taste of her sweet breasts. I quickly assent to her unspoken demand, running my tongue around the rosy circle before flickering it across the nipple.

Catlin flings her head back and squirms. Her movements sharpen the heavy pulse of desire in my cock, making it grow even thicker and harder.

I push her back to gain access to the soft secret folds protecting her woman's sheath. Inserting a finger near the top of the fold, I locate the small pleasure point. With a few gentle strokes, she's twisting and moaning upon the bed.

I continue to stroke and thrust, pushing two fingers into her in a rhythm matched by the teasing of the small button of delight. She shivers and her tight sheath squeezes against my finger.

With one swift movement, I settle her on her back. The surprise in her soft blue eyes amuses me. If I'm a prisoner, I have no intention of being a quiescent one. I'll give as well as take tonight.

Spreading her thighs, I lean forward and tease her with several gentle, languorous strokes of my tongue across the tender skin. Finally I can't resist the temptation, and I put my lips to the soft folds of her womanhood.

I maintain the tempo of lick, suck, and thrust, savoring the sweet nectar I discover between her legs. Catlin squirms beneath me, arching into my mouth, begging for me to continue with soft purrs of encouragement.

Finally, she arches her back and cries out. There isn't time to let her savor the moment, for now my own need screams for release.

I lift myself on my elbows and kiss her lips to hold her captive beneath me. With one hard thrust, I'm sheathed within her. She squeezes me with the slick tightness of her body.

I want to prolong the bliss of our physical joining, but bringing Catlin to satisfaction awakens a sharp agony of need within me. I withdraw only to plunge again into her deep, wet, warmth, shuddering with the delicious sweetness of our lovemaking.

With a final push into her depths, I find my release and cry out in a delirium of pleasure. I would have collapsed upon her but for a quick moment of coherence that made me fall to the side.

I struggle to capture my breath, my chest heaving in an effort to fill my lungs with air. I shake with the emotions flowing through me. When I turn to gaze into Catlin's beautiful soft eyes I'm shocked by the vacant stare she returns.

"Catlin?" I lean on my elbow to watch her movements. "Is there something wrong?"

She blinks at me and rises quickly from the bed.

"Where are you going," I ask, bewildered by her strange and distant behavior.

"I shall return," she says in her strange, lilting voice. She dissolves suddenly into the golden light.

A warning flickers at the edge of my awareness, but I quickly dismiss it.

This is a beautiful, sensual dream, and I hope to never wake up. My skin prickles at that thought and I'm unsettled.

I close my eyes and relax, hoping this dream will continue. With luck, my phantom lover will return. As far as I'm concerned, any world with the beautiful Catlin Glyndwr in it is perfect.

***

"Is he still breathing, Mistress?" Bitsy sat next to Catlin, a worried expression on her face. "He seems right still were ye to ask me."

Although his breathing was shallow, Griffin's chest rose and fell. Blessed be, Catlin thought. While he was in Dream Time, he'd be unaware of any pain. She'd cleaned and dressed the stab wound and packed it with some precious spider web to staunch the bleeding.

Now she waited. He needed rest, and she'd given him the best opportunity to recover by agreeing to what the *sylphs* wanted most.

Her conscience bothered her, because it was unheard of to send a *sophor* into the Dream Time. What would her sisters say? Of course, with Lord Sheffield demanding she be punished, the storm still raging outside despite her best efforts to calm the wind, and Griffin possibly lost to her forever, her sister's ire didn't much alarm her.

Bitsy rubbed her stomach. "Ye wouldn't have a bit of hardtack about, would ye, Mistress? I'm right starved."

The girl was always famished. For such a tiny creature, she managed to consume a fair amount of victuals.

"We have a bit of the hardtack, and I'll brew you some tea to dip it into. There isn't much to eat in here, as we've been too busy to worry about feeding ourselves."

Bitsy's gaze dropped to the floor and her mouth drew downward. "I'm sorry, Mistress. It's right selfish of me to even ask."

Catlin put an arm around the girl and gave her a hug. "Of course you have a right to be hungry, it's been days since you had anything solid to eat."

Catlin stood up, moving carefully as the ship continued to lurch and dip. She put a small pot of water over the charcoal brazier, then found a packet of chamomile and poured it into a bowl. When the water was hot, she poured it over the herbs. She handed the bowl and a hard piece of the cracker they packed in barrels to serve as bread for crew and passengers to Bitsy. She had also found a small wedge of hard cheese.

"It's not fancy, but I believe it will help tamp down the hunger pains."

The girl nodded and ate silently for a few minutes. The wind howled and the ship tossed and twisted in the stormy seas. Wood creaked and she could hear the moans and screams of the other passengers.

By the time Bitsy had polished off the hardtack, her eyelids were drooping. Catlin hoped the herbs in the tea she'd made would help the girl fall back asleep. More magic was required this night, but Catlin didn't want to perform spells in the presence of another *sophor*.

When Bitsy finally settled down upon the bunk, Catlin rearranged the objects for her altar. She again outlined the shape of the pentacle and this time she arranged the items in a different order. This was not a spell for releasing magic, but one to call upon all the elemental spirits for help and protection against the forces of darkness bearing down upon her.

Finally, when everything was assembled to her satisfaction, Catlin stood at the outside edges of the five-sided star and walked around it to form her circle.

"Guardians of the Watchtowers, I call upon thee. From the North I call the elements of Wind, from the East I call the elements of Water, from the South I call the elements of Fire, and from the West I call the elements of Earth. Spirits created by the Mother, she who gives us life, Lady of the Moon, Guardian of the Night, and Queen of Heaven, I summon thee forth for help. Hear my plea!"

Catlin clapped her hands three times.

The candles at the cardinal points flickered, and the flame rose. The wind still howled, but the sound was less fearsome and somehow more comforting. The ship stopped tossing and instead seemed to roll across the sea as if gliding. Catlin closed her eyes, and one by one the elemental spirits appeared to her. The fire dragon representing the element of fire blinked at her lazily and disappeared. A tiny undine swam through her consciousness, followed by a small, hearty figure Catlin knew to be a gnome. Finally, the glow of a *sylph* appeared.

Catlin called upon these creatures to share their magic. A spark of brightness fluttered through her and built, the cone of power rising higher and higher until the pulsing energy of magic transformed her. Now she was a vessel, seeking to release the energy she contained.

With her willow wand, Catlin traced several sigils in the air, and they each glowed with a powerful magic of their own. She sprinkled the water and tossed the salt onto the altar. Finally, she stood in front of the small brazier, holding a sprig of dried angelica. She touched the dry leaf to the flame, and it flared.

"I call upon all the creatures of the Lady for help and protection. There is one who seeks to do me evil, and so I weave this spell to ward him from his foul intent."

She tossed another handful of the salt in the air.

"I call upon the water to calm the waves and keep this ship safe on its journey." She sprinkled more water on the altar.

"I call upon the wind to grant us speed to our destination." She waved the smoking herb in the air.

"I ask fire to protect me from evil, to burn away the threat and light my path." She lit two more candles and set them in holders at the center of the altar.

"Finally, I call upon the earth, to hold the one I love safely within your bosom. Protect Griffin Reynolds from harm."

She pulled the bodkin from her hair, and with a sharp poke, drew blood from the lifeline crossing her hand. She held her hand over the small copper bowl and let a few drops of her blood fall into the water.

"So have I said, so shall it be."

Exhaustion overwhelmed her, but before she could rest she needed to open her circle and release the elemental spirits. She traveled around the circle widdershins before pausing to create an opening. She thanked the elementals for answering her call and released them.

Finally, even though her throat ached and her head pounded, she gathered her magical tools together and put them back into her trunk to safely lock them away.

The storm had passed, for the wind no longer roared and the ship sailed calmly through a gentle sea.

The women continued to sleep soundly. Griffin seemed dangerously pale, but he was breathing. There was nothing more she could do this night. She placed a thick rug on the floor next to Griffin, lay down, and pulled the coverlet over herself.

The noises of the creaking ship, the other women breathing in the room, and the gentle cadence of Griffin's heart beating next to hers acted as a soothing lullaby. Within moments she fell into an exhausted sleep.

She didn't cross over into Dream Time, although she tried. Instead of a beautiful garden awaiting her, she found only a thick, solid gate blocking her way. A lock prevented her from opening it. Whatever mystery lay beyond her reach, it would remain a secret until she called Griffin back to her.

What would she do if he refused to heed her call and remained in Dream Time? Humans could choose to stay there, unaware that their bodies would waste away and die in this world.

She shivered and wrapped her arms more tightly around him. She could only hope that love would be enough.

But could love truly be enough to save a soul?

Chapter Twenty-Four

"Catlin Glyndwr, by order of the Master of this ship, you are to open this door!"

The pounding Catlin thought was in her head woke her with a start. One by one the women stirred and sat up on their pallets.

Bitsy jumped from the bunk, her bright green eyes clear again. "Shut up ye bloody rogue, for the ladies are not yet properly dressed and we won't be opening this door 'til they're presentable."

"Well, then, when you are presentable, we expect this door to be opened." The man on the other side of the door responded.

"Ach, keep yer breeches on. I'll open the door when I'm damned ready and not a moment afore. Heave off and let these ladies have a chance to clean themselves up." Bitsy had planted herself in front of the door with both hands on her thin hips. Her smile held a trace of rebellious triumph.

"I reckon they won't be back fer a bit." Bitsy stomped across the room and scooped some of the water from a wooden bucket into the copper bowl. She set that upon the small brazier and leaned forward to blow on a few hot coals still glowing underneath. Soon a small fire blazed.

"How did we come to be in your cabin?" Dorothie Colebank asked. "And is that Sir Griffin Reynolds asleep there?"

Catlin stood up and shook out her gown. How in the name of the Goddess could she explain all that had happened?

"We was all taken ill, prob'bly with the fever or mebbee even the plague, but Mistress Glyndwr here, she nursed us back to health," Bitsy said. "She saved our lives and likely at her own peril, what with all them worthless sorts on board who'd just as soon let us die." She spit on the floor. "God take their souls and send them straight to hell."

"Is this true?" Dorothie asked. "Are we here because we took ill and you've been caring for us?"

Catlin nodded. "There are some on board who did not agree with my methods of healing. They tried to stop me from helping you, and Sir Griffin intervened." She looked down at the form curled up in the corner of her cabin. "He was badly wounded in an altercation with some of the crew."

The women's expressions indicated their horror at the story.

Finally, Dorothie stepped forward and grasped one of Catlin's hands before falling to her knees. "We are all most grateful for your healing skills, Miss Glyndwr." She rose and the next woman repeated the gesture. When Bitsy finally did the same, Catlin was choking back tears.

"You are all going to recover. We can offer prayers of thanks for that." She nodded at the water now steaming in the pot. "I suggest we have a bit to eat, then we shall all get cleaned up as best we can."

She licked her lips and pointed at the door, trying to control her trepidation.

"Once everyone is ready, I'll open the door."

The women each took up a different station. Dorothie set out several pottery bowls for tea. Bitsy broke the last of the hardtack into fair shares. Lydia, the younger Colebank sister, sliced the sliver of cheese while Catlin and Sylvie, the Whitmans' servant, arranged the pallets so there was more space in the cramped cabin.

Finally, they stood around the small table to share the tiny repast.

"Do you think Sir Griffin will recover?" Dorothie asked.

Catlin hated to be so brutally honest, but they should all be prepared for the worst. "I really don't know. He lost a great deal of blood, but his color seems much improved today. It's best to simply let him rest and wait for him to awaken on his own." She tried to smile. "As they say, time will tell."

A gloomy silence hung in the room. Catlin didn't want to be so blunt, but much had transpired on board this ship while these women were under Lord Sheffield's evil spell. She must somehow warn them of his wicked purpose.

"I believe the man responsible for the wounding of Sir Griffin is Lord Sheffield." She paused. "In fact, he was most insistent that you all be moved from this cabin, despite the fact that you were extremely ill and unconscious."

Lydia's brows knit together and her lips formed into a thin smile. "I allowed that man to become much too familiar, and I now regret my impulsive foolishness. Be assured, my brother shall hear of all that has happened, and he's a man of great influence in the Virginia colony."

Catlin nodded, but in truth, she feared that once the door to her cabin was unsealed and opened, her own chances of making it to the colony were slight. Lord Sheffield wasn't the sort of man who enjoyed being thwarted over and over again. He intended to take possession of her and her magic by any means possible.

And he'd made it clear that if he could not control her and her magic-- no man would.

"You should be warned," Catlin said, "Lord Sheffield has accused me of using witchcraft to cast a spell upon you and make you ill."

"How dare he slander you with such an outrageous lie!" Dorothie folded her arms in front of her ample bosom. "Most certainly when my brother hears of this deceit he shall enjoin the Governor to send Lord Sheffield right back to England in chains." She sniffed. "I've never heard of such foolishness in all my days."

"Witches is all ugly with long noses and nasty warts, don't his Lordship know that?" Bitsy said. "Even the smallest child knows there ain't no such thing as a beautiful witch."

Catlin grinned at her scolding rebuke. "Indeed, even a child knows such a thing," she said. "But, despite that, I expect to find Lord Sheffield on the other side of this door when it is opened." She sighed deeply. "No doubt he shall be calling for me to be punished. I don't know what will happen, but if I'm taken prisoner, I shall rely upon all of you to serve as my witnesses."

The chattering voices assured Catlin she needn't fear losing their support. They pledged to stand with her against the accusations of witchcraft.

Catlin hoped their testimony would be enough to save her. Lord Sheffield's animosity was palpable. His hate circled her like a great bank of fog upon the sea.

Catlin was truly beginning to fear for her life.

***

I lift the gold cup to my lips and savor the taste of the sweet honey wine. Although I drink heartily and often of the mead, I never feel drunk. In this place I can make love, eat, and drink all I want, yet I'm never satiated.

Catlin sits opposite me, naked as she eats and drinks with me. My dream vision isn't at all comparable to the real Catlin. In fact, this woman is only a shadow of the true Catlin Glyndwr. Still, my desire for her burns hot. Even an imaginary Catlin can fan the heat of my passion.

"I shall be sad when this dream finally ends, for it's been a most satisfying interlude." I pick up a strawberry and pull the stem off before taking a bite. "But 'twill be most interesting to introduce the real Catlin to some of the rather imaginative techniques you've taught me."

I rub my wrists where the silk ties had lashed my hands to the bedstead. The dream creature gazes off into space and frowns as if she is seeing something that does not please her.

With a sudden quick movement, she springs from the bed in a blur of motion.

"Where are you going, cariad?"

She melts away, just as she's done countless times.

"Damned dreams are useless if I cannot control what happens."

Leaning back against the soft feather pillows, I wonder if I should try to sleep. I've considered it after one of our more vigorous bouts of coupling, but I fear that to fall asleep in his dream would mean I'd soon wake up in the real world.

I'm enjoying this lusty interlude too much to rush back to the world of sickness, treachery, and death. If this is only a brief respite, I'll relish it as long as the night keeps me captive. Morning will arrive soon enough and rob me of these delightful fantasies.

I sit up at the sound of a woman's voice coming from a great distance.

"Griffin, you must return to me, my love."

Catlin's voice—the real woman, not the wraith I found in my dreams.

I stand and try to walk toward the voice. A large oak door appears, but when I search for a handle to open it, there is none.

"Griffin, you must hurry. There is danger here and I need you."

"I'm coming! Keep talking and I'll try to follow your voice."

I grab the bedclothes to cover myself. If I am in that murky place between dreams and reality, I don't want to find myself on the upper deck of the Lady Bountiful in front of the passengers and crew without a stitch of clothing.

"You must find a way out and I cannot show you the path."

I pound against the door, but it doesn't budge. I walk the perimeter of the room, but no other exit exists. I slide down the length of the door when I return to it, my heart is thumping as I recall Catlin's plea, and I sit with my head bowed. I want to bang my fists against the wood, but I know it is useless.

I'm a prisoner in this place, and I'm trying to wake up. Yet, for some reason I cannot return to reality.

"Time grows short, my love. Come back to me." Catlin's voice is plaintive.

It breaks my heart, but I know I'm still dreaming. Catlin has never called me her love. My heart's desire is forming her words.

I storm around the room like a madman. I'm tired of this whimsy and ready to return to the woman I love. But I'm imprisoned in a labyrinth. Every way I turn is the wrong way.

Why can't I snap myself awake, like I did so many times when I was a child having a nightmare?

"If you cannot come to save me, I fear I shall die," Catlin cries.

The words chill me to the marrow. Even in a dream I can't accept the specter of death haunting the woman who is so precious to me. I pound my fists against the door again. It doesn't budge.

I fall to my knees, exhausted. I have to find a way out, for every moment I remain in this dream state I grow more concerned for Catlin's welfare. I can't shake the sense that she truly is in danger.

"Find a way to come back to me, love. Please." Her voice trails away.

The room seems to grow colder and darker.

I stand and shake off the coverlet. This is foolish nonsense. A man can wake up when he chooses. I close my eyes.

"I'm asleep," I say aloud. "But when I open my eyes, I shall be in my bunk with my cariad." I feel an odd impulse to clap my hands three times, as I've seen Catlin do.

"You cannot make magic happen with a simple wish!"

The unfamiliar woman's voice shocks me. When I open my eyes, a beautiful older woman with golden hair stands a few feet away from me. She has intense blue eyes that remind me of Catlin.

"I beg your pardon, my lady, but I thought all magic was based on wishes."

"Pah," she nearly spits. "All magic is based on desire and intention. When you truly want something to happen, you must first put everything else aside to manifest that desire. A wish is something you hope will happen, but true magic is something you make happen."

I frown at her, trying to understand. "To escape from this dream, I must put all my other desires aside and concentrate only upon that which I want more then anything else?"

She smiles, and her expression softens. "Precisely. Magic isn't made from simple wishes for things we want. It's manifested when we understand our heart's deepest longings."

I understand. This woman is a guide, helping me solve the puzzle of my dream.

She hands me a baldric and sword. "Sometimes you must fight for what your heart demands. It is often the only way to find your destiny."

I take the items and discover I am fully clothed at her touch.

"You must go to her, my young Eagle-Lion, for the one who has captured your heart is in grave danger. But remember this— that which you seek in the darkest of places is most often illuminated by love. Always trust your heart, for it shall not lead you astray."

She gives me a push towards the door. I pause, unsure, then realize her intention. Of course, I have to release myself from this prison of shadows and dreams.

With a huge sweep of my arm, I draw back the sword and strike the ancient wooden door.

Instead of the sharp reverberation I expected, the sword cuts through the door as if it is formed from fog and clouds. No splinters of wood fly toward me, instead the door collapses in a whirl of light and sparks.

A scream pierces the air. It is from Catlin.

Without a thought to my own safety, I thrust the sword before me and jump through the space that only an instant before had been a heavy wooden door. If I plummet to my death, it matters little. My only thought is for Catlin. She needs me.

The aching fear that seizes my heart tells me so.

Chapter Twenty-Five

Catlin stood on the upper deck, a light breeze teasing the unruly curls that had escaped from the tight chignon she'd carefully arranged earlier. The sun warmed her cheeks, and usually this was exactly the kind of day that would bring her topside to enjoy the freedom of the ship skimming across the waves with a sturdy wind filling the sails.

Unfortunately, as Lord Sheffield stormed across the deck in front of her, haranguing her about the many foul deeds she'd undertaken in the name of the devil, she found it impossible to find even a tiny slice of delight in the fresh air. The assembled passengers and crew scattered about her seemed more entertained than fearful about the proceedings. How often had she observed the same expressions of amusement at the hangings in Shrewsbury, when innocent women had been executed for the charge of practicing witchcraft? A mob could turn deadly at any moment.

Sheffield manipulated the innocent encounters between Catlin and other passengers into a diabolical plan to recruit minions for Satan.

"And this evil consort of the devil even called upon the demons of hell to attack me in my cabin." He pulled up the sleeve of his linen shirt to display deep scars on his arm. "See what her cursed familiar did to me! It was a monstrous black cat, with eyes glowing red in the night."

"Lock her in the brig to keep her from hurtin' any other innocent God fearin' folk," said the crew member who had accompanied Lord Sheffield to her cabin several days before.

She could offer no words in her defense, for she was gagged and chained to the midden mast, a necessity Lord Sheffield assured the Master was to prevent her from using her magic to call upon the demons that served her.

In her mind, Catlin had begged for Griffin's help. Yet she had no way of knowing if her pleas were effective. For all she knew, he was still in the thrall of Dream Time, enjoying the many pleasures available to him in that magical realm.

Even if her petition had somehow pierced the veil between the worlds, she couldn't be sure he would respond to her plea.

"We all know what the Bible says. 'Thou shalt not suffer a witch to live'." Lord Sheffield pointed at her. "By her actions, this woman has shown she practices the art of witchcraft. The law demands she be punished!"

Members of the crowd muttered and nodded.

"'Tis a sin against God," one woman yelled.

"Blasphemy," added another.

"A bunch of nonsense and palaver," a voice called from the crowd. Dorothie Colebank emerged, her sister holding her hand. "Miss Glyndwr is one of the sweetest, kindest women on board this ship."

"And it is expected that you would believe so." Lord Sheffield circled the two women like a bird of prey anticipating an attack. "She has put the mark upon you, held you prisoner in her cabin while she converted you, and now you have joined her evil minions!"

The mood of the crowd grew more anxious. Some of the people moved away from the two sisters.

"They've been strange since she kept them locked up," an ancient crone suggested.

"Why wouldn't she open the door? Mayhap these women were possessed by devils, went flying about, and were not even in the room," someone else said.

"Punish them, punish them all," another harsh voice cried out.

Lord Sheffield held up a hand to demand silence. A sinister glow flickered in his eyes.

"We should not blame those who have been captured by black magic, for they are innocent of any wrong doing." His frosty smile settled upon the two Colebank sisters. "It will require prayer and a constant vigil to insure these two still possess their eternal souls."

He waved in the direction of a crewman. "Take them below and secure them in a cabin, for 'tis not safe for them to wander about on board the ship."

Tears pricked at the edges of Catlin's eyes. She'd worked so hard to maintain a calm and composed demeanor during the proceedings, but time grew short. Sheffield had devised a plan he intended to use to punish and ultimately control her.

"Hang her, she's a witch," came a cry from the crowd.

"Hang her," several more voices joined in, until the entire crowd assembled on the deck chanted, demanding Catlin be executed.

Lord Sheffield drew closer to Catlin, the glint of satisfaction evident in his eyes. "What say you now, my little witch?"

Catlin's mouth went dry and a sharp metal taste coated her tongue — the essence of fear.

She couldn't draw on her powers without invoking a spell, and with her hands tied and her voice silenced, that was impossible. She was truly at the mercy of a man she recognized as having no mercy whatsoever.

Sheffield turned and spread his arms. "I invoke the punishment of the sea. Let us lash this witch and pull her beneath the ship. Keelhaul her and let the water determine her guilt or innocence!"

The crowd roared approval.

"I object, my Lord." the Master stood on the bridge, looking down at the crowd. "We are close to shore now. Let the authorities in Jamestown deal with this matter."

Ioan Purdy, the arrogant Earl of Sheffield, crept closer to the Master's perch. "I am the wounded party here, sir, for I am the one who has been accosted by demons, attacked in my own bed, and all because I refused to surrender to the seductive wiles of this woman." He turned back to the crowd. "I wonder how many men on this ship have been milked by her and the succubus demons at her beck and call. How many men have spilled their seed in the night with visions of this blue-eyed beauty haunting their dreams?"

Grunts and nods of acknowledgement buzzed from several men scattered around the edges of the crowd.

The nobleman then appealed to the women standing on deck. "And can we allow this to continue, even for a few days, without punishment?"

Howls from the women on deck demanded Catlin be severely penalized for her sins and transgressions.

Catlin was shocked at the way Lord Sheffield managed to easily manipulate the members of the crowd. He was using a spell or enchantment of some kind, but she couldn't tell how he was doing it.

"Bring her down here," Lord Sheffield demanded.

Catlin was quickly released from the mast, only to be wrapped in rope and taken to the bow of the ship. The crewmembers behind her laid out the lines that would haul her beneath the ship. Several men would work a pulley to wench her from one end to the other.

She would not survive being submerged in the icy ocean water. It was a rare man who could endure being keel-hauled, and Catlin didn't have the strength or stamina of a burly seaman.

She shuddered as hands lifted her to the railing. Her feet slipped on the wet, uneven surface.

Her mind numbly called to Griffin once more for help. She closed her eyes and imagined his beloved face. If these were to be her final memories, she wanted to make them good ones. Her only regret was that fear had prevented her from saying the words of love she longed to share with him now.

"Release her," she imagined her lover's voice demanding, "Or I shall slit Sheffield's throat where he stands."

Her fantasy was so real, she even envisioned the crowd growing silent.

"Stand away."

Her spirits soared as her fantasy lover continued to bark orders. Even the hands that held her fell away to release their hold.

This is a fine death, she decided before stepping off the edge of the ship to plunge into the sea far below.

As she twisted and turned in the air, a voice cried her name. Catlin opened her eyes to see Griffin gazing down at her, the color of his skin blanching as she dropped away from him.

Before the rope snagged her, a sharp blade cut through the air and sliced the rope holding her tethered to the ship.

Griffin flung himself over the railing after her.

Then the sea opened and swallowed her, sending her down

into the deep, dark depths of the ocean. Still bound by the rope, she tried to kick her feet to rise to the surface, but her heavy brocade gown and thick cotton petticoats pulled her deeper. Light faded as she sank farther and farther away from Griffin.

She held her breath, but knew there wasn't much time. With all the strength she could muster, she called to her *sylphs*.

Within a heartbeat, hands grasped at the fabric of her clothing. The soft, dreamlike faces of mermaids swirled about her. Long, golden strands of hair floated around them as they gently lifted her to the surface. They were breathtakingly beautiful, each movement like a ballet through the dark water.

The mermaids gave her one final push and she surfaced, coughing and choking on the sea water she'd swallowed.

Struggling to stay afloat, Catlin searched for the elemental water spirits who had rescued her. Although she couldn't see them, she sensed they still guarded her — a warm and comforting thought.

An arm grasped her from behind and she fought against the hold, afraid Sheffield was taking her prisoner again.

"Catlin, *cariad*, don't fight me!"

Griffin's arm circled her waist and pulled her through the water. She stopped struggling, as relief washed through her. Her heartbeat slowed, and despite the icy cold of the ocean, she was warmed by the thought that Griffin had answered her plea. She was shivering, but her heart sang because he lived, and he'd returned to her.

Finally, they bumped up against a boat and Griffin's strong arms lifted her up. They'd been rescued by the ship's sloop.

A flash of terror gripped her. Was she headed back into imprisonment? The faces of the men around her signaled she had nothing to fear. They looked concerned and worried, not triumphant at having captured the malicious witch.

Bile and sea water filled her throat, and she leaned over the other side of the boat, letting the fear purge out of her.

"Bloody Hell, Mistress liked to have died at the hands of that lyin' bastard!"

Catlin twisted her head to find Bitsy seated in one end of the small boat next to a hearty young man who was handling the tiller.

Another man sat near the jibe, sailing them across the waves and away from the *Lady Bountiful*. Catlin looked behind her. Griffin was there, using a cloth to dry his hair. He tossed her a devilish grin.

He pulled her into his arms and used a sharp dagger to free her from the prison of rope that had kept her arms captive. She used her damp gown to wipe her mouth before collapsing into his arms. Happiness to see him alive and well mingled with her sudden awareness of how precious her feelings for him were.

"I love you," she whispered. Then she leaned back to examine him.

"But--are you all right? What about your stab wound?"

His grin widened. "I'm fine, and I'm grateful it only took a knife attack, the threat of keel-hauling and nearly drowning for you to finally admit you love me." He wrapped his arms around her. "I'll count myself a lucky man today!"

Catlin nuzzled into his warmth, marveling at the way his strength revived her. How silly she'd been before, afraid to tell him what she really was, afraid to confess her love for him. She vowed there would be no more secrets between them. Griffin loved her. He'd proven that today when he jumped overboard, following her into the depths of the sea.

"How did you get the sloop into the water so quickly?" She glanced at the other two men seated in the tiny boat.

"'Twas Bitsy who helped us with that. Apparently she's not trusted Lord Sheffield since he pulled her into his cabin and tried to bribe her."

Catlin stared at the girl in horror. "He didn't! Why, the man should be whipped until the skin falls off his back. She's just a poor innocent child!"

Griffin nodded. "I couldn't agree with you more, but he's a rich and powerful man. We'll deal with him another day."

Bitsy pulled her shoulders back and lifted her head. "He didn't reckon on me fightin' him. Near scratched his eyes out, I did. Lucky for me, he was still hurtin' from his injury in the fire. I whacked his burnt arm and sent him to his knees."

Catlin smiled at the note of pride in the girl's voice. She'd come a long way from the starving waif afraid of her own shadow.

"He wanted me to tell lies about ye, Mistress. Said he'd give me silver coins and fancy dresses." She sneered. "As if that would be enough to make me turn traitor on the only folks what been good to Bitsy since her Mam died." She spat out the side of the boat. "May the bastard burn in hell!"

"But I still don't understand how you managed to get the sloop away from the ship without anyone noticing." Catlin turned her head from side to side to look at the two strangers. "And who are these men?"

Griffin wrapped a blanket around them before pulling her even closer. Her teeth chattered so much, she could barely speak.

"These are Royal Cavaliers, the King's own men who were on board to search out a plot to depose our good King Charles Stuart and put a Puritan back in power in England."

Catlin gaped at his words. He put a cup of water to her lips, and she suddenly realized how parched she was. After taking several long drinks, the chilblains diminished.

"But, why did they help me?"

Griffin smiled. "They did so at the command of their Captain."

Catlin frowned. "Master Williams?"

The sloop made a turn and land appeared instead of the far edge of the horizon. They must be as close to Jamestown as the Master of the ship had proclaimed.

Griffin put his mouth to Catlin's ear to whisper. "The Captain of their corps, and that, my darling Catlin, is none other than me."

Griffin was still in the service of his Majesty the King? How could this be? "Your plantation, is that real?"

Griffin nodded. "It was a great advantage that I had the opportunity to come to the colonies under the guise of settling my Uncle's estate. Hawthorne Hundred is real, and I look forward to settling this affair so I can enjoy my new life there with the woman I love."

Catlin's heart leaped at his words, though one fear niggled at her. Would Griffin blame her for disrupting his mission for the King?

"I'm sorry," she whispered. "You'll never know who the traitor is because you had to abandon the ship."

One of the other men grunted, but he concentrated on his duty and said nothing.

"Do not be concerned about it, for we learned everything we need to know. In good time, the traitor shall be revealed." Griffin tucked the blankets more snugly around her. "Lean back against me and see if you can sleep. We should reach my plantation by morning."

Exhaustion overtook her. The day had certainly been eventful. Now that she was safely in the arms of her beloved Eagle-Lion, she could rest.

"I thought I'd lost you to the Dream Time," she mumbled, already slipping into the throes of slumber.

Chapter Twenty-Six

When she woke, they were sailing down a river surrounded on both sides by heavy foliage and woods. The sound of buzzing insects mingled with the chirping of birds filled the air.

Huge oak trees raised their thick limbs to the sky, while flowers and bushes blazing with bright colors delighted them. Butterflies flitted from one dazzling blossom to another.

She blinked, unsure if she were in the Dream Time or if this were actually real.

A body shifted next to her. She still lay within the strong embrace of her lover.

"Griffin," she whispered, gently touching a finger to his face. His rough beard was foreign to her touch, so she stroked his skin, enjoying the sensation of the whiskers.

He opened his dark eyes, his look growing heated as she continued to rub her fingers gently across the skin of his face.

"I would not do that, my love, for your very touch arouses me."

Catlin gasped at the heat of his words, yet she was aware her gentle strokes had ignited warmth within her own depths. "I've missed our stolen moments together," she said, her cheeks warming.

He leaned forward and brushed his lips against her hair. "I've missed you too *cariad*. By evening we should be at my plantation, and after some rest we can once again renew our intimate acquaintance."

Catlin squirmed uncomfortably, aware the others might overhear. Bitsy was curled up in a large coverlet, sound asleep. The man tending the tiller kept his eyes focused ahead, intensely studying the water stretching before him. The other man was stretched across the bow, also fast asleep.

"Have we traveled far?" Catlin asked.

"Far enough to be safe from Sheffield. The Master will ensure that the *Lady Bountiful* moves slowly into the bay, and he is sure to set anchor tonight before venturing onto the river tomorrow or the next day."

"Is Master Williams also a man for the King?"

Griffin nodded. "A trusted naval man who took the assignment aboard the *Lady Bountiful* when her previous commander went missing."

Catlin frowned. "Is that man dead?"

Griffin laughed. "Hardly. I'd venture that with the gold he's been paid to remain on land, he's enjoying a rather luxurious holiday."

Catlin yawned and stretched with a lazy smile. Her stomach growled.

"By chance you don't have any food, do you, Griffin?"

He tousled her hair. "'Tis a good sign when an appetite returns. God's tears, but I was afraid the unpleasantness on board the ship might leave you in a malaise. I'm relieved to see you have come through it with all your wits intact."

Catlin grinned. "You might be wrong about that, for some would say I didn't even board the ship in possession of all my wits."

Griffin pulled his leg from beneath her and reached across the small boat to grab a gunny sack. "And when your good humor returns so quickly, it only proves you are a most extraordinary woman." He pulled a large chunk of cheese and some hardtack from the sack. "I shall be relieved to find food other than these ship's rations at the end of our journey." He broke off a piece of the hardtack and handed it to her. Using his dagger, he sliced some of the cheese to share with her too.

"Are you so sure there will be foodstuffs on your plantation? I've heard rumors tobacco is so dear that little land can be set aside for the purpose of growing food." She took a bite of the cracker and winced. She too was weary of eating the tasteless stuff.

Griffin waved his hand in the direction of the rich foliage surrounding them. "My Uncle assured me in his letters that he was never so foolish as to rely upon England for his sustenance. He planted a good kitchen garden and corn for trading with his neighbors."

Catlin stretched again, aware that the cramped quarters of the small boat provided no comfort and even less privacy. She'd removed her gown beneath the blanket, but her shift was still damp and clammy. She felt sticky and coarse and found herself anticipating even a tepid sponge bath to remove the salty brine from her skin.

They continued to eat in silence for a while, enjoying the peacefulness around them as the sloop sailed up the river. Finally, after a sideways glance at the man tending the tiller, Griffin leaned forward again to whisper in her ear.

"Did you see them?"

Catlin turned to study his expression. She suspected she knew what he was talking about when he said, *them*.

"The passengers?"

"No."

"The crew then," she suggested.

Griffin frowned. "I think you know what I mean when I ask about, well. . . *them*." He pointed over the side of the sloop in the direction of the water. "I know you must have seen them. They were surrounding you when you surfaced."

"The mermaids?" she said.

A huge smile spanned his face and his eyes lit with delight. "Yes, of course." He laughed. "I can't fathom how they could be real. Yet if you also saw them, they must be real." A dimple appeared at the edge of his charming smile. "They were so beautiful, I swear, their long hair was the color of starlight.

Men had always been an easy target for these magical female creatures of the sea. Had Griffin only heard one of the mermaids sing, he'd be lost to her forever. Their power to enchant *sophor* men was legendary. Catlin struggled with how much information to share with Griffin.

"I believe they heard my plea for help and decided to assist me. I've never seen one before, and while they're the loveliest creatures I've ever seen, I've heard their hearts are as cold as the depths of the sea they dwell in."

"It makes me wonder if other magical creatures are more than legend and nursery tales."

"Such as dwarves, fairies and dragons?" She kept her expression as innocent as possible.

"Exactly," he muttered. "If you can be wrong about one thing, then it simply follows all patterns of logic that there can be many magical creatures we rarely see, and therefore dismiss as legend."

"I have long thought that simply because we cannot see a thing doesn't necessarily mean it doesn't exist." She raised an eyebrow in his direction. "Even a Vicar can agree to that, don't you think?"

He nodded, and she thought he would have continued the conversation if he'd not spied a jut of land before them. He drew a map from his pocket and surveyed it carefully before handing it to the man at the tiller.

"I believe that's Raven's Point, one of the landmarks I was told to watch for." He grinned at Catlin. "'Twill not be far to Hawthorne Hundred now. We should be there before dusk."

Catlin nodded, aware that this was neither the time nor the place to disclose her true nature. The fact that Griffin had responded to the mermaids with more curiosity than fear reassured her.

Still, observing a fey creature was very different from sharing a bed with an elemental witch. While he might think the idea of a mermaid charming, accepting that he slept with a powerful magical creature might be a bit more challenging.

She sighed deeply as she settled herself upon the bottom of the sloop. While it would be easy to simply blurt out the truth to him, she needed to consider her words carefully when she finally revealed the extent of her powers to Griffin.

Each day those powers grew stronger and she was quickly becoming an elemental adept. He knew she was more than a healer but he couldn't even begin to suspect the nature of the magic she controlled.

An odd screech, louder then any bird she'd ever heard, echoed through the woods surrounding them. For some reason, Catlin recalled her dream of the creature with eyes like coals, feet of fire, and a huge maw of a mouth. She shivered from the cold air.

Windago.

The *sylphs* whispered the name Catlin did not recognize.

Danger. The Windago is a ghost who walks here in search of men. She seeks to destroy those who would take what is not theirs.

Catlin shivered again, this time from fear.

***

Catlin had read many tracts about the settlements in Virginia, and expected a small wattle-and-daub cottage to be the main house on Griffin's plantation.

Hawthorne Hundred plantation boasted a stately brick mansion with multiple chimneys and narrow casement windows that could have been in a manor house in England. It was neither small nor rough, and she couldn't hide her astonishment.

"By God, 'tis not what I expected to find waiting for me." Griffin grinned. "But, I'll not complain that my Uncle was too reticent in his descriptions of the estate." He tugged on her hand to pull her up the sand path behind him.

Catlin laughed, delighted to see him so happy and relaxed. "Lud, now that you're a rich landowner, I expect you'll throw me over for some wealthy lady who can endow you with more then her simple wit and nominal charms."

Griffin pulled her into his arms, his dark eyes glowing with warmth and tenderness. "I shall never forsake you, my cariad, for you are the Queen of my heart. Even royalty could not displace you."

Catlin's breathing grew shallow, her lungs tightened with the emotion he stirred within her. His honesty brought tears to her eyes. If only she could be as truthful with him.

Her family had been forced to hide their secret from *sophors* for generations. Caution and silence had protected the Glyndwr witches from the terror of the witch hunters. She would tell Griffin of her true nature, but first she wanted to enjoy watching him take possession of his lands.

A gathering of people stood in front of the house, and Catlin surmised from their garb that they were indentured servants. One tall, thin man stepped forward as they reached the portico guarding the front door. He removed his hat before bowing.

"I ken ye are Sir Reynolds," he said.

Griffin nodded. "I am the new owner of Hawthorne Hundred, and I hope you will find me an easy man to understand. If you are honest and hardworking, you shall find me a fair master.

The Scotsman dropped to one knee, and the others gathered around him and followed his lead.

"We made our pledge to your uncle, and we'll do the same to ye. We're all loyal and honest. We ask only to be treated with a fair hand."

"I shall endeavor to be as fair to you all as my uncle has been in the past. Nothing needs to change here at Hawthorne Hundred, for it appears that even without a master the plantation is thriving." He smiled at the gathering.

The expressions on the faces of the servants relaxed, and one by one the Scotsman, Hugh MacDonald, introduced the others.

Catlin's head swam with the names, until an ethereal dark beauty stepped from behind the crowd. The others parted for her. Her hair was as thick and dark as Catlin had ever seen, and her skin glowed a golden shade in the late afternoon light. She moved with an undulating grace.

"This is my wife, Kanti." Hugh took her hand in his. "Her father was a great chief and she's an Indian Princess. She's taught us many things about growing tobacco and has helped make this plantation successful."

Griffin stepped forward and bowed to the dark-haired beauty. "I am most grateful to you, Kanti, for your assistance."

Without turning, he beckoned for Catlin. "I hazard a guess that you are of the same age as my companion, Catlin Glyndwr."

Catlin made a stiff curtsy to Kanti, for an Indian Princess could well be considered royalty. Her curiosity stirred as she wondered how this lovely woman had ended up married to a Scotch bondsman. Kanti smiled and Catlin relaxed.

"We have hot food and a soft bed ready for ye, Master." Hugh indicated the direction of the door. "Kanti will send a lassie up to yer rooms with some buckets of hot water, for I'm sure ye would like to scrub a bit o' the sea grime off ye."

Griffin slapped the Scotsman on the back. "We surely would. There are several men and Catlin's serving girl following behind us. I trust you to settle them while we make our ablutions."

Hugh nodded and opened the great oak door with iron hinges. With one swoop Griffin gathered Catlin in his arms, and laughing heartily, he carried her across the threshold.

"We're not newly married," she whispered harshly, embarrassed by the laughter following behind them.

Griffin settled her upon the stone floor of the great hall and took her chin gently in his large, roughened palm. "'Tis only a technicality, *cariad*, and one we shall remedy as soon as we find a clergyman." He touched his lips to hers. She expected a brief, perfunctory kiss, but once their lips met, the fire between them sizzled to a blaze. The kiss deepened and Catlin curled her arms around Griffin's neck and pulled him closer. He hardened as he leaned against her. The fierce attraction they felt for each other possessed a magic all its own.

Griffin finally pulled his lips from hers, but he continued to hold her within his embrace. Catlin put her head against his chest, content enough to purr like a kitten.

Griffin gazed down at her, the love evident in his eyes. "This is our home, Catlin, in a new and exciting world." He shifted for a moment, turning her so she could see the great hall before them and the winding cage newel staircase rising to the floors above. "We will be wed in this hall, and our children shall fill the chambers above." He kissed her hair. "And if there be need, we can add more rooms to house our big, prosperous family!"

Catlin scanned the huge timbers of the ceiling and admired the brick fireplace at one end of the room, large enough for her to stand in, until she finally let her gaze wander up the staircase. Calm warmth suffused her as she remembered her mother's prophetic words.

In the new land there is opportunity and hope.

For the first time in a very long while, Catlin Glyndwr felt like she was home.

Chapter Twenty-Seven

Catlin stretched across the feather-bed, enveloped in a sense of peace and contentment. A small breeze teased her naked breasts, and she smiled at the wave of pleasure that rolled through her. She felt wild, wicked, and wanton.

Griffin stood across the room, still garbed in his breeches. He'd removed his linen shirt, and she admired the way his body glowed in the light of the late afternoon sunlight. He resembled a statue of a Greek God, the taut muscles of his arms sculpted as if from marble. He sipped claret while giving her an appraising grin.

"You are a demanding woman, *cariad*, and I can only hope now that I've introduced you to the pleasures of the flesh, I can continue to satisfy your ravenous appetite."

Catlin raised one knee provocatively. "'Tis your own fault, Sir Griffin, for until I became your pupil, I was an innocent maiden, unaware of the proper use for a man's tarse." She threw one arm over her head, making her breasts jut forward in a more appealing way. "Now I crave a good swive as much as a common jade."

Griffin laughed, set his goblet upon the table, and crossed the room. "Perhaps we should expand upon your education a bit and try something different."

A pulse of white hot heat shot through her body. A new game? Her lover could be unpredictable and creative. "You are always so imaginative, Griffin."

He withdrew several lengths of silk from the waistband of his breeches. "Tonight, *cariad*, you will be my helpless slave and do all that I bid of you."

Catlin shivered at his words. She trusted Griffin implicitly. Yet, the idea of being totally under his control excited and frightened her at the same time.

He wrapped one wrist with the silk and fastened it securely to the bedstead. Within moments he'd repeated the gesture with her other hand, then he fastened her ankles in the same manner. Catlin was spread-eagled on the bed, unable to escape.

Butterflies fluttered in her stomach, and her skin prickled with goose bumps. Her nipples ached for his touch, and between her legs, she could already feel the dampness of her woman's honey.

Griffin prowled around the bed. "What do you want, *cariad*?"

"To please you," she whispered in a husky voice. Though Griffin hadn't yet touched her, the play aroused her. She shivered with anticipation.

He opened the carved wooden chest at the foot of the bed and removed several items. He held a thick, bushy ostrich feather as he sat down beside her.

"Aren't you going to remove your breeches?"

"Not yet. I want to drive you mad with wanting me before I make love to you."

His words sent a flutter through her blood, heating her with sensual warmth.

He traced the feather across her lips, and she giggled. "You already drive me mad with wanting you," she said.

He drew the feather lower and tickled each hard, pink nipple. He swirled the feather across the soft, round mounds of her breasts, delving into the valley between them. Catlin moaned.

She twisted on the bed, her body aching for his touch. A molten path at every point he touched.

Griffin leaned forward and suckled each pebble-hard nipple. She writhed at each stroke of his tongue and yanked against the silken ties binding her to the bedstead.

"Loosen the silks so I can touch you too."

A devilish grin spread across his face. "Not tonight. I warned you, love. I shall show no mercy."

Catlin twisted her bottom against the coverlet, her skin hot and her brow beaded with perspiration. Her fingernails bit into her palms as she fought to maintain control. Each tiny sensation he evoked made her delirious with passion. Griffin brought the feather lower and swept it across the tiny bump of her belly. He traced the outline of her Venus mound and parted the thick, dark curls guarding her womanhood with one finger.

Catlin moaned and closed her eyes, savoring each touch of the feather as it created a trail of heat down her body.

Griffin flicked the feather across the small, sensitive bud at the top of the slit between her legs.

Catlin's bottom rose from the bed, her muscles contracting and aching from the strain of pulling against the bindings still holding her captive.

Griffin's hands gently kneaded the flesh of her upper thighs and his mouth moved closer to the place that now ached with need. She wanted him, nay- she needed him. Every movement only ignited her passion more.

"Please," she begged.

He set the feather aside and grinned. "I am most happy to oblige you, my little *diafol*."

Catlin smiled at the playful endearment. "Little Devil indeed, if you loosen my . . ."

Her words were lost as a new explosion of sensation rocked through her body. He'd replaced the feather with his tongue, and now as it swirled and eddied about her sensitive nub, waves of pleasure rolled through her body. He inserted several fingers into her molten hot depths, and her muscles clenched against him.

"Please stop, you're driving me mad," she whispered.

"You cannot object to anything, *cariad*, because you are totally under my control." He slathered his tongue against her again, and she trembled.

"Trust me," he said.

The ministrations of his tongue and finger incited her passion higher and higher. She writhed against him, even more eager for each gentle swoop of his tongue and each plunge of his finger. He sucked and licked her until she bucked against him. When she thought she'd topple over the abyss and dissolve into a pool of intense gratification, he pulled away.

He removed his breeches, his tarse thick and hard as it pointed at her, the member almost demanding she pay attention to its majesty.

"Come here," she begged. "I want to feel you deep inside of me."

He grinned. Climbing back upon the bedstead, he loosened the bonds securing her ankles and lifted her legs and placed them on his shoulders, a move that shocked her.

The tip of his tarse nudged against her opening and teased her with its closeness.

"Now," she cried, tugging against the bindings to no avail. He ignored her plea.

Griffin leaned down to touch his lips to hers, his throbbing, hard tarse still poised to enter her.

"I promised to satisfy you in all things, Catlin." He rubbed against her now aching womanhood. "You must trust me, for I can introduce you to greater pleasures then you can even imagine. But only if you truly place your confidence in me."

Catlin knew he was testing her. Could she actually trust this man with her body and give over all control to him?

She shuddered. If she didn't demonstrate her complete and utter confidence in him, it could tear them apart forever.

She relaxed against him, and then lifted her bottom in invitation.

"I want you," she said, her voice husky with desire, "and if you tell me you shall never hurt me, I believe you."

His dark eyes shimmered with flares of silver light. He leaned forward to gently touch her face.

"Thank you, love." He swiftly tilted his hips to thrust into her. With one quick plunge, he was deep inside her sheath.

She gasped as shivers of delight rippled through her. As his movements repeated the quick thrust, pull rhythm that was pushing her to the edge of her pleasure, she fought against the bindings still holding her captive.

"Harder," she whispered,

He complied, and Catlin dissolved into a shuddering wave of fulfillment. When her eyes slammed shut, small, fluttering bits of light scattered on the backs of her eyelids. She was swept away on a sea of pleasure.

"So tight," Griffin moaned.

Griffin's strokes grew longer, harder, and Catlin lifted herself again to welcome him deeper inside of her body. With a few more intense thrusts, his breathing caught and she knew he was close to exploding in pleasure.

Griffin drove into her once more, then moaned and his hot seed burst into her slick sheath. His heartbeat marched in a swift tempo that matched her own.

He finally collapsed, taking pains to support his weight on his elbows so he wouldn't crush her. She could still feel his throbbing tarse inside of her.

Finally, Griffin loosened the silk ties, releasing her from captivity. He kissed each wrist gently.

"You were most obliging, *cariad*, and I thank you for giving me so much pleasure."

Catlin took his face in her hands. "I was afraid, Griffin, and yet your promise to never hurt me helped me overcome that fear." She pulled him to her, eager to taste his lips.

When he stretched out next to her, the cool late afternoon air rustled the curtains at the window. Catlin closed her eyes. She needed to be honest with Griffin, but for now she enjoyed basking in the afterglow of their lovemaking.

They lay in silence for a while, and a symphony of birdsong filled the air outside. She marveled at the peace and tranquility surrounding her as she discovered a new life in this raw, vibrant colony. Adventure filled each day. She loved walking the land with Griffin, exploring the fields, woods and riverbank.

"I must leave for a few days, *cariad*."

His words shocked her from her reverie. "Leave? Why?"

He climbed from the bed and snatched his breeches from the floor. "'Tis business I must attend to, for being one of the wealthiest men in the colony comes with certain expectations."

His voice still had a deep, smoky note left over from their lovemaking. A dark purple glow radiated around him, alerting Catlin he wasn't being totally honest about the reason for his absence. Did his leaving have something to do with his mission for King Charles?

While she couldn't tell him how she'd discovered his ruse, she could try to get him to take her along. After all, a witch could be a convenient companion in times of trouble.

She cleared her throat. "I should be delighted to see more of this country, for I am ever anxious to learn about the Virginia colony."

Griffin didn't turn around. "I'll need to travel quickly, so 'tis not a convenient time to take you with me."

His brusque tone pricked her pride. "Was I such a loathsome burden then on our journey across the ocean?"

Griffin whirled to stare at her and frowned. "Of course you've not been a burden. But this country is dangerous, and I would never wish to put your life at risk." He sat sit down next to her. "You are precious to me, *cariad*, and I cannot bear the thought of something happening to you."

Catlin leaned forward and slid her fingers through the thick, curling locks of his hair. "Of course nothing shall happen to me, for I have your love as the greatest protection of all." She sighed. "I would dearly love to travel with you, but of course, if you deem it too dangerous I'll remain here and eagerly await your return."

Griffin gently pulled her into his arms and across his lap. "The thought of you waiting here shall certainly encourage me to return as quickly as possible."

Her conscience niggled at Catlin. She should tell him the truth. It was far beyond the time when she should have been totally honest with him.

"I must confess something to you, Griffin." She tried to twist out of his arms, but he held her fast, refusing to release her.

"Is it that you worship and adore me?" An arrogant grin spread across his face.

"No," she said, and giggled as his grin turned into a scowl. "Oh, you proud, conceited dunderhead, of course I love and adore you." She paused to take a deep breath "But this is truly important."

Griffin put his chin in one hand, dropped his mouth into a serious expression and sighed deeply. She giggled.

"You must listen carefully," she said. "Probably there are some things you are not going to like hearing."

"Am I flatulent in my sleep?"

Catlin rolled her eyes. "Stop teasing and pay attention, please."

She wished he'd release her, because pacing and wringing her hands seemed more appropriate than sitting propped upon his knee stark naked.

"I am ashamed to confess that I've tricked you." She held her breath and waited for his reaction.

His gaze moved from her face, down her body to her breasts, then lower. He shrugged. "Your assets are quite visible at the moment, and therefore I find it hard to believe you've hidden anything from me."

Catlin slapped him upon the shoulder. "I tricked you into bringing me with you on the journey to Virginia." She steeled herself for his angry reaction.

Instead he shocked her with robust laughter that shook his broad shoulders. "Tricked *me*? I confess, I conspired from the moment I first set eyes upon you in that gaol to figure out how I could get you into my bed and seduce you. In truth, Catlin, I couldn't believe your sister wanted me to be your chaperone."

Catlin rose from his lap and gawked at him, her hands upon her hips. "My sister cast a spell upon you, using her Fire Dragons. You didn't want to bring me with you, she *forced* you to bring me."

Griffin fell into another fit of raucous laughter. "She cast a spell, eh?" He gulped for air. "Using her Fire Dragons."

Catlin frowned. "Tiny but dangerous creatures, and of course you'd not know she was doing it, for she's a Fire Adept."

Still he laughed. Catlin's temper flared.

"You do not believe a word I am telling you, do you, Griffin?" She stared out the window. The evening sunset blazed vivid reds, bright oranges, and deep yellows against the blue of the sky, reminding her of the elemental fire spirits.

"'Tis true, Griffin, whether you choose to believe it or not. My sisters and I are all elemental witches, and each of us has spirits to help us cast spells and use our magic."

Griffin stopped laughing, but the silver sparkle edging the dark center of his eyes showed he thought she was telling him a nursery tale.

He pulled her back upon his lap. "I do believe you, *cariad*, for you have certainly bewitched me." He traced one thick finger from her earlobe down her neck to her breast. Her skin prickled at his touch, and a flutter warmed her belly. "I would love to hear more of this tale, but I shall be late to meet my companions."

"You travel at night?" A tremor of foreboding snapped through her. "Isn't that dangerous?"

Griffin waved away her concern. "We sail upon the river, and only to the next plantation. We should arrive well before night settles in, for 'tis nearly the solstice and the days lengthen."

He set her upon her feet, stood, and put his arms around her. "Do not fear for me, *cariad*, for I'm protected by a great and powerful witch!"

Before Catlin could give him another slap, he kissed her cheek and hurried out the door.

The way he'd so quickly dismissed her words irritated her. Surely he'd seen enough of her rendering magic to convince him she held true powers. Of course, any man with his wits about him would refuse to admit real witches walked amongst them. That very fact had protected Catlin's family for centuries.

She grabbed a silk dressing gown and donned it. His absence would provide her a perfect opportunity to observe the solstice ritual. She'd need to gather her tools and find a secluded place safe from curious eyes.

Catlin couldn't frighten the good folks who worked at Hawthorne Hundred. This place and its people were quickly becoming precious to her, and she'd do everything within her powers to keep them all safe.

Chapter Twenty-Eight

The next evening at twilight Catlin gathered a basket filled with her ritual tools and slipped out of the main house. She slid along the shadows of the smokehouse, and then crossed the yard, eager to make her way into the forest edging the clearing.

"Stay away from the woods at night," a lilting female voice warned her.

Catlin turned to find Kanti watching her from near the chicken coop.

"I'm only going for a short walk, to settle my meal."

"'Tis not safe out there." Kanti pointed toward the dark stand of trees edging the fenced garden that provided fresh vegetables and herbs for the plantation. "You should not go there alone."

A frisson of fear slid down Catlin's backbone. "Are there others out there who would harm me?"

She feared the answer. In her lifetime there'd been a horrible massacre of colonists by the naturals living in the area. Although she'd been told that those people were long gone, Kanti's warning awakened slumbering terrors.

"Not others like you and me," Kanti said, taking a few steps closer to Catlin. Her dark eyes were shadowed with fear. Her bottom lip trembled.

"We call it *Windago*. I have no word in your tongue." She paused. "My husband would say--*bogie*."

Catlin frowned. If the Scotsman called it by that name, then Kanti must be talking about...

"Ghost?" Catlin said, and the tremor in her voice was evident even to her own ears. "You believe there's a ghost in the woods."

"*Windago*," Kanti repeated, forming her hands into claws over her head. "It will eat you."

Her *sylphs* had warned her of the *Windago,* and an icy trickle of fear splashed through her body. While she'd encountered any number of different spirits, the idea of a ghost terrified her. Her mother had lectured her daughters about the unpredictable nature of a creature held to earth by a need for revenge, for settling a score, or to make peace with a loved one. A ghost would be a frightening intruder during her solstice ritual. Especially a man or woman eating ghost.

"Ghosts can't eat you, they have no—" How could she make this woman who had limited knowledge of English understand her? "Teeth." She circled her fingers around her lips to pantomime.

"*Windago* have teeth. Knife teeth."

Catlin stood at the edge of the woods. They grew darker by the moment. Should she postpone the drawing down of power tonight? It might be her only chance to observe the seasonal ritual, because Griffin would return tomorrow. The timing was perfect to make an offering to the Lady and cast her circle.

Catlin straightened her spine and lifted her chin. She would not let an ancient Indian legend stop her from celebrating the summer solstice. She believed in many beings, but not cannibal ghosts that haunted the woods beyond the plantation. If any such creature had ever existed, she would have heard of it. Her family had been Elemental Adepts for ten generations. Her grimoire held a record of the different magical creatures that roamed the earth. She'd never read nor heard of any creature called a Windago before arriving in this new land.

"I have herbs to collect beneath the full moon. It's very important that I do it now."

"You are Pauwau." Kanti twisted her mouth and shook her head. A frown creased the smooth skin of her forehead. "I have no words, but you are." She folded her arms across her chest, her mouth set in an expression of annoyance.

"Kanti, I'm not afraid." Catlin stood as tall as she could. "I can protect myself."

"Pauwau!" Kanti repeated, pointing at Catlin. "*Windago* eat you."

Not a pleasant thought, but in reality Catlin was more frightened of panthers and bears. She imagined a ghost almost manageable when compared to some of the creatures roaming the wild country of the Virginia colony.

"I shall be fine." She motioned for Kanti to return to the house.

The other woman shook her head vehemently, stepped closer to Catlin and handed her a large, bone-handled knife. "*Windago*," she repeated, then turned and hurried back to the house.

Catlin's steps dragged as she left the safety of the yard surrounding the house. Even though she dismissed the story, her conversation with Kanti made her wary of entering the dark shadows looming before her.

It's a story told to remind children not to wander away, she assured herself. People everywhere had similar stories. Her own mother had told her and her sisters many such tales.

The crunch of her footsteps on the trail reassured her. Animals shuffled in the underbrush and night insects buzzed. A flock of bats wound through the trees on their way to hunt.

Many creatures roamed the woods tonight, and all were part of the rhythm and swirl of life. Catlin felt no alarm at any noise she heard. Enough light still shone for her to make her way through the trees on a thin, almost invisible path.

When she reached the small clearing she'd chosen earlier in the day to cast her circle, she set her basket down and pulled several candles from the bottom.

With the knife Kanti had given her, she made four indentations in the ground, marking the cardinal points of north, south, east, and west. Catlin pulled the other items from the basket and created her altar space in the center between the marked points. With a few strikes of her flint, she built a fire with some dry kindling, and then lit the candles before setting them at the points.

Night had settled upon the forest. She listened for any sign of a strange presence in the woods, but only the rustling of animals met her ears.

With all of her tools arranged in front of her, Catlin took the pine branch she'd carefully hidden earlier and prepared to cast her circle.

"This night of changing seasons, set by the moon
 Brings a summer's bounty, a feast and a boon.
 I offer to our Lady, my head, my hands, my heart,

All I ask of her, is my wish for a fresh start."

Catlin carefully swished the makeshift pine branch broom along the ground and cast her circle as she walked around the burning candles. Strange shadows danced behind her, but she ignored them. Once the circle was set, she could begin the ritual.

When she completed the circle, she returned to her small altar in the center. She drew a consecrated knife through the air and called upon her *sylphs*. Within moments tiny glowing lights appeared.

Pausing in front of the copper pot holding fresh water she'd carried in an earthenware bottle, she spoke the words offering her thanks to the water spirits who had assisted her when she'd jumped from the *Lady Bountiful*.

Another few steps and she offered words of thanks to the earth spirits, for the safety and beauty of Hawthorne Hundred Plantation. She wished she could communicate with Seren, her youngest sister, who often expressed a heartfelt desire for such a home. Perhaps the gnomes of her element would somehow let the young woman know that a safe sanctuary existed for her beyond the great, wide ocean.

A flicker of the candle enticed Catlin to look up, but the moon had not yet risen. Only a ceiling of stars glowed far, far above her.

Finally, she came to rest before the flame of the candle that represented her eldest sister's element. Fire, so dangerous and yet so tempting. How many times had she watched the death dance of a moth, drawn to the flame, enticed, dancing with danger only to find its own life extinguished? Fire. An element so treacherous that any Elemental Adept who mastered it held the highest rank amongst them. Fire—so like her older sister's raging tempers and unfulfilled desires. Aelwyd possessed a hot and blazing heart waiting for the right fuel to set her aflame.

Catlin laughed at her own folly. Perhaps love was making her wish everyone could find what she'd found with Griffin.

The very thought of him made her ache with longing. A day had never seemed so long before she met him, but now it stretched to an eternity when they were apart.

A stick crunched, and she startled. she caught herself before crying out in alarm. Had Kanti followed her?

Another twig snapped from the edge of the clearing, and Catlin jumped. Despite her show of courage, the story the Indian woman shared unsettled her.

"Kanti, are you there?" She made her voice sound as assured as she could. "Please come out."

More rustling followed.

"Don't bother to hide. I know you're there."

Now she'd have to draw back her circle because a *sophor* had appeared. She had no intention of performing her ritual with a witness nearby.

"I know you're out there, so please just show yourself."

A chill of terror swept through her when she recognized the figure walking out of the depths of the forest. The arrogant walk, the aristocratic air of entitlement, and the aura of angry, dark magic made her blood run cold.

"I warned you, witch." He took a step closer, and Catlin sketched a sigil of protection in the air. He could not enter the circle unless she created an opening and invited him in. Still, her fear of the Earl of Sheffield took hold. Her knees shook nearly bringing her to the ground. Her heart beat against her ribcage, and the knife she held in her hand shook uncontrollably.

"You cannot hurt me," she whispered, backing closer to the center of the circle.

"You're right about that, but perhaps we can negotiate a truce." He snapped his arm out to point, and several heavy thuds echoed just beyond the darkness. A bound man jetted forward and slammed against the ground with a bone-shattering crunch.

Catlin gasped and almost left the protection of her circle when she recognized Griffin's bruised and beaten face. Her hand flew to her mouth, tears pricked her eyes.

Blood seeped through the rough shirt he wore. Her hatred for the Earl of Sheffield blazed hot and fierce, a thirst for revenge tempted her to use dark magic to wound him. To destroy him!

"He's nothing to you. It's me you want. If you release him, I'll do whatever you say."

Catlin hated to beg this evil, dark magician, but she couldn't do anything to help Griffin until she secured his release.

"I warned you if I cannot have you, no man ever would." Lord Sheffield prowled around Griffin and gave the prone body a hard kick. He grinned when Griffin moaned.

"Stop it!" Catlin raced to the very edge of her protective circle.

Lord Sheffield raised an eyebrow. "So, the Cavalier who is your lover touches all those soft, gentle places within you."

He gave Griffin another hard kick and Catlin bit her bottom lip. She ached to raise her hand and cast a spell to destroy Sheffield. Tears coursed down her face, and she clutched the knife, prepared to rip the evil magician's heart out if he hurt Griffin any more. Blood roared in her ears.

"What do you want?" Her voice quaked, the edge of hysteria making the sound weak and pitiful. "Just tell me, and let him go."

"You are the rose, the key to finding the treasure." He whispered roughly. "Your father was a great alchemist, and my order has assessed all of his work. But, we never found the key to transforming matter."

Her mouth went dry at the mention of her father, for she and her sisters knew the key had been her mother's magical abilities. No chemical formula could work without the addition of their elemental magic. But, he'd never put that into his diaries, because it would pose a danger to his family.

The Earl of Sheffield laughed, the sound echoing through the woods. "Why should I let him go? Are you willing to trade yourself to save your lover?"

Catlin worked to regain control. She knew nothing would prevent the earl from taking her as his prize. She could only bargain for Griffin's life now.

"You want me, to control my powers and use me for your own purposes. If you release him, I'll do as you ask."

The earl paced around Griffin. Finally he pulled a pistol from the thick leather belt cinched around his waist and aimed it at Griffin's head.

"'Tis a sad truth, but the only way you will ever truly be mine is if I kill your lover." He raised the gun. "His death offers a permanent solution to our little predicament."

Catlin screamed and the ground shook beneath her. The earth rumbled, and she raised her hands to the dark night sky and gathered all her magical powers. She pushed out against the stars, out to Grandmother Moon, and out to the Queen of Heaven.

"You will not do this!" Her words swirled the magic within her. The bright crystal lights of her *sylphs* danced above her. The wind roared and crashed through the trees on its way to do her bidding.

Lord Sheffield cocked the pistol, but her *sylphs* whirled around his hand like a swarm of angry hornets. He tried to shake them away.

"I'll kill him and then I'll have you." He bellowed.

The energy of the stars pulsated in Catlin's body. The magic roared through her blood, giving her a strength that made every muscle flex. She tossed her head back, and howled as the wind slammed into her. She rose into the air, spinning in a tight circle. The knife fell from her hand, and she drew a sigil in the air that flamed into life. It hung just before her, glowing red and gold like a coal in the middle of an inferno.

An entity bobbed just beyond the edge of her vision—a presence she recognized as strange and foreign. She sensed she should be terrified, yet the power screaming through her body made her confident. She didn't fear this creature.

A bloodcurdling scream shattered the night air. Catlin recognized the pain within the cry, and she sent out a burst of welcoming energy.

Come, she invited, come to my circle! I bid you welcome.

Lord Sheffield stumbled. The shadows thrown by the candles grew longer, and another horrifying scream echoed through the dark, gloomy night.

"What are you doing, witch?" Lord Sheffield took a step toward her and aimed the gun. "Let us see if your powers can save you from a bullet."

Before he could fire, a horrible apparition ripped the air apart. A huge creature flew at Lord Sheffield. It had a great, red maw of a mouth filled with dagger sharp teeth and eyes that glowed like fiery coals in the night—the *Windago*.

Catlin felt no fear. The *Windago* wouldn't hurt her, because it had come from the depths of the darkness when she called for help. The poor, tortured creature had answered her summons. Magic sang though her body, making her strong and confident.

She closed her eyes as Lord Sheffield screamed in agonized

pain. When there was finally silence, she opened her eyes to discover she was alone in the clearing with the badly injured Griffin.

She quickly created an opening to her circle and dragged an unconscious Griffin into the space.

As she prepared to reseal the circle, the *Windago* appeared at the edge of the small clearing, hovering. A high keening noise came from the creature, and Catlin was filled with pity. An ache wrapped around her heart and there was thickness in her throat. Whatever had happened to this monster, she had nothing to fear from it.

Catlin stared at the ghost a moment before nodding. "You are welcome here," she said.

The *Windago* entered the circle and Catlin sealed the doorway. The *Windago* transformed into a beautiful young native woman with large ebony-hued eyes that spoke of endless pain and suffering.

Catlin didn't have time to pause and consider her actions. "We must help Griffin, or he will die."

The other woman nodded, and Catlin gathered the ritual tools to begin a healing ceremony.

They said nothing more as they went to work. The darkness surrounded them, and silence filled the night.

Chapter Twenty-Nine

I stand next to Griffin in the realm of Dream Time. Somehow my spell has transported us here.

My mother paces across the wildflowers carpeting the garden. Her brow is knotted.

"Daughter."

The sharpness of my mother's voice forces me to stand taller. I anticipate a harsh judgment. I've broken serious rules governing the uses of magic. But, I never expected to face the consequences with Griffin by my side.

"You have performed spells and used your magic in the presence of a sophor, is that not true?"

One look at my mother's expression signals this is no time for petty excuses.

"I humbly apologize for doing so."

"Apologize?" My mother scoffs. "As if that shall make any difference." She gazes up at the cloudless azure sky. "I seem to remember you have always been most skillful at creating an apology once the deed has been accomplished."

I know it would be wise to remain silent, but I cannot stand to be humiliated in front of Griffin. "I was only doing as you directed, Mother."

My mother scowls. "I doubt I ever told you to endanger your sisters, perform spells in front of a sophor, take this man as your lover, challenge a dark druid, or bring a bwgan and a sophor to the Dream Time with you!"

I swallow. Her list of transgressions is quite long.

My mother taps one silver-slippered toe in agitation.

Griffin stands in the stiff pose of a soldier facing his commander. His face displays an expression of bland indifference, as if facing a powerful dead witch in the magical between realm is an everyday occurrence, hardly worthy of notice or alarm.

"You, sir, have acted in a most disrespectful manner towards my daughter. You have seduced and dishonored her!"

Griffin swallows. "I love Catlin, my lady, and would never do anything to harm or dishonor her."

My mother pauses in front of him. "I must know what your intentions are in regard to my daughter."

Griffin smiles. "My intention is to make her my wife and the mother of a brood of mischievous and delightful children."

I'm tempted to laugh out loud, but adjust my expression when my mother's cold gaze settles upon me again.

"And what do you say to this, daughter? Will you become this man's wife and fill his house with my beautiful and talented grandchildren?"

The question startles me and I laugh. I lunge forward to wrap my arms around my mother, then remember she is a shadow. My happiness is tinged with a moment of sadness.

"Yes," I say, turning to Griffin, "yes to the proposal and yes to the plan for our children." I step away from my mother. "In fact, I suspect the grandchildren part might already have been set in motion."

Griffin's face explodes in a wide grin. He wraps me in his arms. "I'm delighted to learn of it. I've been most distressed I've not yet managed to get you with child. I must be looking to my heir."

"But," my mother says, "we must make certain those children are well-protected."

"Sir Griffin Reynolds — " She raises an arm, and a sword appears in her hand, "I gave you this weapon once before, but you managed to lose it."

"He was trying to save my life," I object. "He had do drop it to rescue me from drowning."

My mother frowns. "Be silent, child!" She commands.

"This sword honors you, and now if you will bend down, I shall make you a knight of the Mystic Moon. Do you swear to protect the life of my daughter and her children? Will you honor the rites of her family and take a vow to the Queen of Heaven?"

Griffin falls to one knee. "I give my oath that I shall do as you ask of me."

My mother raises the sword and touches it to each of Griffin's shoulders, then hands it to him. When he rises, the sword is bathed in a strange, cold blue fire.

I blink as tears flood my eyes. I take a step closer to Griffin, nodding my thanks to my mother.

Pride shimmers through me, and my heart beats a slow, steady cadence. My lover, my husband, my protector. Griffin is all that to me, and more.

I turn to the woman who has been transformed from the Windago. She stands in the shadows of the garden beneath a willow tree.

"What's to become of her?" I ask my mother.

My mother shrugs. "I know not, for her curse is strong. I cannot release her, but I shall send her back with you to act as a guardian while I study upon it."

"Will she continue to kill?" I don't regret the deaths of the vile Lord Sheffield and his henchmen, but I do care about the people living on Hawthorne Hundred. If this creature presents a threat, I need to find a way to protect them.

My mother shakes her head. "This creature seeks only those who would hurt the innocent or destroy the land. You have nothing to fear from her."

Griffin takes my hand in his and we both drop down on our knees to ask for my mother's blessing.

She raises her hands. "By the power of the wind, I give your union strength. By the power of water, I give you perseverance against evil. By the power of the earth, I bless your home with prosperity. By the power of fire, I give you passion and love that shall sustain you for all your days."

She places her hands gently upon our heads. "So have I said, so shall it be!"

Griffin helps me to my feet and puts an arm around me. He carefully takes my chin in his other hand to lift my face up to meet his gaze. His eyes glitter with good humor.

"You have truly bewitched me now, cariad."

I grin up at him. "The magic has just begun."

Before I can say any more, he silences me with a tender kiss.

Epilogue

"How are you feeling, *cariad*?" Griffin's arms encircled her slightly bulging waistline and Catlin sighed deeply.

"Incredibly happy, deliriously in love and hungry."

Griffin chuckled. "Kanti is making supper, we'll eat soon." He gently kissed the top of her head. "And I'm glad you are deliriously in love and happy."

Catlin leaned back against the muscular chest of the man she loved. She couldn't keep the satisfied smile from her face.

"I sometimes feel guilty about all the happiness I've found here in the New World. I worry about my sisters."

Griffin pulled her tighter against him, and she felt a hot pulse of desire whip through her. Despite long passionate nights of making love, she simply couldn't get enough of this man.

"As soon as possible, we'll bring them all here. You sent the letter inviting them to come and stay with us, didn't you?" Griffin said.

Catlin twisted around to look up at him. "You don't think filling your house with a passel of women is going to make your life a bit difficult?"

Griffin nodded his head, an exasperated sigh escaping from his lips. "I imagine it will. Since I'll be dealing with a fire witch, earth witch and water witch in addition to my lovely air witch, I expect my life will consist of one strange incident after another."

Catlin blinked at him, she wasn't sure if he was teasing her. Then his handsome face split into a grin.

"And I wouldn't have it any other way my darling, Catlin. After all, I'm now a Knight of the Mystic Moon." He lifted her and swung her around. "I take my vows seriously and in a few days our wedding vows will be repeated in front of the Priest."

Catlin touched his face with one finger, astounded that somehow this wonderful, kind warrior had accepted her and everything she was with no reservations. When he finally set her down she turned to lean her back against him again and watch the final rays of the sun burn orange and red at the edge of the early evening sky.

She heard the soft murmur of voices as the field hands came in from their chores. The smell of cooking filled the air and she sniffed. Her stomach gave a slight groan as the aroma of roasting venison reminded her that she was starving. Lately, she was always starving. She hoped their kitchen garden and the hunting parties could keep her fed this summer as her pregnancy seemed to keep her ravenous.

"It's a good life here," Griffin said.

Catlin nodded, grasping his hands in hers and placing them gently over her belly.

"It will be a fine life for our children and when my family finally arrives, they'll see it's just as my mother predicted-- our destiny lies here on the shores of this new colony."

"Do you think the child will be born with, well -- powers?" His voice was flat, but Catlin could feel the concern behind his words.

"It will depend, because all the females of our line have possessed special powers. But if they are males, it is not as predictable." She tried to reassure him. "Generally no magical powers are apparent in children."

He nodded. "Then I suppose we will just have to wait and see what happens."

She laughed. "And isn't that the important lesson we've had to learn? We must take each day as it comes, welcome new things and rejoice in all the happiness that is offered to us."

Griffin turned her around and pulled her closer, lifting her chin to gaze deeply into her eyes. Her arms slipped around him. Her heart beat slow and steady within her chest but she felt a tickle of pleasure slide up her spine as she snuggled against him.

"I'm looking forward to every sunrise that I'll share with you, *cariad*." Griffin whispered.

"And at every sunset I'll whisper a prayer of thanks to the Goddess for bringing you to that gaol the night I was arrested." She replied.

His mouth hovered over hers. "As we have said, so shall it be."

The End

About the Author

Sibelle Stone is the pen name for award-winning romance author Deborah Schneider. Deborah writes Western romance, but Sibelle writes stories filled with magic, strange creatures, mystical events and fantastical machines. They both live near the Cascade Mountains in the Pacific Northwest. Deborah won the Molly Award for the Most Unsinkable Heroine for her book, *Beneath A Silver Moon,* and the EPIC Award for Best Western Romance for her book, *Promise Me.* She was also named Librarian of the Year by Romance Writers of America. Sadly, Sibelle hasn't won any awards yet but she remains hopeful!

For more adventures, free short stories, good gossip and other lovely things. . .

Visit Deborah and Sibelle on-line.

http://www.sibellestone.com/

http://www.debschneider.com/

Facebook

Discover other titles by Deborah Schneider at Amazon.com

Beneath A Silver Moon

Discover other titles by Sibelle Stone at Amazon.com

No Ordinary Love

Acknowledgements

I want to thank my critique partner, Sheryl Hoyt (Saralynn Hoyt) for her unfailing patience as we worked through this manuscript. She reads everything I write and I'm thankful to have a friend who tells me the truth, even when I don't want to hear it and shares my enthusiasm for creating stories.

My editor, Helen Hardt has worked on two books with me, and her advice, editing and observations always smooth out the edges of a rough work. I appreciate her commitment to make every work the very best.

My thanks to the librarians at King County Library System for their assistance in researching this book. Special thanks to Alene Moroni for help with proper titles and forms of address. Any errors in this book are mine, and I take full editorial responsibility.

Special thanks to to my Beta readers, Darcy Carson, Danijo Avia and Christel Dujardin-Terry for their observations and advice.

Coming in Fall 2012
Embers at Dawn - Book Two of the Mystic Moon series

Thank you for purchasing this book. If you enjoyed reading it, please consider submitting a review at Amazon.com or Goodreads.

Made in the USA
Charleston, SC
11 April 2014